POWERBALLS

JIMMY CLIFTON

First paperback edition June, 2021

ISBN: 978-0-578-86745-8

www.jimmyclifton.com

For
Donna

Prologue

June 22, 2020
Biloxi, Mississippi

I can't say I was surprised when Jimmy Clifton went over the side in heavy weather that night last May. A clumsier, more careless crew member never walked the deck of the *Miss Rosie Mae*. As usual, he had ignored the order to clip onto the safety wire and Porter, the last man to see him, said he'd seemed even drunker than usual. Of course, we came right about, and a Coast Guard chopper got out there too a few hours later, but in those swells and with the current running five or six knots you'd just as soon find a black cat in a coal cellar.

Well, sir, we'd been short-handed, or I never would have brought Clifton aboard, but he said he'd made an Atlantic crossing or two crewing yachts, so I took him on. He'd seen better days and fishing's a young man's game, but he still looked capable enough. I even challenged him to tie a rolling hitch and he passed with flying colors.

Jimmy never did a lick of work, though. He was clearly down on his luck so I cut him some slack but that doesn't go over well on a working shrimp boat. The thought crossed my mind that maybe old Jimmy didn't go over by accident, but most of the crew seemed pretty shaken up about it, so I put that thought to rest.

The question of contacting next of kin came up the next day. We were still three days out from Biloxi, so the crew gathered round and I broke open his footlocker. I have to admit, anticipation was running high. There was something about Jimmy you couldn't quite put your finger on, and most of the crew held that he'd come from money, whether ill-gotten or otherwise. The crew was sorely disappointed when we lifted that lid. You'd expect to find the usual assortment of things that a man accumulates over time, but there wasn't much in that footlocker but empty Mount Gay rum bottles, a loaded .45, some old NOAA nautical charts, and a stack of tattered five-star notebooks. You hate to see a man's life reduced to such meager possessions at the end, but there it was.

Luckily, Lemieux, who knew Jimmy best among the crew, took a look at one of those notebooks out of curiosity as he was getting ready to load them into the marine incinerator. Turns out Jimmy's notebooks were actually book manuscripts, all written in a bold, confident hand that you wouldn't have guessed Jimmy possessed.

I'd never seen any of the crew reading anything more thought-provoking than *Popular Mechanics,* but pretty soon those manuscripts were making the rounds and work was slipping. I asked Lemieux about it and all he said was, 'That old boy sure could spin a tale, Skip. Like po' boys and gumbo, you can't quite get enough.' High praise indeed coming from a Cajun.

Well, here we are a year later. Never did find Clifton. I like to think the currents and his rummy's luck carried him to shore and he's on a beach somewhere sipping on a rum and coke and still putting pen to paper. But Lemieux was right. Old Jimmy's books are hard to put down. This first one's called *POWERBALLS.* A cautionary tale if there ever was one about the perils of sudden wealth, and what the almighty dollar can do to a man's, or woman's, soul. In the immortal words of Jimmy Clifton, *Be careful what you wish for.*

We think you'll like it.

John Henry Thibodeau, Captain, the *Miss Rosie Mae*

Part I

Be careful what you wish for.

The Best Laid Plans of Mice and Men

Henry Ball wanted his boss dead.

A pleasant little tremor rippled down his spine. Given the chance, he would kill Dexter Schmidt in a heartbeat.

Of late, plotting Dex's demise was the only thing that brightened his days at PharmaSolutions. Dex wasn't about to drop dead from natural causes, of that Henry was certain. The evil bastard was a world class athlete in his prime. As a testament to his physical prowess and narcissism, Dex even kept a life-size cardboard cutout of himself in the corner office that had once been Henry's, immortalizing his triumphant swim-stage victory in the Chicago triathlon.

No, if he wanted vengeance, Henry would have to take matters into his own hands. His imagination ran wild with scenarios. In one of his favorites, Henry pictured himself in scuba gear, lying in wait deep below one of Dex's early morning Lake Michigan training swims. As Dex's steady crawl propelled him along the surface directly above, Henry would launch himself off the lake bottom, shoot upward with a few powerful kicks, and drag a terrified Dex down into the dark, cold depths.

He almost burst out laughing as he imagined reading about it the next day in the *Chicago Tribune*: . . . *the accomplished Chicago triathlete drowned early yesterday morning within yards of the North Avenue beach. Betty Kravitz, out for her morning walk, witnessed the event from shore. "The way he was flailing about, I never would have guessed the man was an athlete," she said, still badly shaken from the event. "He seemed completely out of his element."*

While it seemed like the perfect death for Dex, Henry had to admit there was a high probability the younger man would turn the tables on him as they struggled below the surface. Years ago, in college, Henry had spent his summers lifeguarding, but of late even walking up a flight or two of stairs left him winded. The potential for failure reminded him of an old adage:

If you strike at a king, you must kill him.

Dex's death had to be foolproof.

Then how about curare? Henry smiled. The slow-working neurotoxin used by native tribes in the Amazon to poison their arrows would be the next best thing. Just a few drops slipped into one of Dex's espressos would almost certainly do the trick.

Henry stifled a laugh as he imagined Dex panicking as the poison took effect and even taking a breath became impossible. He imagined looking down at a helpless Dex in the ICU as he wrapped his arms consolingly around Dex's new girlfriend, the beautiful Samantha Tarleton. Then he would lean over and whisper in Dex's ear, *Sweet dreams, asshole—I win!*

"BALL!"

Henry's reading glasses went flying as his head snapped up from the report he'd been pretending to read. Dex, who was leading PharmaSolutions' monthly cashflow assessment meeting in a windowless conference room with ten others from the finance department, stood glaring down at him from in front of the whiteboard. The development of a promising new treatment to arrest the effects of Alzheimer's, code name Shield, had encountered serious setbacks in the clinical trials stage and was now months, perhaps years away from FDA approval. Wall Street had heard the rumors and PharmaSolutions' high-flying stock and market cap were teetering on the verge of free fall. With the future of the company at stake, a full-court press was on to stem the flow of red ink and Dex, as the newly-minted CFO, was hoping to 'make his bones' by saving the company millions. The fact that Dex had, in typical fashion, lowered the temperature in the room to about 60 degrees hadn't prevented Henry from drifting off.

Now, as Henry sheepishly looked around the room, even some of his longtime allies were stifling smiles, knowing what was to come.

"Nice of you to join us, Henry," Dex said, with mock politeness. "If you have a moment, and if it's not too much trouble, perhaps you can shed some light on the cost of our paper clip consumption or whatever it is you're working on at the moment."

There was some nervous laughter. Even Samantha Tarleton, his former protégé, had turned away and was looking down with embarrassment.

"People," Dex said, "we need to shave $5 million off our monthly burn rate or heads will roll." He looked directly at Henry. "Any idea where we should start?"

Rose Ball wanted to make love to her boss.

She flushed at the thought. She strongly suspected Dr. Nick Cohen felt the same way about her. Rose had begun to detect a heightened level of attentiveness a few months earlier when most of North Shore Urology's doctors, nurses and Rose, the office manager, had gone to the annual Leading Edge Urology Conference in Las Vegas.

True to form, the doctors attended one early morning 30-minute lecture and then spent the rest of the day at the exclusive Shadow Creek golf course courtesy of the pharmaceutical reps who circled the doctors like sharks. It was a welcome three-day respite from the pressures of a practice reaping the enormous benefits of baby boomer demographics. A surprisingly inebriated doctor had perhaps summed it up best in a pithy dinner toast one evening as he raised a glass and struggled to keep his balance: "Thank God for ED!"

Million-dollar salaries softened the blow for the doctors, but for Rose and the other staffers working 60 hours a week, the comparatively meager salaries and rare perks seemed increasingly inadequate. But if the natives were getting restless you would not have guessed it poolside at the Mirage. Perhaps no other profession let its hair down so quickly and as thoroughly as the RN. Rose and the nurses spent their days relaxing alongside the vast pool, drinking an endless supply of mai tais and margaritas, and fending off the clumsy if harmless advances of the high rollers known as *whales*. It was, as one of the nurses yelled out of nowhere, "Just what the fuckin' doctor ordered!"

By the time the docs arrived at the poolside bar in the late afternoon, no one was particularly sober, and the usually discrete and very professional Dr. Cohen seemed enamored with Rose. It would not have surprised the casual observer. Rose kept herself in great shape and her lithe, 50-year-old body in a simple black two-piece compared favorably to women 20 years her junior. There was something of a 'come hither' quality about her too that was hard to define. Perhaps it was the way her thick, wavy auburn hair fell seductively just above one eye, made all the more alluring because she seemed so completely unaware of its sultry effect.

While nothing had happened, later that evening she had been squeezed cozily against Dr. Cohen as five or six of the doctors packed tightly into an elevator after a raucous dinner, and he seemed to welcome the contact.

Dr. Cohen was certainly the most handsome of the clinic's partners. Rose particularly liked his calm demeanor, which seemed to get even calmer in crisis (her husband Henry was excitable and seemed to take pleasure in over-reacting); his intelligence (Henry was bright too, well-read and witty, but his interests now seemed limited to the Discovery Channel, Animal Planet, and ESPN rather than the theater and the other arts that Rose had a passion for); and, well, his great body (Henry was taller but had begun to slouch a bit and sport the noticeable gut that seemingly every middle-aged American male gets when he's thrown in the towel on any pretense of athleticism).

Rose yawned, rubbed her eyes, and laid her head down on the tall stack of file folders in front of her. Vegas seemed like a lifetime ago. Who could blame her if she took just a minute to catch her second wind? Most of the staff were still at lunch. She wasn't one to indulge in fantasy but now, overcome by weariness, she succumbed to a favorite daydream.

She imagines returning to the office after the staff has left that evening. She's fallen weeks behind and now hours of pure drudgery awaits. She's changed out of her usual business casual into something more befitting the long, dreary night ahead: vintage Chicago Bears sweatshirt and a pair of ancient Kappa Delta sorority sweatpants dating back to college.

Shit! As she logs into the office server, she suddenly realizes she's left her iPhone at home and there's not even Puccini's "Tosca" to help get her through another hellish evening at North Shore Urological.

But wait. As if on cue she hears what sounds like the unmistakable voice of the renowned tenor Roberto Alagna coming from down the hall. Intrigued, Rose walks to her office doorway and peeks around the corner. Only it's not Alagna; it's Dr. Cohen. He emerges from his office, hesitating for a moment as he masters the role of Cavaradossi and the most difficult of Puccini's arias. He lifts his arms heavenward and the pictures in the hallway rattle with the power of his crescendo.

He grins a bit sheepishly when he realizes Rose has been watching him and takes a modest, self-deprecating bow. She notices that he's exchanged scrubs for a tux and now he strides down the hall with all the je ne sais quoi *of James Bond (the Connery version of course).*

Rose ducks backs into her tiny office. She's in a panic. She looks like hell and her office is in a shamble. She begins to straighten the mountain of file folders on her desk, but it's too late.

"Never mind all that," Dr. Cohen says as he comes up behind her, then sends the file folders flying across the room with a powerful sweep of his arm. He lays a dozen long-stemmed red roses in their place.

"We've got to hurry, Rose, Lyric Opera starts in an hour," he says, holding up two tickets. "Limo's waiting outside."

"Dr. Cohen," she starts to respond.

"*Nick,*" he says. He looks her up and down. "*Hmmm. I hope I guessed right. Size six? Couldn't be sure if you liked Valentino or not, but I took a chance.*" He hands her a garment bag.

He starts toward the door but then turns. "*Oh, almost forgot, here, give me your wrist,*" he says. "*This was my grandmother's. They say Cartier made just two. The czarina got the other. Thought it would look nice on you. The Ceylon sapphires match your eyes.*"

"BALL!"

The practice's senior nurse, Britt Johannsen, all six feet of her, towered over Rose. Big Jo, as everyone called her, was feared by most of the staff and the more timid doctors. Of late a palpable hostility had grown between the two women, and Rose strongly suspected it had a lot to do with Dr. Cohen. Big Jo seemed particularly enamored with him, and while Rose doubted there was any mutual interest, she had to admit that Big Jo could be considered attractive if you went for that big-breasted Swedish dominatrix-nurse look.

Rose lifted her head, looked up at Big Jo, and returned the fake smile. "Yes, Jo, how can I help?"

In what Rose imagined was a subtle act of intimidation, Jo sat down on the edge of Rose's desk and leaned uncomfortably into Rose's personal space; so close in fact that Rose noticed that Jo smelled of a rather sickening blend of tic tacs and antiseptic soap.

"Ball, these records should have been converted to EMR and uploaded to the cloud months ago," Jo said, gesturing toward the stack of blue folders on Rose's desk. "When that task got delegated to you, I feared the worst. Now it's costing us. I don't know who you're playing footsy with around here, but who do you think the docs will keep when given the choice: a highly trained nurse practitioner or a glorified bookkeeper well past her prime?"

With that Jo stood, casually smoothed the front of the pristine white scrubs that somehow accentuated her evilness, smiled at Rose and walked off. Rose settled for a mild flipping of the bird at Jo's back. It had taken all of her willpower not to have leaped onto Big Jo's back and throttled her with any of the six different choke holds she was expert at.

"In some cultures, age and experience are revered!" Henry railed later that day at lunch at Murphy's. It was a popular strip mall eatery with faux Irish pub décor and a sort of canned *Cheers* bonhomie, just one of the many watering holes in close proximity to PharmaSolutions and the dozens of other promising young start-ups that had sprung up along the northern edge of Cook County. Henry was already on his third beer, a personal best for a Friday lunch, and alcohol tended to make him louder and even more excitable.

"But not at big pharma! Now it's all about youth, and bastards like Dex rule!"

Heads turned at several of the adjoining tables. Murphy's was the go-to Friday lunch spot for many of PharmaSolutions' employees, and the place was packed. Not even the Jimmy Buffett soundtrack could lift the somber vibe, a far cry from the raucous Fridays of just a few months ago when Shield and stock price were both flying high. Henry's best friend Arnie Schlecter from IT smiled and held a finger to his lips.

"You know, I have a theory about that," Arnie said, seeking to diffuse the situation. "In the old days everyone had a trade. Blacksmith, carpenter, bricklayer, all requiring great skill and years of experience. Now, technology is the most important trade."

But Henry wasn't listening. Arnie followed his gaze and saw that Dex and Samantha had just walked in. It was a raw, blustery early spring day and Samantha re-arranged the luxurious blond mane that had blown down over her startlingly blue eyes. Dex nodded in their direction and said something to Samantha that made her laugh. Henry watched as Dex helped Samantha out of her coat, her back arching a bit and shoulders thrusting back.

"Henry get a grip, you're drooling," Arnie said.

Henry leaned toward Arnie. "I can't help it, Arnie, she's like Circe, turning men into swine." He glanced in their direction. "What does she see in Dex anyway?"

"Have you seen that life-size cut-out in his office?" Arnie asked. "The Speedo? No shrinkage in evidence there, even after 30 minutes in Lake Michigan."

"Arnie, you've no doubt heard of Photoshop?" Henry asked. "With a bit of work, I'd be a dead ringer for Brad Pitt."

Arnie was too good a friend to hit the hanging curveball out of the ballpark. Instead, he changed the subject. "More importantly, have you heard about the Powerball? Up to $1 billion and change. The drawing's next Tuesday."

"Arnie please, I'm an accountant. It's mathematically more probable that we'll both sleep with Angelina Jolie."

"Oh, come on Henry, live a little, let your hair down," Arnie said, his eyes going inadvertently to Ball's receding hairline. "Life can't all be about playing the percentages. Just think what you could do with that kind of money." He nodded in Samantha's direction.

The Game's Afoot

"Oh, for God's sake Henry, live a little," Rose said, leaning in close to the vanity mirror to apply her makeup.

It was Saturday evening and Henry was dreading their long-scheduled dinner with Victor and Suzanne Black. Suzanne was Rose's best friend, dating back to their freshman year at New Trier High School. Victor had recently been on the cover of *Crain's Chicago Business* as the poster boy for a new breed of swashbuckling investment banker under the title, "Victor Black: Cashing in On Climate Change." Twice a year, the two couples got together on the women's birthdays. It was Suzanne's birthday this evening, and Henry had just remarked that the slow torture of the type the Zulu once practiced on their captives—encasing them in an earthen body cast and baking them alive over a slow roasting fire—was infinitely preferable to dinner with Suzanne and Victor.

"Here's how the night will play out," Henry said, slumped across the bed, still unshaven and in his jockeys. "Su ZON will let it slip that she ran into your old high school boyfriend Eddie Reynolds and that he is absolutely killing it in commercial real estate. Then Victor will pile on, suggesting that if I can pony up the

$250,000 minimum, he'll get me in on the ground floor of a new company putting in oilfield pipelines in Nigeria—knowing full well that I'm only $249,000 short. Oh, and at some point tonight Victor will say, 'Once you've gone Black you'll never go back.'"

Henry rolled off the bed, came up behind her, and began gently rubbing her shoulders. "You always get a little tense when I get around those two," Henry said. "Why don't we stay home tonight? I'll light some candles, put on a little Stevie Wonder, and open that bottle of Korbel that's been at the back of the refrigerator all these years."

Now, as they looked in the mirror, it was a bit of a shock to both of them to see how great Rose looked compared to Henry in his underwear, revealing the 20 extra pounds he'd put on over the winter, thinning hair going gray and a bit disheveled, and salt-and-pepper stubble.

"Just a quickie to at least make the evening tolerable?" Henry asked hopefully. "We can share the occasional secretive glance during dinner, knowing that just a few hours before I'd ravaged you."

Rose freed herself from his grasp and pushed him away. "Henry, maybe later but now we're going to be late," she said, smoothing out her dress. "Would you please quit belly-aching and get in the shower?"

It was Henry's turn to pay for dinner, and Victor had of course picked Chez Paul, the hot new Chicago north side restaurant taking reservations a year in advance. Victor's investment banking firm, Fitzgerald, Black & Partners had a standing reservation, so getting in was only a problem for the *commoners* as Victor liked to say.

Chez Paul was surprisingly small, very crowded, and decorated in an austere, French bistro style that belied its popularity and the recent bestowment of a coveted Michelin star. Paul, a short, swarthy, harried-looking man was barking orders at the waitstaff when he saw them waiting to be seated. He hurried over. "Ah, mesdames et messieurs, bonsoir," he said, shaking hands with Victor and air kissing Suzanne on both cheeks.

Paul openly appraised Rose with a hungry look that Henry guessed some women might find flattering but knew Rose, equipped with one of the world's great bullshit detectors, wasn't buying into. Victor asked a question in French and Paul, clearly pleased, responded in kind. Henry didn't speak French, but he imagined how the conversation was playing out:

Paul: *"Is this the douchebag you were talking about, the one you're sticking with the tab?"*

Victor: *"Yeah, Paul, I don't want him walking out of here spending less than two grand. He can't tell the difference between a '58 Margaux and a Mad Dog 2020, so have the sommelier pick out something good, but really overpriced."*

Paul: *"You got it, you old sumbitch."*

Henry had limited experience with the very rich, but he'd found they generally fell into one of two categories: either they never mentioned money, or they could seem to talk of nothing else. Victor of course fell into the second category. His theme tonight seemed to be how best to cash in on global warming, and how his firm was making big bets on companies profiting from drought, pestilence, famine, tsunamis, and the other *opportunities.* "What difference does it make, Henry," Victor said at one point, shrugging off Henry's opposition, "we'll all be gone by the time the ocean swallows up Florida."

While Victor alternately held court and oversaw the serving of one of Chez Paul's legendary full 21-course dinners—"Don't worry, Henry," Victor winked, "it's prixe fixe, only gonna set you back about a month's pay."—Henry let his mind wander.

He had to admit Victor and Suzanne made a striking couple. As an undrafted free agent out of Princeton, Victor had made the Chicago Bears as a back-up tight end before the inevitable ACL injury ended his career after just a few years. But there had been no shortage of well-healed Bears fans willing to roll the dice on a neophyte investment banker with ivy league and professional football player pedigrees. Now in his mid-50s, Victor had thickened a bit but still carried himself with the casual swagger of a man supremely confident in his physicality. Even his trademark hair still looked great, Henry thought, a full, tawny blond mane with just a hint of gray swept back and worn just long enough to suggest the man might be a bit of a pirate. Suzanne, by contrast, was petite but with a voluptuous, Rubenesque figure that gave both men and women pause the first time they saw her.

After an hour or so, there was a brief interlude between the caramelized quail, seared duck foie gras, and a second bottle of Chateau Margaux, when even Victor was forced to push his chair back and loosen his belt another notch.

"By the way, Henry, sorry to hear about Shield," Victor said. "We made a bet on you guys, but the news on the street isn't good, so we might have to pull out."

Victor was of course fishing and a question seemed to hang in the air. Henry looked around the room and, emboldened by the wine, leaned in toward Victor and Suzanne, lowering his voice conspiratorially. "We've got something much better than Shield in the pipeline, but it's top secret and if word leaks out, I'm a dead man."

"C'mon, Henry, I didn't get to where I am in this industry without being discrete," Victor said. He reached over and filled Henry's glass with yet another healthy dose of the Margaux, like the head of the Gestapo administering a powerful truth serum to an important member of the underground whose resistance is fast weakening.

"Well, we're early in the game, but this drug is a game changer," Henry whispered earnestly.

"Interesting," Victor said, glancing over at Suzanne. "Go on."

"We call it Maximus," Henry said. "For obvious reasons. Imagine the market potential of one pill that does it all: lowering cholesterol, raising testosterone, solving ED, and, well, producing more pleasurable results." He winked at Suzanne. "We've got secret labs in India where we're testing Maximus on rhesus monkeys and the results have been spectacular. These monkeys are living twice as long and screwing like teenagers on prom night."

"Henry!" Rose whispered, furiously. "Keep your voice down!"

"Good God, Henry," Victor said, interest obviously piqued. "It's like the pharmaceutical Holy Grail. Someone could make a killing on it."

"We've only got one problem," Henry said suddenly.

"What?" Victor asked, a hint of concern creeping into his voice.

"Miniaturization."

"Huh?"

"Yeah, right now in order to get all the results you'd have to find a way to ingest a pill about as big as this loaf of bread." Henry held up the large baguette they'd been served.

Victor and Suzanne stared at Henry for a moment and then Victor forced a laugh. Henry caught Rose's withering look out of the corner of his eye and he knew there'd be hell to pay later, but it had been fun to nudge Victor and Suzanne off their high horse, if just for a few minutes.

The payback came an hour or so later, just after they'd finished dessert and a bottle of the 40-year-old tawny port that Victor favored. When the check arrived, Victor pointedly slid it Henry's way. Henry nonchalantly glanced at it, set it down, waited a beat, and then excused himself. Fortunately, no one was in the men's room as he fumbled for his wallet and cell phone to call the 800 number of his last functioning credit card to check his balance. The friendly, automated voice expressed not the least bit of concern that Henry had an available balance of $862.00—not even close to the $1,855.00 he'd need to cover dinner.

Henry returned to the table. Options ran through his mind. Lost wallet? Mugged in the men's room? Feign a sudden grand mal seizure? But the check was gone and the three of them were already standing and he could tell by Rose's embarrassed expression that Victor must have taken care of the bill.

"Victor, I got this, my turn," Henry started to say, but Victor smiled and lazily waved a hand as if to dissipate any lingering unpleasantness.

"No worries, Henry, just keep us posted on Maximus and all is forgiven."

He put a big arm around Henry and gave him a hug, pulling him close. He whispered in Henry's ear. "Someday, and that day may never come, I'll want a favor."

Outside the valet pulled up with Victor's car first, a brand-new white Bentley Flying Spur. Victor saw the look on Henry's face. "Yeah, a bit over the top but with the bulls running my year-end bonus was pretty healthy."

"Yeah, mine too," Henry replied.

"Jelly of the Month Club membership?" Suzanne asked innocently.

Just then, the other valet pulled up in Henry's car, a battered forest green 2005 Dodge Town & Country. He took the five dollars Henry handed him with a look of disdain and, having evidently been on the losing end of a bet, handed it to the other valet.

It was one of the few times in their marriage that she had asked for the car keys. Henry meekly complied, put the passenger seat back and feigned sleep.

Rose glanced over at him. "You were certainly in rare form tonight. Code Name Maximus? What the hell, Henry, Suzanne is my dearest friend. I can't take you anywhere without you making some kind of scene. What's gotten into you anyway these days?"

Henry chuckled. "Well, you certainly got me back. It feels like someone took a nightstick to my shins," he said. "But I think your aim was a little off, thank God."

She suddenly reached over and gently grasped his hand. "Henry, go out tomorrow and get some Powerball tickets. I've got a feeling."

Henry groaned. "God, Rose, don't tell me you've got the fever too? You know the odds—we could buy one ticket a day for a million years and still have only a 50-50 chance of winning. With the way our luck's been running these last few years? There's not a chance in hell."

But Rose wasn't listening. "Imagine what we'd do with the money, Henry. How our lives would change. Oh Henry, I so want to be rich."

Henry looked over at her. Something in her voice was different, and there was a strange, far-away look in her face now. "Just think of it," she said, excitedly. "The freedom to travel anywhere in the world at a moment's notice, the ability to buy whatever your heart desires. Dream big Henry, we're now worth a fortune! Go for it. The world's your oyster. What would you wish for?"

"Hmm, you know, I've always wanted a pony," he said.

"Don't be a horse's ass, Henry."

"Okay, I guess a yacht would be nice," he said, yawning. "An adventure or two. Seats on the ice at United Center. What about you?"

"Well, first we'd do the right thing, of course," she mused, happily. "Set up a charitable trust, college funds for all our nieces and nephews, maybe a million each to my brother and—"

Henry snorted. "Over my dead body, Rose, your brother's not getting—"

"Oh relax, Henry," she said, impatiently. "Then, maybe a lakefront mansion in Lake Forest, a little *pied-a-terre* on the left bank in Paris, someplace south on the ocean for the winters. A private jet." She giggled. "Hmmm. Jewelry of course, nothing too decadent. A box at the Lyric Opera."

There was no response. "Henry?"

Henry had begun to snore softly. Rose shook her head.

"And, most importantly, romance!" she whispered.

A Disturbance in the Force

"Die, motherfuckers, die!"

The blood-curdling scream seemed to come from the lower level. Henry leaped from his easy chair, scattering the Sunday *Chicago Tribune,* and ran to the staircase.

"Zach is that you?" he yelled. He began running down the stairs. "What the hell's going on down here?"

Zach lay sprawled on the couch in the rec room in nothing but his boxer shorts, fingers dancing madly across the keyboard in his lap. Henry could see an army of zombies advancing toward Zach's heavily-armed avatar on the big computer monitor in front of him, and he was blowing off arms and heads and legs with an assortment of small arms and rocket fire.

"Have you tried negotiating with them instead?" Henry joked.

"Dad, you can't negotiate with the undead, you know that from all your years working for corporate America," Zach scoffed.

Henry stood for a moment behind the couch watching his son. Like Bradbury's *Illustrated Man,* new tattoos seemed to sprout across Zach's powerful torso and arms almost weekly. *Ah, there's a new one,* Henry thought, a skeletal hand holding up playing cards—a royal flush in spades splayed out across the back of Zach's right deltoid. Henry had to admit it was artfully done and fit nicely between what looked like a Viking wielding a battle axe and a hand grenade with the pin hanging precariously from it. Henry smiled. He couldn't explain the fascination this generation had for tattoos and piercings, but Henry was something of a non-conformist at heart and secretly endorsed Zach's many eccentricities.

Rose on the other hand was, as Zach liked to say, a real *ball buster*. Zach's long and costly college tenure, checkered work history, and most recently, playing no-limit Texas hold 'em online around the clock had been the source of continuous friction between Henry and Rose. "But you can't argue with the results," Henry had reasoned a few days previously with the arrival of a DHL package containing Zach's most recent tournament winnings.

"Good lord, Henry, eight years of college tuition, three degrees, two wrecked cars, and enough student loans to build a wing on the science building, and all you can say is, the results are promising?" Rose had responded, pointing at Zach who was rifling through the refrigerator looking for leftovers.

"With a better education than Einstein and a higher IQ, he's living in our basement playing poker all night, weight-lifting all day, and eating us out of house and home! Oh, what's the use?" She stormed out, leaving Henry and Zach doing their best to stifle laughs.

But Henry had to admit Rose did have a point. Zach was beginning to resemble the cuckoo bird that steadily outgrows its adoptive but loving parents until they're finally forced to abandon the nest.

"So, I take it from the new tattoo that the poker's going well?" Henry asked, as Zach exited out of the game.

Zach laughed. "Dad, it was so sick." He leaned back on the couch. "I'm at the final table and the only thing standing between me and winning $10k is that Russian SOB Boris."

"Boris?"

"Yeah, a real Russian mobster. He and I are always going mano a mano," Zach said. "Anyway, I've got ace 10 of spades pre-flop, so I check looking to trap. Naturally, Boris raises big. I re-raise, Boris calls, so game on."

"I have no idea what you're talking about, but sounds exciting, go on."

"This is where it gets good." Zach rubbed his hands together. "The flop comes king jack of spades and king of diamonds. I bet a standard half the pot, Boris raises and next thing you know we're both all in. The turn comes king of hearts and then boom! I river Boris with the queen of spades!"

Henry shook his head. "Huh?"

Zach looked at him with disbelief. "C'mon, Dad, between delivering pizzas and chasing Mom around campus didn't you ever play poker in college? I caught a royal flush on the last card. Boris swears revenge in the chat box. 'Spend it quickly. I find you. Pull out fingernails one by one. Then skin alive.'"

Henry smiled at Zach's Russian accent. "Well, don't tell Mom. She'll insist that you start paying rent. Given your recent windfall, maybe it's time?"

Zach yawned and closed his eyes. "Dad, throw that blanket over me will you, I've got a big tournament in a few hours and I'm seriously behind on my REM sleep."

"On another topic—are you coming with Mom and me to your Uncle Larry's 60th birthday party today?"

"That tool? Not a chance."

If ever there was a poster boy for the state of Illinois' catastrophic financial condition, Rose's older brother Larry Flynn was it, Henry thought, as they pulled up in front of Larry and Liz's brick colonial in Deerfield, a rung or two higher up the suburban ladder than the modest Glenview split-level Henry and Rose lived in. Henry had feigned a sudden bout of food poisoning earlier that afternoon, but the look on Rose's face had made it clear that any hope of appeal was clearly out of the question after his performance at dinner the night before.

It was an open family secret that Henry and Larry despised each other. Henry was like a highwire walker who had spent years balancing precariously over the private sector abyss, the mirage of security and a massive payday shimmering just beyond his out-stretched hands. Larry, a Northbrook school district administrator, had plodded along on much safer career ground and been richly rewarded with an early retirement and fat state pension.

Rubbing salt even deeper into the wound was Larry's recent election as president of the Illinois Federation of Retired Teachers. He'd given a surprisingly fiery acceptance speech, vowing the state would have to pry the retirees' mandatory cost of living raises and healthcare perks out of his cold, lifeless hands. His YouTube video, seen by millions, had even made him a bit of a progressive cause célèbre.

To no one's surprise, their casual sparring had become even more heated in recent years, particularly after Larry and Liz had bought a second home in a Florida retirement community called The Enclave. Meanwhile, Henry and Rose were still digging out from under the rubble of a disastrous few years when, between jobs, Henry had finally scratched his entrepreneurial itch and hung out his shingle. He'd built a small, loyal clientele for H. Ball Accounting, but wasn't able to temper his dreamy ambition with the single-minded ruthlessness that characterizes the successful entrepreneur. Slowly, inexorably, H. Ball Accounting, like some giant anaconda, had quietly squeezed the life out of Henry's dreams and what was left of their savings.

"Rose, do you realize that Larry and his gang of moochers stole an extra $7,400 from us last year?" Harry said suddenly, and he could feel the anger rising. "So, tell me again—why are we here helping celebrate his 60th birthday?"

Rose looked at him appraisingly. When Rose went this quiet, Henry knew to be careful. There was even now the dangerous half-smile on her face that he'd seen only a handful of times before, but he couldn't help himself.

"This is the man that now spends six months and one day in Florida every year to avoid the 67 percent increase in Illinois state income taxes that he personally helped engineer." Henry's voice rose. "So, while you and I were slaving like stevedores this past winter, Larry and Liz were leading the conga line of all the other Illinois early retirees now living down at The Enclave off the sweat of our labor!"

As Henry's voice reached a crescendo Rose's left arm shot out and she grabbed him hard by the earlobe. Rose's natural athleticism and ten years of twice-weekly training with Suzanne in Krav Maga, a little-known but highly effective Israeli self-defense system, now paid off handsomely. As Henry reached up to try to dislodge Rose's grip, she grabbed his hand and twisted it with one of Krav Maga's many submission holds, designed to subdue even much larger adversaries. As Henry cried out in pain Rose swung a leg over and pulled herself into a straddling position over Henry, and their faces were now inches apart. It had all taken under five seconds.

"Rose, what the fuck?" Henry gasped in pain, a look of shock and fear evident. He winced as Rose twisted his wrist even harder for emphasis.

"Henry," Rose said quietly. She released her grip suddenly and now took his face in both hands. She had never before laid a hand on him, and now they both seemed to appreciate the gravity of the situation. "I hope to God the wonderful man I fell in love with all those years ago is still somewhere inside, because all I see of late is this imposter. What is happening to you?"

"I'm beaten down, Rosie." He reached up and wrapped his arms around her. "Financially, emotionally. This isn't how we envisioned it would be at this point in our lives is it? I thought we'd be well off by now."

"Spending our winters in the south of France?" Rose smiled sadly. She kissed his forehead. "Oh, Henry, you always were a dreamer."

"What are you looking at?" Liz said, as she came up behind Larry, who was leaning just far enough to look around the living room picture window curtain.

"It's Rose and Henry," he said. "They've been sitting out there for ten minutes. There's something going on, but the windows have steamed up. PharmaSolutions probably fired his ass, with their stock plummeting. Rose could have married so much better."

After the usual forced pleasantries, Henry had done his best to placate Rose by avoiding Larry. There were enough of Larry's and Liz's friends, former colleagues, and neighbors in attendance for Henry to blend in and strike up a conversation here and there, flirt innocently with a pleasant-looking blonde, and talk about the Bears' previous woeful season with the Deerfield High football coach. Once or twice he felt like he was being watched, and he turned to find Rose looking at him, signaling with a playful hand gesture that her eyes were on him. Henry smiled but he had the uneasy feeling that after their fight earlier, the balance of power had somehow shifted in their relationship.

On Henry's fourth trip to the beer cooler sitting out on the sun porch, as he dug down through the ice and a largely-depleted stock of generic soda pop and off-brand domestic beer—the cheap bastard—Henry felt the hair rise on the back of his neck. The tap on his shoulder confirmed Larry had finally seized the opportunity to corner him. Larry extended a hand. Henry pretended not to notice.

"Henry, thanks for coming," Larry said. "I was hoping we'd have a chance to talk. I feel horrible, just horrible, about what's happening at PharmaSolutions. To think that this was going to finally be that big payday you've been working so hard for all these years. That really sucks. Maybe it will all work out?"

Henry straightened and opened a beer. He'd guessed that Larry would lead with something about PharmaSolutions. Schadenfreude practically oozed from Larry's pores, and it seemed to Henry that Larry had always taken special pleasure from the many career misfortunes that had befallen him, as if a testament to the inherent inferiority of the private sector.

Henry gave a furtive glance in both directions, put his arm around Larry's shoulders, and drew him closer. "Well, Larry, thanks for your concern, but no worries. I got in on the ground floor of something that will make penicillin or the cure for polio seem like Absorbine Jr. by comparison," he whispered. "Can't say too much about it yet—but we call it Maximus. Suffice to say that once we get you on Maximus, Liz will be happier than she's been in years."

Henry felt something jab him firmly in the middle of his back. Rose stood behind him, a stern look on her face, holding their coats. "Time to go, already?" Henry said innocently. He turned to Larry, who now looked a bit crestfallen. "Thanks Larry, and happy 60th. I'll get you a sample." Henry gave him an exaggerated wink.

They reached the front door. Larry kissed Rose on the cheek. As a demonstration to Rose of his new-found magnanimity Henry extended a hand, bracing himself for Larry's typically limp and clammy handshake. "Great party, thanks again, Larry," he said, sounding jovial but with just a hint of over-the-top bonhomie that he knew would have Larry wondering about his sincerity later.

A sudden thought crossed his mind. "Got your Powerball ticket yet? You never know." He glanced back at Rose. "If either of us win, let's agree to give the other $5 million, deal? Drop in the bucket, but a great way to increase our odds."

Larry smiled blandly. "Yes, Henry, I've got a ticket, who doesn't? Sure, happy to give my little sister $5 million if we win. Thanks again for coming. Drive careful." He waved as Henry and Rose walked toward their van, then closed the door with a bang.

"What was that all about?" Rose asked, as they got in the van.

"Not sure," Henry said. "It was weird. I had a feeling out of the clear blue that Larry was suddenly, and in the not-too-distant future, going to come into a lot of money. Just hedging our bets. Maybe Larry will pay us for a change, rather than the other way around. Oops, sorry, old habits die hard." He held up a hand in defense.

Rose patted him on the arm. "You two seemed to be getting on fine. Thanks for trying. Don't worry, Henry, I'm not going to rough you up—at least not right now."

Henry managed to force a mirthless laugh, hopefully sufficient enough to cover the growing sense of anger he felt over his recent emasculation. Rose seemed not to notice. He put the car into drive and pulled away from the curb.

In Flagrante Delicto

The first time Suzanne had caught Victor in the act, it had cost him a flawless 15-carat, antique brilliant emerald-cut diamond.

Suzanne upped the ante when she caught him a second time. In exchange for another 'Get Out of Jail Free' card, Victor was only too happy to write her a check to launch Maasai, Chicago's hot new Africa-themed boutique located at ground zero on Chicago's Magnificent Mile.

When Maasai had thrown open its doors to great fanfare just months before, no one had seen anything like it and there had been the usual naysayers. But Suzanne's instincts and timing had proven prescient: authentic African art, jewelry, clothing, and furnishings produced by talented but impoverished third world artisans were suddenly très chic—and checked off a 'global social justice' box for her recently woke clientele.

"Spoils of war," Suzanne said happily, as she linked arms with Rose and guided her through the boutique, still crowded with shoppers. They weaved through the lush, tropical décor. The pungent smells of tropical flowers, wet earth and, improbably, campfire, filled the air, and a deep rhythmic tribal music pulsed in the background.

Suzanne stopped suddenly to reach up and adjust the bright red shuka cloth that barely covered a strapping young man dressed as a Maasai warrior standing en garde next to a display of what Rose presumed was authentic Maasai jewelry. Beautiful, Rose thought as she leaned down to look at an exquisite, beaded necklace. But that was odd, no price tags. "This is nice, Suzanne, how much?"

"Come on Rosie, if you have to ask you can't afford it, and anyway the best things in life are free." Suzanne turned and winked at the Maasai, who smiled broadly in return.

"Recognize him?" Suzanne asked, as she linked arms with Rose, and they resumed walking. "Dominique Jones. He plays forward for the DePaul Blue Devils. Almost all my Maasai are college athletes. I pay them well and they get a little taste of 'the life' as they like to say. Don't tell anyone, but I hear one of my Maasai has been seeing a lot of that hoity toity bitch Veronica Miles. They're never seen together in public of course. Not surprising. I doubt her husband Ned's had a hard-on since the Reagan administration."

Rose felt a bit apprehensive as they walked up to Maasai's lounge and coffee bar, set up to resemble a luxury safari camp under a large canopy and complete with folding camp chairs, tables, and even a vintage Land Rover. Rose was the most recent addition to Suzanne's monthly book club, and tonight she would be leading the discussion for the first time on the novel she'd recommended: Fitzgerald's *The Great Gatsby*.

Of course, based on past experience, Rose knew she had little to worry about. Discussion about even a literary classic like *Gatsby* would likely be cursory at best and the evening, fueled by a surprising amount of alcohol, would quickly progress in stages: raucous banter, gossip, accusations and the opening of old wounds, and finally, tears.

Still, Suzanne had insisted that Rose join if, for nothing else, "To get you out of that little house and away from that man!"

And Suzanne had been right; Rose did enjoy these rare evenings out, perhaps more than she cared to admit. She had little if anything in common with Suzanne's coterie of friends: a local news anchor, several of Victor's partners' wives (no trophy wives allowed, however), and an assorted mix of six or seven other prominent members of the upper tier of Chicago society. They all shared the perfectly coiffed, lightly tanned, heavily jeweled uniform that instantly identified them as 'one of us' in all of the wealthy's far-flung enclaves.

There had been a few quizzical, 'look what the cat dragged in' glances and raised eyebrows that first evening when Suzanne had introduced Rose as her oldest and best friend. Rose, in an act of defiance, had actually dressed down for the occasion, wearing old Levi's, biker boots, and a Chicago Cubs 2016 World Champions hoodie. The women sized her up and, with her appearance discounting any potential threat, took her in almost as a novelty.

A bar had been set up and several of the Maasai were serving drinks and hors d'oeuvres. Dinner was to be catered in shortly. The women gradually gathered at the big camp table, pulled their folding chairs up to the table, and the discussion began.

"Let's begin with our initial thoughts about what is widely regarded as one of our greatest American novels," Rose began. "Who would like to start?"

There was silence. Rose looked around. A few of the women glanced at one another. One appeared to be stifling a laugh, and Rose caught another rolling her eyes. Finally, Gloria, one of the partners' wives raised her hand.

"Yes, Gloria, what did you think? What did you like best about Fitzgerald's masterpiece?" Rose asked, relieved that the ice had finally been broken.

"Well, you know how they say the book is always better than the movie," Gloria said. "In this case, I thought the movie was actually better than the book."

"Which version, DiCaprio or Redford?" someone asked.

"Both!" Gloria, replied.

Then the gloves came off.

"Oh my God, what a stinker. Nothing ever happens!"

"At least Gatsby gets it in the end. What a loser!"

"Daisy never would have dumped Tom for Gatsby. Totally unreal."

"I was forced to read it in high school. Why would I want to put myself through all that again?"

"And worst of all—no sex!" Suzanne shouted after a few minutes of withering critiques. "C'mon ladies, dinner's here," and she draped her arm around Rose's shoulders.

"Don't worry about it, Rosie," she whispered in Rose's ear. "Remember what Nick tells Gatsby near the end: *You're worth the whole damn bunch put together!*" She kissed Rose on the cheek.

Among this group Rose was considered almost a teetotaler, but she proceeded to get about as drunk as she ever had outside of a college party or two. This rare debauchery went largely unremarked by the others until Rose, late in the evening and out of nowhere yelled, "Fuck it!" and leaped off a table onto the back of one of the towering Maasai.

Suzanne gently talked her down, but nothing breaks up a party of socialites like a sudden lack of decorum.

"Love shack is a little old place where we can get together." They sang the old B-52s' song in unison as they stumbled out of Suzanne's limousine.

Suzanne, with some difficulty, steered Rose toward the entrance of 999 North Lake Shore Drive, where James the doorman held the door open for them. "Evening, Mrs. Black, can I be of any assistance?" he asked casually, too well-trained to show even the slightest surprise at the sight of the two obviously very drunk women.

With James' help they made it to the private elevator that took them to the Blacks' penthouse. The elevator opened in the foyer of the penthouse, and Suzanne walked Rose to the vast living room with its floor-to-ceiling wall of glass and 180-degree panorama of the Chicago lakefront 25 stories below. Light traffic snaked along Lake Shore Drive, and over the lake six or seven inbound airliners were descending on their final approach to O'Hare to the west.

"Kinda like my place!" Rose said as she curled up on the couch. "Shitty view, though. Rosie wants more wine!"

Steely Dan began playing in the background. Suzanne brought a bottle of wine and glasses. *Kick off your high heel sneakers it's party time. The girls don't seem to care . . .*

She sat next to Rose, poured two glasses, handed one to Rose, and proposed a toast: "To men. Can't live with em."

"Can't kill em!"

"But if you could?" Suzanne asked, leaving the question open.

Rose lay her head on Suzanne's shoulder. "What am I going to do, Suzy? I'm so tired of it all."

"Dear, dear Rosie," Suzanne said. "Look, you're young enough to make a new start. Still beautiful, smart. I know a dozen eligible men—rich, single, a few that won't be around much longer. Isn't it time?"

"Huh? For what?" Rose muttered, sleepily.

"Rose, Henry's a . . ."

"Loser?"

"Not exactly, more like a liability," Suzanne said, stroking Rose's hair. "You deserve better. You know it, I know it—hell, the American people know it!"

Rose turned suddenly to Suzanne. There were tears in her eyes. "I'm going to leave him, Suzy. Got to. He'll be all right. Long as he's got cable TV. And beer. He'll land on his feet. I want to live. See the world. Get wined and dined. Before it's too late." She began sobbing.

Suzanne gently took the wine glass out of her hand and helped Rose stretch out on the couch. She slipped her shoes off and laid a throw over her. "You're doing the right thing, you'll see, baby," Suzanne whispered, as "Deacon Blues" played softly in the background.

Reversal of Fortune

"Fuck!"

The Town & Country's low fuel light and warning ping had ceased functioning years ago and the fuel-starved van sputtered and lurched. He doubted he could milk the last few miles home out of what little gas was left. Fortunately, there was a Kwik Pump convenience store that sold gas just ahead on Waukegan Road and he coasted to a stop right next to a pump just as his engine died. Henry shook his head and let out a loud, maniacal, cackling laugh that had a touch of desperation to it. "Yee hah!" he yelled as he got out of the van. The woman at the pump next to his hurriedly got in her car, started the engine, and drove off.

"That's right lady, I'm one crazy fucker." Henry pantomimed giving her the moon when he saw she was looking back at him in her rearview mirror.

He opened his wallet. He didn't trust any of his credit cards, and he was down to his last $20 after stopping at a roadside tavern earlier for a burger and a few beers. Rather than risk being considered stingy, he'd over-tipped a pretty but disinterested waitress who barely acknowledged his largesse. The pump indicated that cash

30

payments had to be made in advance, so he went inside to pay with what little cash he had left.

"What the hell!" Henry said loudly, as he took his place in a surprisingly long line of ten or so people. "Like lemmings lining up at the cliff!"

The line ignored him. There seemed to be something going on of great interest at the front counter, because everyone was peering around the person in front of him or her to get a better look. Henry resigned himself to the wait, and his mind drifted back over the events of one of the worst days in recent memory.

He'd been poring over a spreadsheet trying to reconcile marketing's forecasting with the sobering realities of PharmaSolutions' actual sales when he heard a soft knock on his open office door. He looked up and Samantha Tarleton stood leaning against the door frame, with that suggestive look that she played to such great effect.

Henry leaned back in his chair. "Well, well, well—Sam Tarleton!" he said with mock enthusiasm. "To what do I owe the pleasure?"

"Good morning Henry, may I come in?" she said, her British accent making the request sound at once both formal and sexy.

He silently studied her for a moment, hoping that his face had just enough of a look of disdain to register his hurt feelings, but not enough to send her packing.

"Oh, come now Henry, don't let's make this so difficult, shall we?" she said impatiently after an uncomfortable pause, seemingly prepared now to call his bluff. "If you can't be civilized." She turned to walk away.

"Here, make yourself at home, mi casa es tu casa," Henry said, realizing the game was up and wanting her to stay. Visitors to his small, windowless office were increasingly rare, so he got up and cleared off a chair stacked with file folders. She sat, and now he caught the faint fragrance that he always identified with her. What was it? Oh yes, Bal d'Afrique she had called it. African dance? Exotic, expensive, picked it up at Harrod's in London last summer.

Reminded her of her time at St. Anne's College at Oxford, and somebody named Clive, she'd laughed, over drinks.

There had been a lot of late nights for Henry and his team in the finance department during the heady days the previous year when PharmaSolutions was the hot new kid on the pharmacological block, with seemingly one promising new product after the other in the development pipeline. Henry, then the finance department's senior CPA, would often join his coworkers for drinks after work—absolutely vital to teambuilding and stress-reduction, he'd explain to Rose after rolling in well after midnight once or twice a week. More often than not, Henry and Samantha were the last to leave.

"There's no easy way to say this, Henry, but you're getting the sack this Friday. You and a few others. No one to blame. Usual belt tightening. Shield's got everyone running scared. I'm sorry, Henry, I wanted to be the one to tell you, for . . ." She hesitated, searching for the right words.

"Old time's sake?" Henry suggested, with a hint of sarcasm.

Samantha seemed not to notice. She glanced at her watch and stood abruptly. "I'll be late for another bloody meeting. Not like the old days, Henry. I do miss our times together. We had such fun."

Henry rose suddenly and came around from behind the desk. While the news hadn't exactly shocked him given PharmaSolutions' precarious financial position and the fact that he had clearly fallen out of favor with corporate, he felt a sense of panic now that he'd never experienced the five or six other times in his 30-year career that he'd been down-sized, right-sized, merged, or acquired out of a job. It went with the territory, he'd always reasoned. In the past, he'd known he would land on his feet. There was plenty of time and his career would stretch on for years and end in pleasant fashion somewhere over a distant horizon.

But that was before. Now the years had come and gone and he was, suddenly, at the age of 53, on the verge of obsolescence. Yes, he would still find something in finance but his career from this point forward would be in an ever-descending spiral of lesser jobs and smaller paychecks and then, finally, nothing.

He reached out suddenly and gently grasped her arm. It was all he could do not to throw himself at her feet. "Look, Sam, do you think I can buy some time, I mean a month or two so we can make this look better and I can arrange for a soft landing?" A note of desperation crept into his voice. "My finances are on life support right now and this couldn't come at a worse time. Maybe you could talk to Dex. Use your considerable charm. Make an appeal. He'll listen to you."

The expression on her face was that of a person who has mistakenly opened the door to the wrong room at a hotel and seen something repulsive. It confirmed what Henry guessed she was thinking: what kind of man would ask a woman to grovel to another man on his behalf? He let go of her arm. She brushed her sleeve as if to remove an unpleasant residue and gave Henry a final appraising glance over her shoulder as she walked out the door.

There was one customer in line in front of him now, an elderly woman who asked for a pack of Virginia Slims, a pint of Canadian Club, and a Powerball ticket.

"With about a minute to spare," the woman behind the counter said, pointing at the clock showing a few minutes to nine.

"Oh, good night, left my wallet in the car!" the lady said as she rifled through her purse. "I'll be right back." She turned, brushed past Henry, and scurried out the door.

Henry stepped up. "Pump three," he said, and put his last $20 bill on the counter.

"Thirty seconds to nine," the woman said suggestively, as she took Henry's $20. "Got time to sell one more Powerball. It's been crazy!"

"You getting a commission? Oh, what the hell, give me one," Henry said. "After gas, that leaves me with exactly zero dollars to my name. A fitting conclusion to yet another red-letter day for the Ball family."

He could hear the machine outputting his ticket. She slid the ticket across the counter. "This could be the one. Good luck, fella."

Henry put the ticket in his empty wallet. "Luck? You know the old line, if it wasn't for bad luck, I'd have no luck at all."

Fate Takes a Hand

He'd read somewhere that most suicides were preceded by a sleep-less night.

Henry sat at the small table in their breakfast nook in an old pair of boxers and T-shirt, staring out at a dreary gray morning. A weatherman cheerfully predicted rain for the rest of the day from the small TV on the kitchen counter. Rose had stayed downtown the night before for her book club, and now Henry sat alone, run-ning through his few options.

Gunshot to the head had some appeal: fast, painless, and usually foolproof. But he didn't, unfortunately, own a pistol.

Next.

Slit wrists? Yes, easy enough to do but very messy, and there was the chance that Zach, against all odds, might wake before noon to raid the refrigerator and find Henry still alive and call an ambulance.

Or, just run. Start fresh, somewhere warm. Live on a boat. Rob a grocery store or two, maybe a bank branch in some small town, steal a car, and drive to Mexico. Slip across the border, hitch-hike down the coast, join the other expats sure to be hiding out in some sleepy Mexican coastal village.

Start a new life.

Right.

Henry rubbed his eyes. He knew he didn't have the will, or the energy, to run. So, it was suicide. The only honorable thing to do. Oddly enough, the thought didn't particularly frighten him. All right then. How about car exhaust in the garage? You just went to sleep. And the end was just ambiguous enough. The party line might be that Henry had had a heart attack or stroke while getting ready to leave for work. He'd have to get dressed, find his keys. Hopefully he had enough gas in the tank.

And Rose? She'd be fine. Better, in fact. Tough, resourceful Rosie. They were right: she could have married so much better. He felt a sudden sharp pang in his belly. Should he at least leave a note? He would have a hard time coming up with anything more than a simple, "I fucked up."

"The hell with it," Henry said, and he rose from the table.

In the background the local weather had segued into the *Today Show*, and the perky talking heads ran through the top stories of the day. Now they handed it off to a reporter doing a remote from . . .the Kwik Pump on Waukegan Road?

Henry stared at the TV. "That's right, Laura, I'm here with Kanwar Singh, owner of this Glenview, Illinois Kwik Pump where the single winning Powerball ticket worth a record $1.1 billion was reportedly sold," the reporter said. "Kanwar, how does it feel to be part of history—and the recipient of a cool $10 million for yourself?"

A small crowd of excited Kwik Pump employees and customers had gathered around, high fiving, slapping Kanwar on the back, hugging the reporter and letting out yells. "Only in America!" Kanwar yelled. "Land of opportunity. I'm so happy for us!"

"There you have it, Laura, as Kanwar says, only in America!"

"Let's put that winning number up again," Laura said, as they cut back to the *Today Show* studio. "Somewhere out there, a newly-minted billionaire has the winning ticket with 5, 8, 21, 29, 37, and the lucky Powerball number 6. Can you imagine what that winner must be feeling this morning?" Laura asked her coanchor.

A commercial came on. Henry grasped the edge of the kitchen table. His legs had begun to shake and sweat dripped down his sides. He had glanced only once at the Powerball ticket before stashing it in his wallet the night before, but there was something vaguely familiar in that set of numbers.

He found his wallet and smart phone and returned to the kitchen. "Thank God!" he said, as he removed the Powerball ticket and slapped it face down on the kitchen table. He searched for *Powerball, winning number* on his phone and found a site where the winning sequence was shown. 5, 8, 21, 29, 37, and the lucky Powerball number 6.

He took a deep breath. "Oh God!"

He flipped the ticket over and covered the row of numbers with his hand. His heart was pounding, and he'd begun to hyperventilate. "Jesus, Mary, and Joseph," he yelled, and he slowly slid his thumb to the right and the first number came into view: a five!

"Oh Lord, please don't toy with me!" he wailed. Now he moved his thumb still further to the right. "Shit! A six? No, it's an eight!"

Henry closed his eyes. He knew now that he was dreaming. He would open his eyes and he would be in bed, rain beating against the window, the start of another bleak gray day.

What the hell. He opened his eyes. The ticket was still there. It had begun to rain more steadily. In the background the *Today Show* anchor was fawning over a hot young movie star promoting her new film. Henry took a deep breath and cringed, like a man playing Russian roulette about to squeeze the trigger and slid his thumb off the next number: 21.

He exhaled. He knew with mathematical certainty now that two of the same tickets with the same first three numbers from the winning ticket could not have been sold at the same store. He was like some cosmic safecracker that has worked on a lock for years and finally, with an ear pressed up to the cold steel of the safe, hears the last tumbler fall into place. Now all he has to do is push the heavy door open and step into a completely new life of vast wealth and adventure and travel by private jets and parties on yachts and making love to beautiful women and, most prized of all, box seat season's tickets at Wrigley Field.

Still, Henry hesitated. He wanted to savor the moment but his natural default emotions after so many years of being kicked when down were fear and doubt, and while the math said he had the winning ticket, fate could still take a hand and he knew from long personal experience that she didn't play fair. A low, guttural, primal sound originating deep in Henry's gut became more audible and built to a crescendo and an almost incoherent FUCK IT! as Henry removed his hand from the ticket and revealed all the winning numbers: 5, 8, 21, 29, 37, and the lucky Powerball number 6.

Barry White? No, too cliché. Rose, with her bullshit detector these days set on maximum sensitivity, would almost certainly burst out laughing.

Elton John? Back in the day Rose had liked him but Henry thought the lyrics too melancholy for the occasion.

Opera? He wouldn't even know where to start.

Henry scrolled hurriedly through his library of music, looking to compose just the right playlist. He had a rueful smile on his face as he ran through the 300 or so songs he had at his disposal. Most were like old friends he'd known since college. His music tastes were simple and predictable at best, with classic rock making up the vast majority. Somehow AC/DC, Zeppelin, the Stones or even his all-time favorite—Rush—simply weren't going to cut it.

How about Sinatra? Maybe later, if all went well.

Sting? Perfect! Rose had had a thing for him back in college. The perfect blend of the sexy and cerebral, she used to say.

Henry knew Sting would conjure up a smile on Rose's face and perhaps bring back memories of that glorious, carefree summer in college when, rather than returning home, they'd both stayed in the small college town to build up credit hours and replenish bank accounts for the fall semester. Fortunately, he had three or four Sting and a few of The Police in his library. He connected his smart phone to the Bluetooth speaker that he'd bought earlier that day and got "Brand New Day" playing.

Then he surveyed the dining room table one final time. Martha Stewart he was not, Henry thought, but it would have to do. He'd laid out the little-used china set that dated back to their wedding, lit the new candelabra, filled a vase with 12 fresh long-stemmed red roses, then decanted a bottle of that outrageously expensive Petrus that Rose had seemed to like at one of their dinners with the Blacks. Even the clerk at Binny's Beverage Depot earlier that day had been impressed when Henry went through checkout with two of the Petrus. He'd laughed knowingly when Henry suggested that Petrus must mean *sucker* in some language.

Then he'd returned home and given the last $50 and change from the $822.00 that was all that had been in their checking account to Zach, telling him to make himself scarce for the evening. Zach had stashed the money into his pocket, winked at Henry, picked up Henry's car keys from the kitchen table, and left.

And as for dinner? Rose's favorite of course: Lou Malnati's world-famous Chicago deep dish pizza with everything on it, with delivery just a phone call away.

Henry glanced at his watch. *Where the hell was she?* He leaned over the couch and looked through the curtains. He saw headlights down at the end of the street, but the car didn't seem to be moving. He turned up the volume on the speaker a bit and began singing along with Sting. "Why don't we turn the clock to zero honey, I'll sell the stock we'll spend all the money we're starting up a brand new day . . . turn the clock all the way back I wonder if she'll take me back I'm thinking in a brand new way."

Rose sat in her car, parked along the curb a block away from home. She'd gotten to work about an hour late that morning, courtesy of Suzanne's limo. When she'd sprung up suddenly from a weekly staff meeting and made a hasty retreat to the ladies' room with the sudden onset of flu-like symptoms, it seemed to confirm her excuse for being late. Despite her impaired condition, she was still able to detect a subtle chill in the air. Even the usually solicitous Dr. Cohen was unusually curt the few times they'd come in contact. The signs seemed to confirm Rose's suspicions that big Jo had indeed made good on her promise and delivered an ultimatum to the doctors that evidently had not gone in Rose's favor.

That morning over a hasty breakfast, Suzanne, whose constitution was legendary, seemed even perkier than usual. As Rose, bleary-eyed from three hours' sleep, poked listlessly at her scrambled eggs, Suzanne sketched out the broad strokes of what could only be described as Operation Dump Henry. She had just the right attorney in mind: "Trust me, Rosie, if Henry puts up a fight, Nicky Sambruca will strip the flesh from his bones." And she offered to put Rose up at the Lake Shore Drive penthouse for as long as she needed to either land on her feet or hook a prospective new husband.

"After the usual mourning period of a month or two we'll put the word out and they'll be lined up from here to the lake," Suzanne had said, running down a list of the most eligible bachelors in the Blacks' vast social circle and their respective strengths and weaknesses.

"Hmm, Bernie Birnbaum, 70ish, richer than Croesus, wife passed away a year or two ago, keeps himself fit, no skeletons in the closet to speak of. Plays a lot of golf, so he won't be around much—perfect!"

Rose nodded assent, but the prospect of divorce and then almost immediately embarking on the kind of quasi-military campaign to find a new husband that Suzanne was describing was both overwhelming and depressing. While she appreciated Suzanne's zeal and knew her heart was in the right place, Rose had a much different future envisioned for at least the short-term post-Henry: a small, studio apartment lined with books; an acting class or two at the Steppenwolf; long walks along the lake; volunteering for some worthy cause; and, most importantly, travel.

At heart, Rose simply wasn't mercenary enough to engage in the ritualized mating dance of the type expected from a recently divorced, highly desirable, but seriously impoverished woman. Finding a man with deep pockets who could provide the financial means and security that Rose was so obviously in need of would make perfect sense. But what Rose desired above all else was to be swept off her feet and fall head over heels in love just one more time.

And Henry? Rose's decision that she wanted a divorce would come as a shock, but in time he'd realize it was best for both of them. In recent years they'd been almost like two desperate strangers wandering through a desolate, drought-stricken land, staying together only because it was safer than traveling alone. But the long-awaited rains hadn't come. Now it was obvious that their very survival required that they strike out in different directions. She started the car.

"What the hell?" Rose said, standing in the front doorway. Henry was dancing around the living room and singing along with Sting's "If You Love Somebody Set Them Free."

His dance moves had a herky-jerky quality reminiscent of *The Wizard of Oz's* Tin Man, but he made up for it now with manic energy. When he saw Rose standing there, he danced over and pulled her into his arms, swinging her around clumsily to the beat.

Mercifully, the song soon ended and Henry, a little out of breath and sweating, let Rose go. Rose staggered back a step or two. Henry held up a hand suddenly, evidently having just remembered something extremely important and dashed around the corner into the kitchen. She could hear Henry laughing and the refrigerator door open and then bang shut.

"Henry have you completely lost your marbles?" She looked around the room and noticed now how the dining room table was decorated.

"What is this? I know it's not our anniversary or my birthday, because you didn't forget. A promotion?" she asked, doubtfully.

Henry came out of the kitchen with two beers in his hands and handed one to Rose.

"Better than that, Rose, I'm getting fired on Friday," he said. "Cheers!" He clinked bottles with Rose.

"Oh, and by the way," he said. "We're billionaires."

Rose stared at Henry. "Fired?"

He saw the look on her face and took a step toward her.

40

"No!" Rose, said, shaking her head, and she held up her hands in defense. "I can't go through this again with you, Henry. Not this time."

And then the words began tumbling out, fast and almost incoherently. "We both need a fresh start, Henry, you'll see it's the best thing for both of us. We've grown apart, like a lot of couples. No one to blame. You're a good man, you'll find another woman, someone better suited to you. I'm leaving you Henry, now, before it's too late." She turned toward the still-open doorway, Henry lunged forward, caught her from behind, and held her tightly.

"Five, eight, 21, 29, 37 and the lucky number six," he whispered mysteriously into her ear.

"Huh?" Rose stopped struggling.

"We've won, Rosie, we won the Powerball, $1.1 billion and change," Henry whispered. "I've got the winning ticket!" He pulled the ticket out of his jeans pocket and held it in front of Rose's face.

Rose's legs suddenly went weak, and she began weeping, overcome with exhaustion and by a flood of conflicting emotions ranging from the pure joy of someone rescued from sure death in a burning building, to the deep shame stemming from her plans to leave Henry and what now seemed like treachery. Who knew what the gods had in store for them now, she wondered, her Irish fatalism so deeply ingrained that even happy news of this magnitude must surely be the harbinger of trouble ahead.

"This isn't going to be like the time you invested all of our life savings in that hydroponics tomato factory is it?" she asked, doubtfully. "Or that perpetual motion gizmo that your buddy said would make us all rich?"

Henry laughed and pulled her close, struggling a bit to hold her up. "This time we've made it, baby," he whispered. "We've come through the fire, stronger than ever. Nothing can touch us now."

Payback

High on the list of American male fantasies is taking the controls of an airliner with an incapacitated pilot and landing it safely. Higher still is winning the lottery and telling an abusive boss to, in the immortal words of Johnny Paycheck, take this job and shove it.

Henry arrived at work Friday morning at five a.m. after the third night in a row of sleepless, adrenaline-fueled euphoria. That first night he and Rose drank both bottles of the Petrus, the old bottle of Korbel at the back of the refrigerator that had long ago gone flat, and at least a twelve pack of Bud Light. Rose had finally succumbed, toppling over still fully clothed with a quiet moan across the foot of their bed.

Henry however had remained preternaturally alert, the alcohol serving only to heighten his growing sense of paranoia. What if the house was being watched? Could they have somehow tracked him and the winning ticket from the Kwik Pump? Easy enough to get the convenience store's surveillance camera tapes, trace his license plate, and then rip him off. He had no idea who 'they' might be, but if they could bag an American president from the grassy knoll or stage the Apollo 11 moon landing from a sound stage somewhere in California and get away with it, snatching Henry's unclaimed billion-dollar ticket would seem like child's play.

He'd hurriedly turned off all the lights in the house, waited a bit for his eyes to adjust, and then spent the remainder of the night crawling on his hands and knees so he couldn't be seen through the windows with the night vision goggles they'd surely be using. After a frustrating couple of hours at floor level, he finally settled on pulling up a corner of their threadbare living room carpet and sliding it in under there.

That was three days ago. The winning ticket was now parked securely in a safety deposit box, and ready to be claimed. But first, some unfinished business. If his plans were to succeed Henry had needed to arrive early, before Dex. The odds were astronomical that the anal prick had changed the lock on his old office, but Henry's luck was running good: his key still worked.

He stepped into Dex's office and flicked on the lights. A corner office, about five times the size of Henry's. Spotless of course, and not a file folder in sight; a reminder of Dex's legendary work ethic and efficiency to all who entered. It was a stark contrast to when Henry had occupied it and when the décor, as Arnie had commented one time, was 'early hoarder.' Now, a series of vintage black-and-white photographs of racing yachts tastefully adorned the walls, and a Peloton exercise bike accented one corner. The walls of windows looked out over a county forest preserve to the east, and the credenza behind the desk was lined with photos and mementos of a 'life well lived.' Dex's infamous cardboard visage stood life-size in another corner. Henry rubbed his hands together. This was going to be fun.

He sat down behind Dex's spotless desk and placed the envelope that was in his breast pocket on the desk. He'd also, when leaving home that morning, found and Glad-bagged the very fresh pile that the neighbor's dog had deposited per its usual early morning routine in his front yard. Henry pulled out one of the lower drawers in Dex's desk, detached it from its tracks, removed the drawer and deposited the pungent contents of the bag onto the floor. He then replaced the drawer, knowing that the source of the odor would be almost impossible for Dex to discover and would slowly, inexorably, drive him mad.

Then he kicked back, feet up on the desk. The day before Henry had bought the largest cigar he could find at a small smoke shop up in Highland Park—something called a double Churchill—and now he bit off the tip, spit it on the floor, and fired it up. He swiveled his chair around to get a glimpse of himself reflected in the window: still unshaven after almost a week, hair disheveled, torn work shirt opened sloppily to mid-chest, and an enormous cigar clamped between his teeth. Henry laughed. "My way of sticking it to the man," he yelled out loud, took another hit from the cigar, then blew an enormous cloud of smoke into the room. He looked out through the window. It had begun to lighten along the eastern horizon. It wouldn't be long now.

"BALL!"

Henry woke to find Dex standing in front of the desk and a group of about ten curious on-lookers gathered behind him, Samantha Tarleton and Arnie Schlechter among them. Finding Henry asleep, Dex had evidently summoned the others to witness Henry's ultimate humiliation and demise. From behind Dex a horrified Arnie mouthed a silent but unmistakable "WHAT THE FUCK!" and Samantha's sad half-smile confirmed what must have been a truly pathetic sight.

"My God, what reeks?" someone said as they came into the room. "Holy shit, is that Ball?"

Now Dex took his time, like some sadistic Spanish inquisitor about to apply a favorite torture to a particularly deserving heretic.

"Henry," Dex said pleasantly, playing now to the fast-growing audience behind him, "Before I call security to have you removed from the building, perhaps you can tell us . . . yes?"

Henry yawned, stretched, then gestured at the envelope on the desk. "Open it. Then read the contents out loud. For the benefit of our fellow employees."

Dex wrinkled his nose. "You realize of course that whatever it is you're smoking has burned a hole in my George Nakashima black walnut desk? No worries, I'll just take the cost of refinishing it out of your severance package which, if my calculations are correct, means you'll owe us about $7,700.00 and change."

"Read it!" Henry bellowed.

Dex hesitated, momentarily taken aback by Henry's uncharacteristic belligerence. He glanced around. Most of the others were staring at Henry with a mixture of disbelief and even horror, but Dex saw that one or two had expressions of barely concealed admiration. He made a mental note to put their names on the list for the next round of layoffs that were sure to come. Then, reassured by the thought that Henry couldn't possibly wriggle free from the personal and financial disaster that was about to befall him, Dex opened the letter. There were just four words, in all caps, boldface and 72-point type, and Henry's signature below it.

"FUCK YOU, I QUIT," Dex read out loud.

He set the letter down on the desk. The others in the room all wore expressions ranging from shock to fascination to unabashed envy. This was of course the rarest form of corporate career suicide, and none of them had ever witnessed it first-hand. The onlookers were almost like prisoners on a remote island penal colony watching one of their own, rather than live the rest of his life in servitude, leap boldly off a 100-foot cliff into the shark-infested waters below, with a one-in-a-million chance of survival.

Henry leaned back in the chair, exhaled a huge cloud of cigar smoke in Dex's direction and waited for his reaction. Henry imagined word of his heroic act spreading later like wildfire through the usual networks of email chains, texts, and word of mouth in the cubicles of first the pharmaceutical industry and then the corporate world at large. Over time the urban legend would grow, of a middle-aged man with the improbable name of Henry Ball who had dared to do what millions could only dream about. Pretty soon Henry Ball would become part of the American corporate lexicon, and his name would be used as a verb to describe similar incidents where a talented, hard-working but long-suffering employee had 'Henry Balled' his boss.

Dex stared down at Henry. "Ball, I don't know what game you're playing, but by the time I'm done spreading the word industry-wide about your gross incompetence, lousy work habits, and general sloth, you'll be lucky to get a bookkeeping job with your local Boy Scout troop. Ever heard of LinkedIn? By day's end you'll be an untouchable. And at your age?" Dex forced a laugh. He looked around for any sign of support. None seemed forthcoming.

Henry slowly rose to his feet. He looked around at the others in the room. He paused, thinking he could further burnish his legend with just the right final, inspirational comment. It had to be easy to remember, pithy, and eminently quotable—but with just a hint of mystery, even poetry. There were the usual suspects to choose from, of the type you'd see framed at Office Max or Staples, coupled with a photo of a man standing atop a mountain, arms outstretched, or a magnificent sunset or a majestic lone eagle in flight, like: *Dare Greatly, Live Boldly*, or *Dare to Soar* . . . or Nietzsche's ubiquitous, *What Doesn't Destroy Me Makes Me Stronger*. But they all seemed, well, too corporate. In the end, Henry thought his last words at PharmaSolutions as he brushed past Dex and made his way through his high-fiving, back-slapping former coworkers perhaps missed on a poetic level, but would burnish his legend nicely:

"Try not to step in the dogshit."

An Angel Descends

Isn't it true that most men lost in the wilderness die not of hunger or exposure—but of shame?

Henry suddenly remembered the line from somewhere as he looked up and down the long Lake Michigan beach, bordered by the high bluff where the Balls' mansion, named Lake Cliff, was perched. He had to admit, he was lost. Buck, their new six-month-old pure-bred golden retriever—the breed was de rigueur in Lake Forest—had broken free from his grip and gone racing down the narrow beach, intent on ambushing a distant flock of seagulls breakfasting on the edge of the early morning surf. Henry, bent over and winded after a fruitless half-mile chase, sought to get his bearings.

"Not since Mr. T chain-sawed all the oaks on his property has there been such a stir in town."

Startled, Henry straightened and swiveled around.

The woman laughed and extended her hand. "You must be Ball. Agnes Montgomery. Care for a drink, neighbor?"

She sat and patted the beach next to her. About 80, Henry guessed, but with a surprisingly firm grip and that rare bearing you find in some of the elderly who seem undiminished by and unconcerned with age. She was dressed for gardening, with auburn hair streaked with white tied in a bun under a floppy sun hat, and overalls stuffed into dark green rubber wellies. Her fair skin had clearly suffered over the years from too much sun, but she had surprisingly sharp blue eyes and her gaze was direct and inquiring. He guessed she had been considered a beauty in her youth. He liked her immediately.

He sat down next to her and saw now that she had a thermos with her. She unscrewed the cup and poured out a healthy measure of a brown liquid that Henry guessed was tea, given the early hour. She handed it to him. "Take it for Christ's sake, you're going to need it by the time they're done with you."

Henry sniffed it. "Whiskey?"

She laughed. "Dear boy. Don't be vulgar. At this hour? No, bourbon of course. A little 25-year-old Pappy Van Winkle just seems to start the day off right, don't you think?"

He sipped it. "I could get used to this."

She took a healthy slug right from the thermos. "Remember what Fitzgerald told Hemingway about the rich when they met in Paris in the 20s? 'The rich are different from you and me,' Fitzgerald told him, like they were superior beings from another planet. But Hemingway wasn't buying it. His response was, 'Yeah, they've got more money.'

"Ball, you've got more money, but deep down inside you're afraid they won't like the cut of your jib. That's what they're counting on. Before too long they'll have found a way to separate you from your fortune. After all, how do you think they got theirs?"

"A fool and his money," Henry said.

"Lucky enough to get together in the first place," she replied. They both laughed, and Henry poured himself another healthy dose of the bourbon.

"It took three husbands, two great fortunes won and lost, and a heart-breaking loss at the 68 Westminster Kennel when my favorite Yorkie blew out a hamstring to learn what Fitzgerald could never have known about the rich. And what I'm about to tell you."

"Agnes, I don't think—"

"Let me guess. They lawyered you up on day one, with the best legal team in Chicago, am I correct?"

"Well, of course, Waxworth Barnes is reputed to be—"

"Then, a well-respected investment banker, perhaps a close personal friend—maybe even a beloved ex-football player," she winked, "working in close conjunction with your crackerjack legal team created separate trusts for you and your wife, for your own protection and other assorted liability issues, giving this highly respected, close personal friend power of attorney to make key decisions when authorized by you on your behalf? And most, if not all, of your money now resides in these trusts—generating of course, a handsome income from only iron clad investments in, oh, steel mills, car companies, pharmaceuticals, and other blue chips?"

Henry gazed out at Lake Michigan. The sun was about 20 degrees above the eastern horizon now in a cloudless June sky, and he could tell from the surprisingly flat, oily look of the lake that it was going to be very hot. He leaned back on his elbow and poured himself another bourbon. It was true, he and Rose had called on Victor Black immediately upon receiving their after-tax settlement of $684,000,000 and change—or had he called them? But they'd both agreed: who better to handle their money? Now, most of their fortune did reside in what Victor called high-yield, very conservative investment products that, as Victor said, 'Could only be at risk if another Cretaceous period extinction event occurred.' But the trust was still spinning off a surreal monthly income: "$510,000.00, are you shitting me?"—Henry had yelled, just a few weeks ago, as he ran through their new, mostly empty mansion holding aloft his first monthly Fitzgerald Black statement.

He looked over at Agnes and lifted the thermos cap in a toast. "I get your point. So, what are those hard-earned lessons that Fitzgerald wished he'd have known?"

"He learned them, dear boy, but too late," she said. "He died penniless in LA at age 44, one of our great writers turned Hollywood hack. Just two things to remember: First, your wife. Hear she's a looker. Probably has a good head on her shoulders. Keep her, at all costs. You'll be tempted of course, we all are. But trust me, the ones who will come after won't be worth a damn."

Henry chuckled, appreciatively. "And number two? Let me guess: don't touch the principal."

"More importantly, hide some. Call it a rainy-day fund. Gold. Loose diamonds. Bury it somewhere and don't tell a soul. No paper trails. No safety deposit box keys. I'm talking about a hole in the ground. Someday, it'll come in handy. Might even save your life, and your wife's."

Buck ran up, panting, and began licking Agnes' face. The dog was soaking wet and covered in wet sand, but she laughed and wrestled playfully with him. After awhile, Henry stood stiffly and brushed the sand from his shorts. He reached down and offered Agnes his hand. He helped her to her feet and hugged her gently, her body feeling frail in his arms.

"Thank you, Agnes, it's been a memorable morning." Henry held her now at arm's length and looked into her fierce hawk's eyes. There was something so strangely familiar and comforting about her that he found himself reluctant to let her go.

"I like you Ball. You'll do all right, if you keep your head. Don't let the bastards get you down." She turned and began walking down the beach.

"Agnes," he yelled, "final question: where the hell's my house?"

Trouble in Paradise

Clear head, new life ahead, it's time I was king, now not just one more pawn . . . fly by night away from here, change my life again . . .

The windows shook as a live version of Rush's "Fly by Night" boomed out from the new $50,000 Dolby surround sound system that the installers claimed could deliver 210 decibels with ease; a sound level they said was on par with the eruption of Krakatoa. It would be, the older of the two installers said as he winked at Henry, "like putting your head right up against Pete Townsend's amplifier."

"There's a drive, it could be, it might be." Henry leaped up and gloved the tennis ball that he'd thrown against the two-story foyer wall, just missing the enormous vintage baccarat crystal chandelier the realtor had said was worth as much as the average suburban house.

"What a catch by Ball at the wall!" Henry yelled, mimicking the guttural, slightly slurred speech of the legendary Harry Caray. "There goes the runner at third to win the game and end the Cubs' chances for another pennant. Ball has a cannon for an arm, and he lets fly. It will be close." Henry threw the tennis ball hard across the foyer and down the long hall toward the kitchen. Buck, trying valiantly to gain traction on the marble floor, took off after it.

"Out!" he cried. "Cubs win, Cubs win!" And he danced around, arms outstretched in victory.

Henry glanced at his watch. Only 11:30 a.m.? It was odd, but Henry had noticed the days seemed to be moving at a snail's pace. Time. What was it that Einstein had said about it? Past, present, and future were evidence of man's attempt to explain his surroundings, but didn't in fact exist.

Now, just two months into his new life as a billionaire, Henry felt that, for whatever reason, time had slowed perceptibly. Maybe it was the stage he'd reached. First there'd been the initial euphoria, which had given way to, oddly enough, a mild depression. Now, for lack of a better word: boredom?

Of late Henry had plenty of time on his hands, which perhaps was contributing to his general sense of unease. He'd begun detecting a disturbance in the force, as he liked to say, not a little of it stemming from his growing dissatisfaction with his relationship with Rose.

They had of course gone on a spending spree, but nothing too decadent: his and hers Range Rovers, seasons tickets on the ice at the United Center and along the third base line at Wrigley, a little *pied-a-terre* on Lakeshore a few blocks from Victor's and Suzanne's place, and of course the jewel in the crown: the massive 32-room red brick Lake Forest mansion built just before the market bust in '29 and known, famously, by the cognoscenti as Lake Cliff.

The mansion had been recently renovated and modernized with a climate-controlled 5,000 bottle wine cellar, six-car garage, master spa bath, 1,500-square-foot his-and-her closets, a vast, fully-equipped exercise room, and all the other amenities considered indispensable by today's most affluent buyers. The $15 million selling price, as their realtor proudly informed them on the day of their closing, was the highest ever paid for a Lake Forest property.

Yet, the transformation, the metamorphosis, the expansion of his life that Henry had expected had not yet occurred. His life hadn't really changed; he'd only added things to it, and he'd found the initial rush of new-found wealth to be transitory. He was still

Henry Ball, living much the same life but in a strange, gigantic new house and with a golden retriever as his closest companion. Not even Zach was around now to enjoy Cubs games and cold beers with him from the best seats in Wrigley. He'd finally flown the nest for Vegas and the professional poker circuit, courtesy of Henry and a mid-six figure 'grub stake'. Henry longed to fill the void with something that he felt must be lurking just over the horizon; an exploration of wild, unexplored country and adventures fit for a daring man of means.

Making matters worse was the fact that while Henry now seemed at a loss for how to spend his time, Rose's days seemed filled with endless activity, as if she were trying to catch up for a lifetime of lost opportunities and unfulfilled dreams. Most of her time of late had been spent with Suzanne and a new coterie of well-heeled friends. In fact, Rose was flying off the very next day with Suzanne on one of Fitzgerald Black's private jets to Palm Beach for a few weeks because, as she'd said giggling over dinner the night before, "Suzanne wants to see if old money likes the cut of my jib."

And, admittedly, he was having a surprisingly hard time getting over what he perceived as his diminished manhood, and the barely perceptible shift in marital power that had resulted from Rose's manhandling outside Larry's house months before. Intellectually he knew it was childish. But his wounded pride had somehow cast a pall over his feelings for Rose ever since. He knew he should clear the air, but of late an opportunity for a rapprochement had yet to present itself.

Buck came charging up the hall with the tennis ball in his mouth, sliding across the foyer floor to a full stop at Henry's feet. As Henry tried to wrestle the tennis ball away from Buck's slobbering mouth, Rush was suddenly replaced with Henry's smart phone ringtone cutting in via Bluetooth and booming out over the speakers.

"Alexa, answer my phone," he yelled. Victor Black's voice suddenly came on.

"What the fuck," he heard Victor mutter under his breath. "Henry? Are you there?" Victor asked, sounding a bit exasperated.

Henry laughed, pleased that the smart voice recognition system had worked as advertised and surprisingly happy to be hearing from Victor, who of late always seemed to be the bearer of good news.

"Yes, Victor, you're coming in loud and clear."

"Where are you? Sounds like you're in a tunnel."

"Standing in the foyer, testing the voice recognition feature," Henry said. "Best system money can buy. Microphones everywhere so Alexa can meet my every whim."

"Well, you can certainly afford the best," Victor laughed. "So, about that $5 million that's going to your brother-in-law, Larry? Simplest to wire it to his bank. Or he can swing by here and pick up a cashier's check. We'll just need a day or two notice." There was a moment's silence. "Henry?"

"Victor let me get back to you on that," Henry said, finally. "I'll need to talk to Rose. There might be a change in plans on this."

Victor, with the sixth sense that all the best money managers develop over time to detect when something might be amiss with his clients or, more importantly, their money, saw his opening. "Look, Henry, none of my business, and you and Rose should be commended for your largesse, but $5 million is a lot of money," his voice boomed out over the foyer speakers. "I've seen more than one large fortune whittled down to a small fortune. I wouldn't be your friend if I didn't recommend that maybe you wait until you can pay something like this out of earnings, rather than principal. Give it a few months, maybe make a small partial payment or two."

"Thanks Victor, we're babes in the woods, no doubt about it," Henry yelled up toward the ceiling. "We won't do anything hasty, I promise. Gotta run. Bye Victor. Alexa, disconnect."

It was late afternoon and Henry was on his third PowerBaller when he looked out his study window and saw Suzanne's limo pull up to the front door. He'd invented the PowerBaller just that afternoon: four fingers of Gray Goose, a splash of tonic, a sudden, inspirational dash of Tabasco, and then shaken not stirred with crushed ice and topped off with a wedge of lime. Unlike the pleasant, happy, optimistic buzz he experienced from beer and wine, vodka made Henry feel sluggish and vaguely anesthetized. On the few occasions when he'd had a vodka or two, Rose later claimed that it made him mean. Admittedly, Henry wasn't sure why so many of his generation ultimately seemed to gravitate to vodka as their drink du jour, but the PowerBaller seemed like the perfect choice for this afternoon as he walked a bit unsteadily out of his study and down the long hall toward the foyer.

Just then the heavy front door swung open, its momentum banging it hard into the 18th century Louis XIV side table in the entry way. Rose and Suzanne tumbled in, arms linked and laughing uproariously. They were followed by a powerfully built black man who Henry assumed was Suzanne's driver, laden with shopping bags from Bloomingdale's, Marcus, OSKA, and a few with the distinctive zebra-skin pattern of Maasai. When the women saw Henry, they pulled up short, still giggling.

"It's Henry, we're so busted!" Suzanne said, a bit too loudly. Rose walked over to Henry and threw an arm around his neck and kissed him. He could smell the wine on her breath. She looked down at the drink he had in his hand and up at his unsmiling face.

"Vodka?" she asked, surprised to find a drink in Henry's hand so early before dinner.

"Wine?" he sneered, with barely concealed sarcasm.

"Trouble in paradise? Okay, we're out of here. Carter, set those down," Suzanne ordered, gesturing impatiently toward the man. "See you tomorrow, Rosie, wheel's up at ten a.m., so we'll be here to pick you up no later than eight. Bye, Henry," she said, winking at him.

Rose walked over and kissed Suzanne on the cheek. "Thanks for a great day, girlfriend," she said. "Goodbye, Victor's man." She waved. The black man turned toward Rose, smiled, glanced back at Henry, then closed the door quietly behind them.

Rose was in too good a mood to let Henry spoil it with whatever seemed to be bothering him. He'd seemed particularly cranky of late, easily irritated by even the most inconsequential things. Rose usually shrugged off Henry's complaints, categorizing most of them as what Suzanne called 'champagne problems.' These were the types of things, Suzanne had explained, that could only upset the very wealthy, like when you'd asked the sommelier for a '55 Mouton Rothschild and he returns with the vastly inferior '56. Now, seeking to defuse a situation that threatened to turn ugly, she reached down and rifled through one of the Maasai shopping bags.

"I thought this would look good on you, love." She held up a man's belt and stretched it out in front of Henry's waist. "Hand-crafted from Nile crocodile skin, all farm-raised in Tanzania. Sustainable, humane. Money goes toward schoolbooks, better housing. Got a brochure for you that tells the story. Really interesting. Suzanne says Victor's got one just like it. Wears it everywhere. She said she hid a GPS tracking device in the belt buckle, and I don't think she was kidding." Rose laughed, hoping to break the ice.

"Oh, speaking of Victor, he called this morning," Henry said, matter-of-factly, gazing up. "Voice came out of the ceiling like the word of God. Amazing sound system, I might add. He was wondering how to get $5 million to your brother Larry, so I told him I'd get back to him. Giving Larry $5 million—now, that's a croc!" Henry cackled.

Rose gave Henry a cold stare. "Henry," she said slowly and very calmly as if talking to a petulant child, "I was there when you made the agreement with Larry. If someone won the Powerball, as crazy as that sounded, each of you would give the other $5 million. It's the right thing to do. We're going to make good on a promise you, like an idiot, made. Anyway, with Victor's help, we'll make that back in no time." She hurriedly began gathering up her bags.

Rose sensed danger, knowing that Henry, fueled by vodka and his hatred for Larry, would now ratchet up the stakes. She dreaded a fight, one of those epic, exhausting, no-holds-barred donnybrooks, as her father had called them, that ultimately required one party to capitulate so the other could save face and life could go on as before. There had been relatively few in their relationship, and Henry had usually been the one to accept blame and work to salve the open wounds. But she doubted now that it would be business as usual.

As she reached down for the Maasai bag, Henry gave it a kick that sent it flying across the foyer, scattering its contents. She dropped the remaining bags and stood.

"Are you telling me that your asshole brother really expects to get paid?" Henry yelled, incredulous. "You can tell that fucker to go fuck himself! No fucking way. He doesn't get a nickel, do you hear me, Rose? Not one. Fucking. Cent. Where was Larry when I got sacked from National Dynamics, or when H. Ball went belly up? How about when you got laid off at Mercy General? Any offer of help? Any chance that the mooch, the pig wallowing in the fucking government trough would be there for his little sister? Hell no!"

The diatribe went on, increasingly profane and less and less articulate. As Henry reached a state of extreme, almost incoherent agitation, Rose began aping his behavior and mimicking his facial expressions and mannerisms, a simple but effective schoolyard ploy that she'd used on him a time a two before, designed to both make Henry look ridiculous and infuriate him.

"Look at you," she said, her voice full of scorn.

"Look at me? Look at you!" he roared.

"Asshole!" she yelled.

"Bitch!"

"Loser!"

"Fuck you!"

"No, fuck you!" Rose took a few steps back and grasped the neck of one of two 800-year-old blue and white porcelain Yuan Dynasty vases off a table along the foyer wall that the decorator had insisted on and charged them in the low six figures for.

"Not the Yuan!" Henry lunged awkwardly and tried to catch it, but it bounced off his outstretched fingers and shattered on the floor next to him. He looked down for a second and did a doubletake when he saw what looked like the words 'Made in China' engraved in English on the rough, unglazed side of one of the shattered pieces. He looked up and had just enough time to duck the second Yuan vase, which this time he didn't bother to try to catch. She took a step or two toward him. Henry began to step forward too but then thought better of it. Just the other day Henry had peeked in on one of Rose's early morning workouts in Lake Cliff's gleaming gym. Rose had been pummeling the heavy bag with a flurry of kicks, punches, and elbow strikes that left no doubt as to her formidable Krav Maga fighting skills.

"We're through, do you hear me?" Henry yelled, as he retreated into the entryway. "You'll be hearing from my lawyers."

The door slammed behind him. "Good riddance, motherfucker!" she yelled, an act of bravado that she wasn't quite sure she believed.

Rose stood in the middle of the foyer, shopping bags, broken porcelain, and the shattered pieces of her marriage scattered about her.

10

The Plot Thickens

"How'd you like to ride that? And I don't mean the horse."

Suzanne handed Rose her field glasses and pointed toward the horse and rider racing now toward the goalposts at their end of the field. "That's Cisco Torres," Suzanne whispered excitedly in Rose's ear. "He's this year's *it* player. Everyone's talking about him."

Rose watched now as several of the riders at full gallop tried to head Torres off. It looked like they'd all converge at about the same time around the ball bounding toward the goal. The crowd, seeing the potential for either a goal or a catastrophic collision, was on its feet and began to roar. But somehow Torres managed to coax the extra burst of speed his pony had in reserve and got his mallet on the ball a split second before an opposing rider cut him off and sent it flying between the goalposts.

"Francisco Torres scores for Team Victoria!" Boomed out over the PA system.

It was halftime and Suzanne and Rose, following tradition, walked the field with most of the other spectators, sipping Veuve Clicquot and stomping down the divots turned up by the horses' hooves.

"There's Bunny Phipps!" Suzanne said, grabbing Rose's arm suddenly and waving to a woman dressed in an eccentric menagerie of pink jeans stuffed in riding boots, purple sash, cowboy shirt, and a man's blue blazer and pith helmet.

"Best parties in Palm Beach, five acres right on the ocean," Suzanne said excitedly. "Don't let the funky getup fool you. Old money likes to remind the rest of us that they can act and dress however they like. Of course she's a dyke but who the hell cares? Wangling an invite is like getting an audience with the Pope. I'll meet you back at our seats!"

Rose made her way back to their seats. She picked up the program and thumbed through it. Across the polo field she could see Suzanne walking arm in arm now with Bunny Phipps. A photo spread of a young, very good-looking polo player playfully holding a carrot in his mouth to feed an eager pony caught her eye.

"Cisco Kid Is a Friend of Mine," the headline read. The story went on. *The hard-charging, fun-loving Francisco Torres and his improbable rise from Bogotá barrio to the sport's youngest ten-goaler—and why the cognoscenti are saying he might be better than Adolfo Cambiaso, and hotter than Nacho Figueros.*

Rose, interest piqued, had read almost all of the short, glowing article by the time most of the patrons had returned to the stands. Suzanne finally squeezed in next to her just as the next chukker began.

"We're in!" Suzanne said, giving Rose a hug.

She leaned over, catching a glimpse of Cisco Torres' photo. "My my!" she said, appreciatively. Then she looked at her watch and pulled the program out of Rose's hands. "Never mind that. Now, Rosie, we've got about five hours to get our groove on before all hell breaks loose."

She stood suddenly, pulled Rose to her feet, and began to sing the old Bee Gees standby. "Whether you're a brother or whether you're a mother, you're stayin' alive, stayin' alive."

And then Rose who, over the years, had learned to simply play along with Suzanne's often inexplicable bursts of enthusiasm, joined in for the famous refrain. "Ah, ha, ha, ha, stayin' alive, stayin' ali . . . iiiiiii . . . iiii . . . iiiivvvve!"

They laughed and got a round of applause for their impromptu a cappella performance from the nearby onlookers. "See you at Bunny's!" one of them yelled.

"I am one bad motherfucker!" Henry said to himself with a mixture of pride and fear, as he straddled his new Ducati Diavel Carbon superbike. Five hundred high-tech pounds of black steel, chrome, and composites all wrapped around a colossal engine capable of, according to the literature, generating 162 horsepower, more than 900 foot-pounds of torque, and a top speed of just under 170 miles per hour. The Ducati dealership had dropped it off practically at his front doorstep early that morning. Henry had last owned a bike—the ubiquitous Honda 350—in college. Yet the Honda bore about as much resemblance to the Ducati as a housecat does to a Siberian tiger, Henry thought, as he balanced the massive bike upright, kicked up the kickstand, turned the key, and pressed the ignition. The engine started instantly, a low, deep rumble, and he goosed the throttle a few times. He squeezed in the clutch and kicked the shift lever into first gear. Then he cautiously let out the clutch and inched forward a few feet before braking, putting the kickstand down, and killing the engine. When he got off the bike, his legs were shaking. He looked at his watch. They would be here any minute. Just what the hell had he gotten himself into?

Admittedly, when Henry had expressed a casual interest in joining Victor Black's motorcycle club, the Capitalist Pigs, Victor had sought to deflect Henry's interest to more sedate and safer hobbies. "Why not join Old Elm?" Victor said. "Nice golf course, good bunch of guys, little chance of breaking every bone in your body. Not sure you're really Pig material. These boys play kind of rough, Henry. You're, well," he paused, searching for the right words, "more refined."

With the gauntlet thrown down and his manhood seemingly questioned, Henry had proceeded to take a weekend motorcycle certification course, gotten his M class driver's license, then researched and purchased the Ducati which, as one motorcycle publication had described it, was, 'Like strapping on a 500-pound piston-powered black codpiece, with the potential to make every ride like the chariot race in Ben Hur.'

Henry now could hear motorcycles somewhere off in the distance. As they got closer, he could tell they were riding Harleys, with that distinctive, intentionally unmuffled Harley roar—an auditory flipping of the bird to those soulless suburbanites playing it safe in their shiny metal boxes.

They came into view and turned onto Henry's long-winding cobblestone drive, 20 or so bikes, and Henry now could feel the vibration in his feet. Victor was on the lead bike, a massive, low-slung heavily customized Harley with Capitalist Pig insignia—a smiling, rakish razorback hog with eye patch and gold incisors—emblazoned on the saddlebag. They slowly pulled past Henry, arrayed in a semi-circle around the fountain centered in the middle of the cobblestone circular drive, and killed their engines. The men began dismounting, stretching, removing helmets.

Victor waved to Henry. "Hogs, say hello to Henry Ball!" he yelled, evidently still a bit deaf from wind blast and collective roar of the Harleys.

The response seemed tepid at best, with perhaps half the group acknowledging Henry with nods or a wave. A few had lit cigars and others were passing around a flask. Henry recognized several of the riders as former teammates of Victor's and guessed that most of the others were from the clique of wealthy, adventurous entrepreneurs, self-made men, and other assorted bad boys that seemed to compose Victor's innermost circle of friends.

Henry found himself locking eyes with the only black man in the group, an incongruous figure standing a bit apart from the others.

"Boy, what are you looking at?" the man said loudly as he strolled casually up to Henry and planted himself just inches away.

Henry was a head taller, but this man had the shoulders and chest of linebacker. Now with the Pigs looking on with evident amusement, Henry sensed this was a test of some kind and he barely resisted the urge to take a few steps back.

The man chuckled, and began walking around Henry, looking him up and down like a drill sergeant inspecting a slovenly new recruit. "Nervous? I bet this motherfucker's never even seen a black man except in *National Geographic* or shooting a basketball on TV."

Henry managed a smile. "Well, not exactly true."

The man came around from behind Henry, and now stood toe to toe just inches away. "Shit, boy, where you think we're going, planet Mars?" he laughed. "Who wears a suit like this but some kind of astronaut?"

Henry's brand new, bright lemon-yellow single-piece Roadmaster jumpsuit, with Kevlar reinforcement, armored knees, hips, and elbows, and advanced chest and back protective features that would inflate on impact like the airbags on a car stood in stark contrast to the vintage leathers and heavy jeans and boots favored by the rest of the riders.

"And shit, what kind of Powerball-winning, America-hating, motherfucking pussy rides anything but a Harley?" he added, as he waved dismissively at the Ducati.

"All right Pigs, saddle up!" Victor yelled over the laughter and guffaws and cutting short the man's scathing indictment. "Next stop, Jolly Roger's!"

Henry had somehow made it the 40 miles or so to the restaurant on the Fox River favored by the area's biker clubs, but just barely. The scenic route had taken them through the farmlands and small towns west of Lake Forest, on a lightly trafficked two-lane road with plenty of twisties to make the ride interesting. Henry had ridden second to last, carefully negotiating the winding country road at near-idle speeds, then trying to make up lost time on the safer straightaways or when the group slowed going through the occasional town or intersection. Behind him the entire time was his antagonist from the driveway, who seemed to be taking perverse pleasure in tailing Henry.

Henry sighed with relief as he slumped heavily in a chair on the crowded Jolly Roger's veranda that fronted the Fox River. The rest of the Pigs had already staked their claim to several large tables and were loosely arrayed in small groups and chatting up a few of the busty Jolly Roger's waitress 'wenches' who now were vying for the Pigs' attention. The Pigs were well-known as heavy tippers, and Victor's largesse had helped make the Pigs popular amongst even the outlaw one percenters who frequented Jolly Roger's and often entertained themselves by beating up the occasional poseur riding out from the burbs.

Henry's arms and legs felt like rubber after an hour of wrestling with the Ducati. The seat and crotch and armpits of his jumpsuit felt uncomfortably wet now that he'd come to rest. Victor had ordered a round of drinks and pitchers of beer and one of the Pigs offered Henry a mug. He caught Victor's eye, who nodded at Henry with approval and raised his glass in a toast. "Ball, Vegas odds were 100 to one against you making it here alive." Victor laughed. "Salud!"

Henry drank thirstily and then leaned back, eyes closed and basking in the pleasurable warmth of the late morning August sun. Was there anything better than the feeling of having survived almost certain death, he asked himself? Wasn't it Churchill who had said there is nothing so pleasurable as having been shot at with no effect? Henry had certainly dodged a few bullets today. But he had to admit, the terror he'd felt early in the ride had given way to exhilaration toward the end as he had begun to master the Ducati. A hand on his shoulder caused him to open his eyes. His antagonist stood there, hands on hips, glaring down at him.

"Oh God," Henry said.

Suddenly the man broke into a broad grin. "No, Carter Banks," he said, and extended a hand. They shook. "Victor gets a kick out of shocking unsuspecting white folk with the 'angry black man' routine," Carter chuckled. "I have to say, you held up better than most."

The man's threatening gangsta dialect had now been replaced by a pleasant southern drawl and the hint of another accent that Henry thought sounded vaguely Bahamian but couldn't place for sure.

"We met a few days ago when I dropped your missus off after that shopping trip downtown with Mrs. Black." He smiled at the lack of recognition in Henry's expression. "I know, all us black folk look alike, particularly the help."

Henry stared at Carter, vaguely remembering now the man that had helped carry the packages into the house that day. "Sorry," Henry said, embarrassed, starting to explain. "I was a bit distracted that day, nothing to do with . . ."

"Carter, get your ass over here," one of the Pigs yelled. "I've got $1,000 that says you can beat their best guy at arm wrestling."

Carter rolled his eyes. "Children. Later, man," he said, winking at Henry, then he walked over to where a few of the Pigs were negotiating with some particularly burly bikers from one of the outlaw clubs.

Henry watched him go. He had the close-cropped hair, physique, and bearing of some of the managers and CEOs he'd encountered in the corporate world—men who were inevitably graduates from one of the military academies or perhaps former law enforcement. Later, after Henry and Carter had become friends of a sort, his theory would be confirmed. Over many beers one night, Carter Banks' story had reluctantly emerged. He was a 'saltwater Gullah,' descendent from the enslaved Africans who had made their escape and settled in the low country and the barrier islands off the coast of South Carolina. Prodigious athleticism and formidable intellect had led to a full scholarship to the Citadel, the first Geechee ever to have received the honor.

Officer candidate and Army ranger schools and training in long-range reconnaissance and as a sniper had followed. A record shot during Operation Desert Storm—the bagging of an Iraqi brigadier general from almost two miles away—had made Banks' reputation, as well as a few enemies within the tightknit sniper clique still largely composed of white southern 'crackers.'

Growing restless, Banks left the Army looking for new challenges and began a long stint with Chicago PD, steadily rising through the ranks to a deputy chief of detectives. But with the ladder upward to further promotions filled with the beneficiaries of favors being returned, or the friends and relatives of people connected to the Chicago machine, Banks had jumped at the opportunity to handle security for Fitzgerald Black and the 500 percent pay raise that came with it. Over time, he'd become more like Victor's trusted aide de camp with a much broader portfolio of assignments than he could have imagined at the outset.

A crowd had gathered around Banks and his outlaw adversary, an enormous hairy beast in sleeveless leather vest with the name Sasquatch and a snarling simian face tattooed across a massive bicep. Just as they were about to lock hands, Sasquatch raised a hand to temporarily halt the proceedings, chugged a pitcher of beer—spilling about half on his chest in the process—belched, leaned to within inches of Banks' face, and let out a primal roar.

Not to be outdone, Banks also raised a hand, reached for his beer, and took a small, almost dainty sip. He looked over at Henry, winked, and locked hands with the giant.

It was over in about three seconds.

"Most battles are won before they're even fought," Banks said to Henry a few minutes later, after collecting his share of a large wad of cash wagered by the onlookers and helping Sasquatch off the floor. The giant had gone flying out of his chair with the force of his arm being jerked almost out of its socket and pinned to the table.

Henry shook his head in disbelief. "That was an amazing display. How did you do that?"

Banks laughed. "Speed and leverage always works best against larger and, ideally, slightly impaired adversaries, so we pick the biggest and drunkest. Sasquatch has been on our radar all summer. Get the weight moving the right way and, as the man said, down goes Frazier."

"But why do it?" Henry asked. "It can't be for the money."

Banks laughed. "Of course not. Motivation's as old as mankind, Ball. The usual alpha male shit. Victor likes to win. Doesn't matter if it's for a round of drinks or a billion-dollar deal. Got to hand it to the man."

Just then, Henry's phone announced the arrival of a text message. He glanced down. "Dinner?" it read. *The plot thickens.* The sender was Samantha Tarleton.

Beautiful Stranger

"These are your people!" Suzanne yelled in Rose's ear. Bunny Phipps' old ballroom floor, designed a century before by Addison Mizner for a more genteel age and gentler dance steps, shook with the force of more than 500 members of Palm Beach society bumping and grinding as Miami's famous club DJ, Samurai, mixed a heavy base beat and synthesizer into The O'Jays' "Love Train."

"Lookin' hot tonight, Palm Beach!" Samurai yelled over the PA. Rose looked at the crowd, with an enormous disco ball suspended from the 25-foot ceiling slowly rotating and casting a million colored lights on the dancers. It was a surreal, albeit fascinating, scene, and Rose had to resist the urge to burst out laughing. Older men in vintage bell bottoms or leisure suits and shirts open to the navel enthusiastically reprised 40-year-old dance moves like The Bump, The Hustle, The Chicken, and even the odd Twist or two. Mating dances designed for much younger bodies were now being performed in torturous fashion and at greatly reduced speeds, and you could almost hear the creaking of a thousand titanium joints. The women, many considerably younger and seeking more excitement, drifted together here and there into small groups or sought out one of the many polo players that Bunny had evidently seeded the guest list with.

Without missing a beat Samurai segued into The Trammps' "Disco Inferno." The crowd roared with the recognition and Suzanne grabbed Rose's hand and pulled her into the nearest scrum. Rose, who loved to dance but hadn't been anywhere near a dance floor in years due to Henry's self-proclaimed 'white male dance disorder' now found herself swinging her hips in close synchronization and brushing against those of a tall, very tan, and impossibly gorgeous young man dressed in a simple white polo and blue jeans. In the past she might have subtly danced her way into safer territory. But tonight, she felt particularly sexy and in disguise in the vintage black Halston jumpsuit and huge blond fro wig that the concierge at the Four Seasons had helped her score that afternoon. While the outfit was ridiculous, it did show off Rose's athletic, lightly tanned body to great effect.

The man, who seemed to know nothing about disco dance steps but had the natural grace of an athlete, fell into easy rhythm with Rose. When the Bee Gee's "More Than a Woman" began, he took Rose in his powerful arms and she followed his lead. It was more salsa than *Saturday Night Fever*, but they made a striking couple, and word began to circulate. The crowd, recognizing the man and perhaps in need of a breather, formed a circle around them. Rose laughed as the man, playing now to the crowd, suddenly swung Rose out by one hand and then snapped her back with a twirl into his arms. They linked hands and he put a hand on the small of her back to guide her. As they danced in close synchronization, he pressed his surprisingly hard torso against her, and a faint but pleasant smell of cologne lingered. Then suddenly he turned Rose 180 degrees and his hands dropped to Rose's hips and as he pulled her backward into him. The crowd roared their appreciation at the characteristically brazen Latin dance move.

When the song ended the crowd cheered and clapped with cries of "*Bravo, Cisco!*" He smiled as if mildly embarrassed by his performance, gave a short bow, and extended a hand toward Rose to indicate it was she who deserved all the credit. He took her hand then, kissed it, and led her off the dance floor toward the doors at the back of the ballroom that opened onto the vast veranda and the great lawn that ended at the seawall.

They went out onto the veranda. There was a light sea breeze, and it was cool and quiet. Some of the other guests had gathered around the outdoor bar or gone out onto the lawn to sit by a large fire pit burning driftwood.

"Francisco Javier Torres," he said, with a formal bow. "Forgive me. I have the manners of, how you say, a farmer."

Rose laughed. "I think you mean peasant."

He laughed. "Yes, you are right. My English, not so good."

"Yes, but your dancing needs no interpretation." Suzanne laughed as she came up behind them and held out two drinks. "Tito's and tonic with lime for Rose and for Señor Torres, a Cuba libre. At least that's what Bunny says you like when you're not in training. That was a hot workout, and I figured you two would be thirsty."

"You read my mind, Suzanne," Rose said, grateful for both the drink and a chance to gather her thoughts. Torres accepted the drink and gave Suzanne a polite bow.

"Freddie!" Suzanne said suddenly, waving to a huge, disheveled man in a rumpled white leisure suit who had just come out on the veranda and was walking rather unsteadily toward the bar. The man looked around briefly for the source of the voice but kept moving, as if no force on earth could keep him from reaching the bar.

"That's Freddie Guest," Suzanne said to Rose and Torres. "Palm Beach royalty. You couldn't miss him on the dance floor. Literally. Probably sent half a dozen guests to the hospital. Great fun, though. I'll leave you two lovebirds alone," Suzanne said, with a wink at Rose. She turned and walked quickly after Freddie, who'd already plowed into the six or eight people waiting for a drink and sent them flying like bowling pins.

Rose and Torres sat on the low veranda wall and sipped their drinks. Torres seemed comfortable with what most Americans would consider an awkward silence and Rose, rather than risk a comment that might somehow ruin the moment or send him away like a skittish colt, waited for Torres to take the lead. After a few minutes, Torres smiled and took Rose's hand. "I am sorry," he said, apologetically. "I am used to spending time with my ponies. They will tell you much if you listen carefully. A beautiful woman is much the same, no?"

Rose laughed. "I suppose so, but you'd probably find your ponies more interesting," she said. "Really, though, I'm enjoying myself more tonight than I have in a long time. But I think it's time I was honest with you. I'm not perhaps the beautiful woman you think I am." She reached up and carefully removed the big blond afro wig.

Torres feigned surprise. Then he smiled and reached over and gently pulled out the hair pins that were holding up Rose's hair, letting it fall to her shoulders. He gazed at her for a moment and then stood. "On a night such as this, the beach is the place, no?" he asked.

She took his hand, and they began walking toward the steps leading down to the lawn. Rose caught Suzanne's eye as they left the veranda. Suzanne gave her a thumbs up sign. Rose waved and shrugged her shoulders in a gesture acknowledging she was about to enter unchartered waters and helpless to resist the forces at work.

They walked hand-in-hand across the broad lawn. Rose paused for a moment to kick off her retro platform shoes, and Torres followed suit with his espadrilles. A few of the men sitting in Adirondack chairs around the fire were evidently fellow polo players, because they called out in Spanish, "*Cisco, que pasa?*" and "*Hola, Cisco, tener una le bebida!*" Torres gave them a friendly wave as they walked toward the low seawall bordering the lawn.

They found the gap in the seawall and the short staircase leading down to the beach. There was no moon, and a surprising number of stars could be seen in the night sky despite the light pollution from the nearby coastal cities. Out on the horizon, the running lights of what looked to be a large freighter or perhaps a cruise ship were visible. There was a gentle surf, and Torres led her right to the edge. They walked down the deserted stretch of beach and away from the party parallel to the surf in the wet sand, letting the surprisingly warm ocean water wash up just far enough to wet their calves.

When Rose stopped for a moment to roll up the wet legs of her jumpsuit, Torres suddenly began to run down the beach along the surf. He waved, laughing, and yelled, "Come on!"

Rose laughed and began to follow. Then Torres stopped suddenly, pulled off his shirt, turned his back to Rose and dropped his trousers and underwear in a pile. Surprised, Rose turned way, glancing back just in time to see a naked Torres running at full speed into the surf to about waist deep and then diving headlong into the sea. He surfaced a little farther out, waved and yelled, "Come on, Rose, you will love it."

Rose looked about and, seeing no one else on the beach, reached back and unzipped her Halston jumpsuit. She stepped out of it, folded it neatly, hesitated for a moment, and then slipped off her panties.

"I must be nuts," she muttered, as she made a dash for the surf. She dove in, enjoying the feeling of swimming underwater, still familiar after so many years spent out of water, and struck out with a few tentative strokes toward where she imagined Torres would be.

As she surfaced, Torres came up suddenly and embraced her gently from behind, kissing her neck. Treading water, he turned her around and grasped her waist. As he lifted her up, she grasped his powerful shoulders for leverage and straddled his waist. They kissed long and hard, and she could taste the saltwater and a hint of lime from the drink he'd had earlier.

How easy it was, she thought, after all these years of faithfulness to Henry, to make love to this beautiful stranger.

To Victor Go the Spoils

"General Abdul Malik sends his regards," Carter Banks said, as he set a small glass vial of what Victor presumed was sweet, low-sulfur bonny light crude oil on Victor's desk.

Victor smiled. "Next time he'll probably send a body part from what's left of President Mugambe. So, game on, I take it?"

Carter had just returned from two weeks in the sweltering coastal capital of the People's Republic of Equatorial Africa (PREA), a newly-minted democracy with recently-discovered oil reserves of high-quality crude that would someday make it one of Africa's wealthiest nations. Easily exploitable new finds in relatively shallow waters of this magnitude were increasingly rare, and a turf war not seen since the Iraqi oil field auctions of 2009 and 2010 had erupted between the oil majors in the PREA. A relatively unknown consortium of wildcatters out of Texas and their company Javelina Energy had, surprisingly, emerged with the major concession. After a hasty IPO, the young company's stock price had skyrocketed to $300 almost overnight. With production already ramping up to almost four million barrels a day, and reserves estimated to be well in the tens of billions of barrels, Javelina Energy and the PREA would likely be writing one of the last great fossil fuel success stories of the 21st century.

Or not.

The game was definitely on, with Carter handing off the third in a series of $50 million installment payments to the old general and former president, a proud man with tribal scars etched deeply across his cheeks who bridled at the notion this upstart new president from a rival tribe was somehow now in a position to give him orders and slowly, inextricably, strip him of power.

The plan was simple and right out of the time-honored African despot playbook and the dog-eared chapter on coups. If all went well, President Mugambe's plane would experience a catastrophic mechanical failure and plunge into the jungle in about six weeks' time. With the death of the new president, who better than General Abdul Malik to reluctantly step in and restore order with the understanding that martial law was just temporary?

And who would blame the old general if, after the discovery of evidence that the recently-deceased president had received millions in payments from Javelina Energy, he then nationalized PREA's oil industry, thus putting Javelina out of business and, as he would likely spin it, "Safeguarding our sacred birthright from evil colonial powers."

The reinforced custom Herman Miller Eames executive chair creaked under the strain as Victor leaned back, kicked his bare feet onto the enormous five-inch-thick section of highly-polished sequoia tree trunk that served as his desktop, and looked out at the Chicago skyline. A snarling ten-foot-tall Alaskan brown bear was propped on its hind legs with giant forelegs and paws extended in menacing fashion in one corner of the office, wearing an oversized Chicago Bears helmet. Victor had chosen the corner office, with its floor-to-ceiling glass walls 75 floors up in the John Hancock building so he could look south down the lakefront and toward Soldier Field in the distance. He put his hands behind his head, swiveled a bit in his chair, and looked out at the vast inland sea, slate gray under an overcast sky, the Indiana shoreline barely visible to the east.

Victor had to admit, the PREA project was an audacious gambit even for him, but the risks—and there were plenty of them—paled in comparison to the upside, which he'd calculated could be as much as $2 billion in short sale profits when Javelina Energy shares plummeted as they were sure to do. Then there was probably as much to be made when oil prices spiked upward as they inevitably would when PREA went temporarily offline. He was already snapping up calls on the other oil majors from secret trading accounts in London and Hong Kong. He had quietly, and without his partners' knowledge, moved most of the Fitzgerald Black assets in his control into covering these positions, and paying off the general caused Victor a few sleepless nights, but also that indescribable and highly pleasurable rush he remembered experiencing on the eve of a particularly big game. The Balls' sudden windfall couldn't have come at a better time and seemed to Victor to be a harbinger that the gods were indeed on his side. It was money that wouldn't be missed, at least in the short term, and who better to put it to good use?

"Well done, Carter," he said, finally. "This is the Big Kahuna. If we pull this off there's a nice little seven-figure pot at the end of the rainbow for you. You'll be able to go back to that island of yours and buy a few shrimp boats or launch that seafood restaurant you're always talking about or, hell, just sit on your ass in the sand all day."

"Thank you, sir," Carter said. *Fishing boat, my ass.* When the time came, he would be asking for something more in the low eight figures. Real fuck-you money, as Carter had heard Victor's crew call it.

"Now, on to other things," Victor said. "How's my little pet project coming along?"

"Operation PowerBalls?" Carter smiled at Victor's name for the assignment and pulled some eight-by-ten photos from a manila folder and tossed them onto Victor's desk.

Victor leaned forward, his interest piqued. He picked up one of the photos and gazed closely at it. "That's not—no, it can't be."

"Rose Ball."

Victor laid the photos down, shaking his head, a rueful smile on his face. The night vision photography was grainy and shot from a bit of a distance, but it was clearly Rose, straddling what looked to be a young and particularly well-built man.

"I made a run or two at her over the years, who wouldn't, but Rose was always so, well, solid," Victor said. He leaned back in his chair, hands behind his head. "Who's the guy? What do we know about him?"

Carter read from his small notebook. "Francisco Javier Torres. Professional polo player. Rated as a ten-goaler by the time he was just 24. Known for his particularly aggressive, no-holds-barred style of attack. Classic South American rags-to-riches tale. The story begins when a starving kid living on the mean streets of Barrio Santa Fe in Bogotá tries to pick the pockets of one Hector Ramos."

"Hector Ramos?" Victor asked, raising his eyebrows. "You mean Don Hector?"

"Yes, *that* Hector Ramos," Carter said. "Something about the boy's audaciousness must have gotten Don Hector's attention, because instead of ending up in the Bogotá city dump with the others who have crossed Don Hector, young Torres was soon mucking out horse stalls at Don Hector's finca out in the country. Evidently the kid has an uncanny skill with horses, and that's saying something down there. The rest as they say, is history. Gifted young polo player with powerful, well-connected patron quickly works his way up the polo food chain and lands a spot with Team Victoria, the sport's equivalent to the New York Yankees."

"And all the perks that go with it," Victor said, looking down at the photographs on his desk. He looked up at Carter. "Keep an eye on her, Carter. She's Suzanne's oldest friend, not to mention . . ."

"An important asset?" Carter smiled. "No worries, boss, I'll keep you posted. Now, regarding the other half of the PowerBalls, there are some developments."

"I'm not that good."

Samantha's loud moans gradually subsided. "My God, Henry, that was, you were . . ."

"Magnificent?" Henry asked, and they both laughed. *I've crossed the Rubicon*, Henry thought, *the die is cast.* How odd, he thought, that despite all the years of faithfulness to Rose, he did not now feel an overwhelming sense of guilt or remorse. The fact that he was now enormously wealthy must have something to do with it, he mused. *Perhaps Agnes was wrong, maybe the rich are different, and the rules don't apply.*

"Now, would you mind untying my hands, love? Can't feel my fingers."

She'd been surprisingly physical and evidently liked being pursued, and the room was littered with their clothes. They'd had quite a lot to drink at dinner, and on the ride to her apartment in Henry's new Range Rover Sam had, to Henry's surprise, produced a joint. Stoned for the first time in years, he'd been emboldened enough that he bent over to kiss her the instant they'd walked into her apartment. She reciprocated hungrily at first, but then slapped him across the face hard, and the game was on. She ran screaming but Henry made a lunge and brought her down heavily on the couch. As he sought to hastily unbutton her blouse, she elbowed him in the solar plexus and managed to wriggle free. He gasped in pain and as she broke loose Henry made a desperate dive for her legs and just managed to trip her, and she landed heavily on the floor.

He crawled to where she lay, concerned that the game they were playing, one he'd never even imagined playing with Rose, had gotten a bit out of hand. She rolled onto her back, eyes closed and seemingly dazed by the fall. "Tie me, Henry," she muttered. "Use your belt. Tie my hands."

Henry pulled his belt off, straddled her and pushed her arms above her head. He looped his belt around her wrists and tied a makeshift knot. She fought half-heartedly but he had her pinned under his considerable weight. Her face was flushed as he tore her blouse open, revealing her magnificent décolletage and a sheer black lace bra. She moaned. "Oh God, Henry, please, please don't, you're going to spank me now, aren't you? You're going to have your way with me."

He rolled her over on her stomach, struggled a bit to pull off her slacks and panties, and threw them to the side.

"Harder, Henry," she gasped, as Henry slapped her bottom softly and then harder as she cried out in a mixture of what seemed like both pleasure and pain.

After, as he untangled himself from her, she said, "You're not even gone yet, and I miss you. When can I see you again?"

"Right after I get out of the ICU."

Now, with the effects of the pot starting to diminish, Henry was reasonably sure he'd torn an ACL on his last decisive lunge to bring Sam down, and his lower back was beginning to spasm. He crawled toward his pants beside the tattered remains of a new Hugo Boss shirt he couldn't remember ripping off. He pulled a throw off the couch, crawled back, and spread it out over Samantha.

"This is about to get complicated," he said, looking down at Samantha. Oddly enough, he didn't seem to care. *Yes, the rich really are different.*

When Your Ship Comes In

"Come, meet my girlfriends."

Cisco took Rose's hand and led her into the barn. The sun was barely up but it was already quite warm, and the not-unpleasant smell of horse manure, hay, and horseflesh hung heavily in the air despite the big ceiling fans going overhead. A dozen or so horses leaned out of their stalls, ears perked, looking curiously at their first visitors of the day. A few neighed excitedly, anticipating breakfast or perhaps the sugar or peppermint treats Cisco typically doled out for them as a reward the day after a match.

They stopped by one stall and the horse leaned out expectantly over the half door. She was bay colored with a black mane and white face. Cisco stroked her neck and she pushed against his hand in an almost cat-like fashion. Rose, who loved animals but had no experience with horses was a little taken aback by the size of the animal up close but knew better than to show fear. She reached out tentatively and stroked the horse's nose. Cisco offered a handful of sugar cubes to Rose and gestured toward the horse. Rose held them out and the horse eagerly nuzzled Rose's hand, taking them quickly in her wet, gentle, and surprisingly dexterous lips.

Cisco laughed. "Sí, a good sign, Chica likes you," he said. "See how the others watch? She is 12, the oldest. She is, how you say, *la jefa*, the boss. Gentle, sí, but with the heart of a tiger. Do you ride? No? Then we will start you on Chica."

Cisco led Rose by the hand to the next stall. A larger horse, almost jet black, eyed Rose warily. Cisco gave Rose a handful of sugar cubes. She held them out, but the horse took a step back. It stamped a hoof and whinnied loudly, head bobbing up and down.

Cisco shook his head disapprovingly. "This is El Gato Negro, The Black Cat. She is a beauty, no? Fast too, like winged Pegasus. But arrogant. The other ponies, no like so much. She is very jealous of you. Watch." Cisco reached out and stroked Rose's hair, then drew her close and kissed her. El Gato Negro stamped hard and took a few steps toward them angrily. Cisco laughed and drew Rose back away from the stall, wagging a finger at the horse.

"Is there a reason all your horses are mares?" Rose asked as they walked out of the barn into the morning sunshine. Two teenage boys had just pulled up in a golf cart, evidently to feed and water the horses and muck the stalls in preparation for the day's training and exercise regimen.

"Buenos días, Senor Torres," they said almost in unison, respect evident in their voices. Cisco nodded politely and issued a few quick commands in Spanish. As they walked away, both glanced back at Rose shyly, and she could hear them talking about them excitedly in rapid Spanish as they entered the barn.

"Yes, of course, mares are best," Cisco explained. "Smart and brave. Sí, some prefer geldings, but for me, not so much. A mare will listen, a gelding must be told. Others, like the great Argentine, Cambiaso, have their test tube ponies," Cisco said, as they walked toward Rose's car. She detected a note of disdain evident in his voice.

"Test tube ponies?" Rose asked.

"Sí, clones. Every pony the same."

"I had no idea," Rose said. "I've heard of sheep and maybe pet dogs being cloned. But not horses. It's allowed?"

"Sí, allowed, but for many of us it is, how you say, *falso*, something phony. No matter. We will play them this summer, in England, and then again in France, for all the marbles, as you Americans say. His clones against my Chica, the Black Cat, and the others. The old ways against the new. Cambiaso and his clones are very good, no? No one believes we can win. We will see. I think this time we will have lady luck on our side?"

They'd reached Rose's car. She turned to face him. He pressed her gently up against the car and bent forward to kiss her.

"Come with us, Rose, for the season in Europe," he whispered, as he nuzzled her neck. "It is very exciting. My teammates, they are the best, you will like them. Some have their women with them, some not. No matter. We will have such fun. You will see."

Rose looked up at Cisco, surprised and very pleased by his sudden and unexpected offer. What would have seemed like an act of, at best, complete irresponsibility months ago and at worst, self-destruction, now seemed like the perfect thing at this point in her life. The thought of traveling through Europe with this exciting man had great appeal, particularly now that she was unencumbered by money worries for the first time in her life and, for at least the time being, at loose ends domestically. But while she trusted her instincts, she couldn't yet be completely sure about his motivation. She looked into his eyes, searching for answers.

"So, am I to be your latest conquest, just along for the ride?" Rose asked, playfully, but seeking to gauge the sincerity of his offer by his reaction.

"You are the first woman Chica has approved of," he said, seriously. "Until now, I have not wanted a woman along; not wanted, how you say, the distraction. My ponies and me, we are like fighters, always in training. Or a monk, no? But with you, it is somehow different. Come with us, Rose. Say yes."

After a brief moment Rose reached out and took Cisco's face in her hands. "Yes, my love, yes, wherever it takes us," she said, and she pulled him toward her.

"First thing we'll do is buy a bigger boat," Samantha said as she came up out of the cabin, steadied herself on the top step, then carefully carried a thermos of hot tea aft to where Dex stood at the wheel.

The squall had arrived an hour earlier than the marine weather channel had forecast. Dex's vintage 32-foot Herreshoff sailing sloop, with its classic lines that made for speed and particularly nimble handling in lighter air, was struggling to reach Belmont Harbor, fighting a 25-knot headwind and the characteristically short, choppy Lake Michigan waves building now to four or five feet.

Nonetheless, Dex was in high spirits. He relished the physicality of a fight against the elements and had taken in only a little sail. Most importantly, he was about to be a very wealthy man.

Samantha winced noticeably as she sat gingerly by Dex. "Bum's still a bit sore, that wanker."

"Small price to pay for $10 million," Dex said.

"Easy for you to say," she said, pouting a bit.

Dex laughed. "Sorry, babe, I know that couldn't have been pleasant, but imagine the pleasure we get when we fuck Ball out of, who knows, $10 million? Twenty?"

"That does salve the wound a bit," Samantha said. "Anything I can do to help?

"Saw a rough cut of the edited video last night," Dex said. "Billy's a genius. This is right up there with the Zapruder film. We'll have Ball by the balls after he sees it." He laughed, turned to Sam, reached out and stroked her hair, and then pulled her hood up onto her head to give her some protection from the spray.

"Relax, babe, I'll take it from here. He'll pay us. He'll have to. Amazing how much someone's respectability can suddenly be worth."

Carter Banks, sitting at a corner window table in the Chicago Yacht Club dining room, sipped his beer. Victor was a member, if for nothing else than for yet another opportunity to rub elbows with old Chicago money, and Carter had snagged a table and had lunch on Victor's tab. The room was empty, save for a few members playing gin.

Carter picked up his old Army-issue spotter's binoculars and brought the sloop back into focus. The boat was still about half a mile out from Belmont Harbor and seemed to be taking quite a beating, with the waves breaking over the bow as the boat plunged down and then struggled up out of the trough between waves. There weren't any other boats on the water that he could see. He could make out both Dex and Samantha in their yellow wet weather gear in the cockpit aft. He guessed it would be another 30 minutes or so before they reached the harbor, pulled into their slip, and tied up.

He was certain Dex had the rough-cut of the video on board because he'd gone right from that sleazeball Billy Kwiatkowski's apartment to the harbor late last night. Billy—whose rap sheet as video blackmailer, con man, and small-time grifter stretched back so far that Carter had run into him a few times during his days on the force—had given up the original memory card and external hard drive that he'd dumped the video footage onto without protest. Carter had put the nine-millimeter Sig Sauer to Billy's head for good measure, making it clear if the video ever surfaced Billy would also star in a video airing on WGN-TV some night: that of a John Doe being fished out of the Chicago River.

Now, all he had to do was wait. He sat back, sipped his beer, and looked out at the marina. He felt a little sorry for Ball, whom he'd grown to like, cuckolded now by both his wife and supposed mistress but what the hell, having that much money couldn't help but soften the blow.

Yes, my ship is coming in too, he thought as he looked out at the lake and the lone sailboat. *Won't be long now before I get what's coming to me.*

Go Biggs or Go Home

"The sad fact is that the political landscape is changing and it's open season on middle-age white men," Henry said, deep into his third Glenmorangie. "We're in danger of going the way of the Dodo or, hell, the Quagga."

Henry took another puff from his pre-Castro Monte Cristo No. 3, a very expensive, highly prized and, outside Havana, particularly hard to find cigar. He'd selected it from the 50 or so Cuban Monte Cristos, Cohibas, and Romeo Y Julietas that he now kept in his very own humidified locker at the Biggs Mansion, a white stucco, three-story Federalist-style landmark sitting incongruously among the tall apartment buildings and bustling neighborhoods in the heart of Chicago's Gold Coast.

Biggs seemed tailor-made as a refuge against political correctness, repurposed to be, as the owner's mission statement said, *A haven where personal liberty is neither taken for granted nor compromised.*

As the statement implied, Biggs catered to the whims of a mostly male, predominantly Republican membership seeking privacy and relaxation with others sharing a similar interest in fine cigars, 25-year-old single-malt scotch, and perhaps a discrete rendezvous with a generally much younger woman outside the prying eyes of the public. Conversation in the heavily paneled, deeply leathered lounge inevitably centered on the rising or falling fortunes of the Bears, Blackhawks, or Cubs, the most recent events in politics or the markets, a snippet of juicy gossip, or an old war story. In short, Biggs was the place to go for the generally harmless diversions that added spice to the life of the deep-pocketed media and entertainment celebrities, jocks, and traders that made up most of its membership.

Henry had joined on the recommendation of Victor Black, and in fact the Capitalist Pigs considered Biggs to be their informal clubhouse. Henry secretly loved it. He had used a hackneyed old line and gotten a few laughs at a new member 'Biggs Smoker' when he said he'd never join a club that would accept him as a member. But he found himself enjoying the decidedly macho atmosphere and rubbing elbows with men that now considered him, if not a peer, at least worthy of sharing a casual conversation and passing a pleasant evening. Oddly enough, as a lifelong non-smoker, he'd also taking a liking to cigars. He guessed it might be a bit of a Pavlovian response, associated with the immense pleasure he'd felt when he'd ground his first cigar into the top of Dex's desk.

"Quagga?" Carter Banks laughed. He reached over and poured himself another two fingers from the bottle of Glenmorangie. "Damn, this is some fine scotch, Ball."

"Yes, a zebra-like beast once found in South Africa, but only half its body was striped," Henry said. "Hunted to extinction."

It was a warm, still, summer evening, and they were sitting on the Biggs' patio courtyard fronting North Dearborn. The streetlights had just come on. It was a bustling residential neighborhood with a dozen good restaurants within walking distance. The sudden, pungent, and increasingly rare smell of cigars hanging in the air caused some of the male passersby to pause suddenly and peer through the wrought iron fencing at the dim, mysterious figures within. It seemed to Henry that the men in almost every case seemed hesitant to leave for just a split second longer than the women they were with, as though longing to be inside the fence and enjoying one of those increasingly rare evenings when the stifling façade of political correctness can be safely dropped.

Henry glanced over at Carter. *Like a pig in shit,* Henry thought, using one of Carter's expressions to describe the look of contentment on the man's face. The two had struck up a friendship of sorts over the course of half a dozen Sunday bike rides with the Pigs, regular workouts at the East Bank Club that Carter had insisted on, and increasingly frequent nights at Biggs. As was the case with most friendships, Henry found Carter possessed characteristics he both admired and felt were perhaps lacking in himself; most notably, Carter's supreme self-confidence. While Henry suspected Victor had assigned Carter to him and Rose for both their protection and Victor's, he also imagined Carter liked being around him for, if nothing else, a refreshing change of pace from the burden of the constant machismo that was expected of him.

"Carter, you ever been married?" Henry asked. It was the type of question Carter usually fended off, but Henry was feeling the compounding effects of Scotch and Cuban cigar and seeking a subtle way to take Carter into his confidence.

"Shit, no woman worth her salt would want me—a beat up old soldier working hours not fit for a taxi driver," he said. "Maybe when I get back to the island. Too busy now looking after Victor's interests." He glanced pointedly at Henry.

"Settle down with a nice Geechee girl, no doubt?" Henry asked.

"Hell no!" Carter laughed. "Geechee girls work their men like a rented mule and want a houseful of kids. I want a nice quiet life with a woman that will pour me a drink at the end of the day, rub my tired feet now and then, and keep me warm in my old age. Like what you got with Miss Rose. I dig that woman. You best get down on hands and knees and worship the ground she walks on when she gets back in town."

Henry glanced around. "Look, Carter, there's something you should know," he said, lowering his voice conspiratorially. "I'm leaving Rose. Best thing for both of us. We've grown apart over the years. If anything, the money's divided us even more. There was a time when I would have chopped off an arm rather than lose her, but now, well, we both have other interests."

Carter laughed and shook his head sadly. "You referring to an English tart by the name of Samantha Tarleton?"

Henry stared at Carter. "You know?"

Carter sipped his drink. He hesitated for a moment, and then pulled his iPhone out of his inside jacket pocket. "This is going to smart a bit, Henry."

Carter found the video on his phone, clicked on it to begin playing, and held it up for Henry to see. Henry watched expressionless as the cleverly edited video showed Henry assaulting a seemingly terrified Samantha Tarleton played out in graphic detail. The video had been made to look very grainy, and its poor, herky-jerky quality seemed to cover for the fact that there were short sections of video footage and audio that seemed to be missing here and there throughout the video. Still, the overall effect was that of a poor-quality CCTV capturing the sudden, violent assault of a clearly terrified victim who had tried, but failed, to flee from her attacker.

Henry handed the phone back to Carter and slumped back in his chair.

"Sorry, Henry, but Samantha and that boyfriend Dex were setting you up all along," Carter said. "If I had to guess, you would have paid millions rather than have that out in public. Anyway, I got to them first. A few nights ago, on their boat. You can thank Victor. He's got a sixth sense about shit like this. In his immortal words, 'Being a billionaire ain't for the faint of heart.' Shit like this happens all the time. Luckily, guys like me are around to clean it up. There's nothing quite like the persuasive powers of a nine-millimeter held to the side of one's head. You'll be happy to know that Dex was whimpering like a schoolgirl when I put old Sig up to his temple and forced him to give up the one and only copy."

A few hours later, after they'd finished the last of the Glenmorangie, Carter helped Henry up the stairs of the Biggs and lowered him gently into one of the deep leather chairs in the lounge. It was late and the room was empty. There was an old-school turntable and a nice selection of classic vinyl in a rack on the lounge's massive floor-to-ceiling bookcase. Carter, finding one he liked, put it on. "Oh yeah," Carter said, as the soulful voice of Al Green began playing softly in the background.

"I'm so tired of being alone so tired of on my own won't you help me girl just as soon as you can."

Carter sang the melody in a pleasant voice several octaves lower than Al's. When the song ended, he flipped the LP to the other side. "Nothing better than the Reverend Green when your heart's been broken."

"Carter, how much to kill that British wench and her evil boyfriend?" Henry asked, stirring suddenly from his stupor. He was very drunk. "Got a million for you. Make it look like an accident. Two million. Name your price. Gonna make them pay."

"No, Henry, that's not my thing," Carter said. "And anyway, tomorrow you'll wake up no worse for wear, and having learned a valuable lesson: never accept an invitation to tie a woman up."

"Look, I got a few weeks of downtime," Carter said after a moment. "Best thing to do is get away for a while, someplace new, exotic. It'll help you get some perspective. Get back in the saddle. What say we take a trip?"

"I'm in!" Henry slurred.

Carter reached over and spun the enormous antique globe that sat on the floor between them. "Okay, wherever I put my finger to stop the globe is where we'll go, on your nickel of course," Carter said.

"Any place 'cept Iowa City," Henry mumbled, thinking of the popular Iowa college town where he and Rose had spent a small fortune on Zach's eight-year college stint.

Carter reached out and stuck his index finger hard against the spinning globe, stopping it suddenly. Both men leaned forward to see what location fate had selected for them. "Well, I'll be damned," Carter laughed. "Right square on Havana, Cuba. Always wanted to go there." He looked over for a response from Henry, but he'd slumped back in his seat and was already starting to snore.

A Gypsy in Paris

There are the iconic places in the world both natural and man-made that, whether through reputation or literature or long history, loom so large in one's imagination and take on so great a degree of significance that they can't help but underwhelm when actually experienced for the first time.

Then there is Paris.

The woman stopped for a moment on the Pont de Arts bridge over the Seine to get her bearings. She thought that nothing she'd read or seen in photos over the years had adequately captured the city's magnificence. To the northwest she could just make out the Louvre, and there, just behind her and upstream to the east, was the Pont Neuf and Notre Dame behind it. A long river boat with open deck filled with excited Japanese tourists motored under the bridge right below her and when it emerged a few of the people looked up at the woman and waved enthusiastically.

She wore a black beret—*tres bourgoise Americain*—and a dead giveaway of the type of tourist the Parisians seemed to disdain but, c'est la vie, it made her feel, well, bohemian. Judging from her black turtleneck and Levi's and running shoes the woman, while attractive, was without fashion sense and clearly a little down on her luck. Who would have guessed that the utilitarian outfit was a testament to the 'form follows function' philosophy that ran so deeply in her Midwestern psyche, or that she was one of America's newly-minted billionaires?

It was early afternoon on Rose's third day in Paris. An unseasonably warm late October breeze swept down the Seine from the west, bringing with it a delicious aroma that was part fresh bakery, part charcoal grill and just a hint of fish. Rose was suddenly very hungry despite the enormous breakfast she'd had early that morning at her hotel. Paris was a city of walkers, and she knew now how the Parisians, all of whom seemed slight, undersized, and extremely well-dressed by comparison to their American counterparts, managed to eat and drink into all hours of the night with seeming impunity.

Suzanne, in town for Fashion Week, had been surprised and a bit dismayed by Rose's choice of hotels: the simple, quaint, and unknown little Hotel Les Jardins du Luxemburg. It had none of the amenities of the bigger, better-known hotels that Suzanne had recommended, all of which were in much closer proximity to all the great shopping around Champs-Elysees. Suzanne of course was staying in her usual suite at the five-star Hotel Four Seasons George V, a stone's throw from her favorite couture atelier, Chanel, and the Michelin-starred Le 39V, where the *ravioli parmentier a la truffe noir* was, according to Suzanne, even better than sex.

But the Hotel Les Jardins was exactly what Rose had been looking for: a quiet, cozy little place on the left bank at the end of a dead-end street right off the Boulevard Saint Michel and directly across from the Luxemburg Gardens. This placed it strategically between the fifth and sixth arrondissements where St. Germain de Pere and the Latin Quarter butted together. In short: within easy walking distance of the Closerie de Lilas, Les Deux Margots, Café de Flore, and a dozen other of the Lost Generation's favorite haunts.

You couldn't swing a cat in her tiny room, Suzanne had commented when she'd come to pick up Rose for dinner that first night after her arrival, but for 12 euros you got a splendid breakfast of scrambled eggs and bacon, croissants and pain au chocolate, strong coffee, fruit, cereal, and yogurt. The staff was friendly and spoke reasonably good English and there was a tiny zinc bar with complimentary champagne and canapés for the guests at the end of the day.

If you are lucky enough to have lived in Paris as a young man, then wherever you go for the rest of your life, it stays with you, for Paris is a moveable feast.

Rose smiled, thinking of Hemingway's famous line about his favorite city. How true. Paris was a seemingly endless feast for all the senses, one course after the next of the art, food, history, and culture she'd been starved of for so long, and her three days there had done nothing yet to satiate her appetite for more.

Rose leaned against the rail. Paris was well inland, but she sensed the sea, with the sharp cries of the gulls over the river and the low, scuttling sea clouds against the soft, blue fall sky. Rose slipped the Paris street map out of the cross-body Chanel handbag, her one concession to fashion, and spread the map out on the rail.

There was still so much to see in the few remaining days she'd planned on staying in Paris. She'd already checked the d'Orsay off her list the day before with Cisco, gone to the top of the Eiffel Tower, taken a river boat, and a dozen of the other things tourists were expected to do. She'd need at least a full day at the Louvre, another day for Montparnasse, and then perhaps a trip out to Versailles. *C'est beaucoup!* So much left for her to do in this beautiful city.

This morning she had started the day with a brisk, buoyant walk up the Boule Mich toward the Seine. With another day in Paris stretching out in front of her, she couldn't seem to stop smiling, eliciting curious, but not unfriendly glances from many of the typically stoic Parisians hurrying along the wide, crowded sidewalk.

Then she turned down Quai de Montibello to make a long-anticipated stop at the iconic little English bookstore, Shakespeare & Co. She browsed the tight, crooked, musty maze of floor-to-ceiling bookshelves, finally finding an old copy of Joyce's *Ulysses* stamped with the famous "Shakespeare & Co. Kilometre Zero Paris." It was a book Rose had tried once or twice in the past and found almost indecipherable, but now she figured she had the time, and perhaps the right perspective, to finally crack Joyce's difficult code.

Then she'd crossed over the Seine to the Ile de La Cite for a visit to Sainte-Chapelle, the ancient 13th century chapel built to house Jesus' crown of thorns. She arrived just as the rising sun sent light streaming dustily through the high wall of magnificent stained-glass windows.

Finally, a loop up the Quai de L'Hôtel de Ville on the right bank and back to the Left Bank on the Pont des Arts. Now, back to the Quartier Latin for lunch at one of the outdoor cafes—La Grange Aux Canards perhaps?—a glass or two of wine, and a short, delicious nap before drinks and dinner later that night with Suzanne.

Rose started to cross the Quai Conti into the Quartier but the long row of open-air stalls west along the Seine caught her eye. Ah, the Bouquinistes, a chance for a nice original watercolor or perhaps a rare early edition Fitzgerald? Lunch could wait just a little longer. She crossed Rue Bonaparte and turned to walk up the Quai toward the stalls.

Rose was talking with the proprietor of a booth selling vintage postcards of Paris street scenes when she felt someone tug on her arm. A boy whom Rose guessed was around ten years old, with an angelic, filthy face, unruly mop of curly red hair, and wearing an old peacoat several sizes too large bowed theatrically. "Madmoiselle, sil vous plait, come see Madame J'aime," and he pointed toward a tiny ancient woman in a black shawl covering a pronounced widow's hump sitting alone at a small table along the river wall. Rose watched as the old woman picked up a bottle of wine from the ground next to her, pulled the cork and took a long pull. She wiped her mouth with her sleeve. She put a stack of cards on the table.

The boy looked up at Rose and pulled softly on her sleeve. "Madame never wrong, come, English lady, you make little Michelle so happy." He tugged a bit more insistently.

Rose, amused and a bit intrigued by these two who she imagined were Roma, Paris' Romanian gypsies, followed the boy to the table. The woman, lips stained red from the bottle of wine, glanced up and gave Rose a hard, questioning stare as if trying to remember her from some long-forgotten event, and then after a moment nodded toward the chair opposite her. Michelle pocketed the euro coin the old woman had slid across the table, bowed, and then dashed off toward a motley group of similarly ill-dressed boys, evidently planning some new caper and gesturing excitedly for him across the quay.

Rose sat opposite the old gypsy. "Bonjour, Madame," Rose said. "Michelle says the madame is never wrong."

The woman cackled. She reached down, picked up the bottle, offered it to Rose. "Non?" she said, raising an eyebrow. She pulled the cork and took a healthy swig. She set the bottle down and reached forward suddenly, grasping Rose's right hand. She held it with surprising firmness, palm up, and pulled it toward her brusquely for closer inspection. She ran an index finger down the indentation Rose had always thought of as her lifeline. The old gypsy looked up after a moment, and then released Rose's hand.

"Madame J'aime wrong many times, pretty lady," she said, in a thick accent that sounded vaguely Russian. "About the Nazis in '40 when they came to kill, again in '61 when Henri left me for a gadji harlot. There have been other times. No matter. J'aime never wrong when reading the cards."

She laid a black silk scarf on the table and began shuffling the deck of old cards, which Rose could see were larger than standard playing cards and with an illustration of a wolf baying at the moon on the outside of each card. She stopped shuffling. "What is your question?" she asked, looking up at Rose.

"Oh, well, I don't know," Rose said. She had an Irish Catholic's unwavering faith in Jesus but put little stock in the occult or anything even vaguely paranormal. Nor was she, by nature, superstitious, yet there was something about the gypsy and her cards that was a bit unsettling, as if a door were about to open that would offer a glimpse into an uncertain future.

"I guess I'd like to know what's next in my life?" Rose said, finally. "Love, happiness, all the usual stuff. What can the cards tell us?"

"Draw three cards and lay them face down one by one next to each other," the gypsy said, sternly. "They will tell us about the past, present and, future."

Rose drew three cards and laid them out in a row on the scarf. The gypsy reached out and turned the card to her left face up. She seemed surprised. The card depicted a woman on a throne, with a large coin in her lap. "Ah, Queen of Pentacles. Very unusual. Great wealth came suddenly into your life, yes? Abundance, beauty, love, all at once. But perhaps too much of a good thing? Let us see."

The gypsy turned over the next card. "Yes, of course, Knight of Wands," she said, looking down at a card showing a knight riding a horse, holding a wand. "Now is a time of adventure, far-away lands, and a man, *tres belle homme*. A man good with horses perhaps? But also, a time of caution. Knight of Wands, oui, an exciting time, but also *tres risqué*."

The gypsy reached out slowly and turned over the last card. "*Mon Dieu*," she said, quietly. The card showed a skeleton wearing a suit of armor astride a white charger against a black background. The skeleton held a flag emblazoned with a red rose.

Rose looked up at the gypsy. "Death?" she asked, apprehensively.

"Oui, death, in all our futures," the old gypsy said. "But also, when something ends, something new begins. Do not be afraid, beautiful lady, I have seen strength and long life in your hand. Death, but also a new beginning. You will come back many times to Paris, even when you are an old woman like me, of that I am sure. Now, 50 USD if you please?" she said, holding out her hand.

Rose stood, feeling a little weak in the knees, found the money in her purse, and handed the old gypsy two twenties and a ten. As Rose walked away, she glanced back over her shoulder. The old gypsy was still watching her, then reached down for her bottle of wine.

The Beginning of a Beautiful Friendship

It was early Sunday morning, and the little fishing village of Santa Rosa was still asleep as seven-year-old Consuela Morales rode her grandfather's ancient swaybacked gray donkey slowly down the narrow main street. Small tin-roofed shanties with just enough yard for a chicken coop or goat pen lined the street. Strutting, imperious Cubalaya cocks with their harems of hens foraging in the road crowed loudly in protest and begrudgingly gave way to the plodding old donkey.

Consuela grinned. A rare appearance by Chico Sanchez, a local boy with prodigious musical talent who had made it big in Havana, and his Orquesta La Banda had drawn a crowd of several thousand to the small village square. The dancing had lasted almost until dawn. Her grandfather, who had been one of the revelers, had evidently pulled a hamstring during a particularly vigorous salsa with a woman half his age, which had given Consuela a rare chance to take the donkey to the edge of town for grass and water along the creek that ran all the way down to the beach and emptied there into the sea.

She saw the old donkey's ears twitch and perk up, and then she heard a low rumble that grew louder. As she turned, two motorcycles in single file emerged suddenly over the low hill on the edge of town and rode toward her down the main street into the village.

"Los Harlistas!" she yelled, excitedly. She kicked her heels into the sides of the old donkey and urged him out of the middle of the street. The two motorcycles slowed as they approached, and as they pulled up alongside Consuela and her donkey they came to a stop and shut off their engines.

Henry Ball, who had quickly come to the conclusion that the Harley was singularly ill-suited for the primitive roads of rural Cuba, climbed slowly and very painfully off the 1951 Knucklehead that had been part of Battista's motorcycle police escort prior to the revolution. Carter Banks got off his red 1950 Panhead, set his helmet on the seat, and stretched. Both men stripped off their light leather jackets and draped them across their handlebars to air them out a bit in the warm morning sun. Henry fished three bottled waters out of a saddle bag, handed one to Carter and held the third as an offering to Consuela, who shook her head no.

The two men had flown into Havana a few weeks before. Carter, having done his usual thorough research, had struck a shrewd bargain for three weeks' rental of the two bikes with several of the senior members of the Harlistas, a loosely affiliated club of Cuban Harley enthusiasts. The Samsonite filled with 50s-era Harley parts had proven irresistible to the Harlistas, just as Carter had predicted, and the deal had been sealed over a few cases of Bucanero beer. This had been followed by a wild night that started at the tiny La Dichosa and a stop at Café Taberna. By then word had spread of the largesse of the two newly-anointed American Harlistas, and their entourage grew to perhaps 100 or more, including two complete bands with instruments. The evening had finally terminated after an impromptu dance party that lasted until dawn on the cobblestones of the old cathedral square.

"Hola, Señorita," Carter said to Consuela as he walked around his bike, still ticking with heat after a hard, three-hour ride. The two men had set out well before dawn that day after spending a pleasant night in a quiet casa on a small farm just outside Pinar del Rio. By starting early, they had made good time for a change and avoided the usual small herds of goats and cattle or the horse-drawn carts with hay or tobacco or sugar cane or bananas driving two abreast with drivers deep in conversation and who, with typical Cuban pride, rarely gave way to motor vehicles.

So, it had taken them the better part of two weeks to circum-navigate the island and now, heading north on the homeward leg to Havana, they hoped to spend a final day snorkeling and spear fishing on Cayo Jutias, a little-known barrier island the locals were secretive about but when pressed spoke proudly about its spectacular reefs and a beach that put the world-famous Veraderos east of Havana to shame.

Carter gently stroked the old donkey's neck. Spanish, French Creole, and even Arabic had come easily to Carter during his Ranger days, and his months-long postings to the various hotspots of his day that included Panama, Grenada, and the Middle East. He asked Consuela where they might find gasoline, explaining they had already passed through nearby San Cayetano and the gasolinera there was closed and waiting, like the gasolineras and shops seemingly everywhere throughout the interior of the island, for re-supply.

The girl smiled at the man's painstaking, heavily accented Spanish. She pointed down the narrow street. "Sí, there at the harbor, the fishermen share gasoline from a big tank," she said slowly in Spanish so the man could understand her response. "Go to where the street turns toward the ocean. You will find it."

"Gracias, señorita, un momento," Carter said, holding up a hand. He walked back to his bike and fished a small box of crayons out of the saddlebag. He handed the crayons to Consuela and bowed. The girl's eyes widened with delight as she opened the box and pulled out a crayon. She tested it by trying to draw her initials on the donkey's short, coarse coat.

"Adios," the men said, almost in unison, anxious now to get moving before the inevitable crowd arrived and surrounded them so that there was no polite way of leaving.

They bartered for more than an hour for the precious fuel with the small group of fishermen at the marina playing their customary Sunday morning dominoes on the dock. The fishermen had eventually settled for 250 Canadian in return for about eight gallons of gas and directions to Cayo Jutias, an exorbitant exchange rate even for Cuba, but one Carter and Henry were happy to pay since it now extended their range to at least the outskirts of Havana, about 180 miles to the northeast.

After another 20 minutes or so of riding, they turned off the main road as they'd been directed onto a narrow dirt two-track that cut through low, dense manigua thicket down to the ocean and the low, sand-swept causeway that took them out onto Cayo Jutias. They took their time, riding carefully around dangerous patches of sand on lumpy asphalt they guessed had been laid before the revolution.

The road ended abruptly at a small frame building painted deep red with a grass thatch roof. The name *Palmares* was painted on the side of the restaurant, which they'd been told was the only building on the entire cayo, and where they could rent snorkeling gear and spears.

A pristine white beach, with just a few figures sunbathing under umbrellas in the distance, stretched from Palmares to the west for miles. Out well beyond the reef and the line of low surf dividing the sea green lagoon from the deep blue whitecapped waters of the gulf stream, a single vessel was anchored, an enormous pleasure yacht with navy blue hull and white superstructure.

The men parked alongside a '57 Chevy Bel Air, a Lincoln convertible older still, and a Russian Lada, which Carter had first seen years ago along a bombed-out stretch of highway leading out of Kuwait, and what he considered to be one of the ugliest cars ever built. They dismounted and walked into the restaurant.

There was one simple room with a wide wooden patio deck that stretched from the open side of the restaurant toward the beach. A long bar ran the length of the interior wall to the right, and there were perhaps tables for 20 or so.

"Hola," Carter said, and the man sweeping up broken glass from behind the bar looked up from his work. Two men sitting at the bar who appeared to be locals looked up from their breakfast and nodded politely.

"Los Harlistas Americanos, we've been expecting you," the man behind the bar said, in surprisingly good English.

Carter, who by training and vocation seemed always on the alert for even the slightest anomaly in unfamiliar surroundings, smiled and gestured toward a table turned on its side and what looked to be a badly smashed chair in one corner of the room. "Surely Los Palmares is too beautiful and peaceful a place to have had any trouble last night?" he casually asked the man.

The man stopped sweeping and nodded his head toward the yacht anchored beyond the reef. "Sí, crewmen from the ship. Russians," he said with a look of disdain. "As you Americans like to say, they got a little out of hand, but it was not something we couldn't handle." He reached under the bar and pulled out a sawed-off double barrel shotgun with a pistol grip in place of the stock. It was typical of that family of weaponry known as a deck sweeper, a useful tool common to so many of the bars and yachts throughout the Caribbean.

Carter laughed, then reached out and the two men shook hands.

The man, who turned out to be the owner of Palmares and who everyone called Ricky, fixed them a light breakfast of fruit and the most delicious lobster quiche they'd ever had. They sat on the patio deck enjoying a small pot of strong Cuban coffee while Ricky brought out several boxes of snorkeling gear: a hodgepodge of mismatched fins, masks, snorkels and a couple of makeshift nylon catch bags; all of which the men guessed had either washed up on shore or been left over the years by the occasional vacationer that stumbled upon the cayo. With a bit of a flourish, Ricky proudly produced two aluminum sling-type spearguns complete with reels and what looked to be plenty of line.

"Now, let me tell you about the fishing," Ricky said, sitting down at the table as Carter and Henry tried on masks and fins. "There is a strong current and with the tide going out now. You will be careful not to go beyond the reef because it will not be so easy to come back inside. No matter, there will be plenty of good fish that have come in at high tide. Take only small snapper and grouper and a few of the spiny lobster you will see hiding in the coral, and we will prepare you a feast this evening that you will tell your grandchildren about."

Ricky paused for a moment, looking out at the big yacht, where it appeared the crew were using a crane to swing a jet ski out over the transom, and then went on. "Be careful not to spear anything bigger than the length of your arm. You will see of course barracuda and perhaps Ernesto, the big goliath grouper that comes in to feed sometimes when the moon is full. But do not be afraid, he will be full by now, and he has eaten only one or two Americans that I know of."

It was perhaps a quarter mile swim to the wall of coral that rose up suddenly some 50 feet from the seabed to form the reef. They proceeded at a leisurely pace, but as the reef came into sight, Carter gave Henry the thumbs up and then hurried impatiently on ahead. Henry, who had no experience nor any real interest in spearfishing, planned on catching only spiny lobster and had one of the catch bags fastened to an ankle. He stopped, treading water for a moment to clear his mask and catch his breath. He proceeded along the surface toward the edge of the reef, took a deep breath, and dove downward, descending slowly, tentatively like some clumsy, weightless astronaut landing for the first time on an unexplored world filled with brilliantly decorated, benign alien life forms.

Henry had read that the Cuban coral reefs were among the best preserved in the world and had not, as of yet, been subjected to the massive degradation and over-fishing occurring throughout the Caribbean and the rest of the world. But nothing could have prepared him for what he saw. He swam through several schools of parrotfish, grunts, and angelfish, all giving way lazily as if there could be nothing to fear from this strange, harmless land creature so clearly out of its element. As he neared the edge of the coral, he caught some movement out of the corner of his eye, and a heavily-built fish the size of a Mini Cooper that he guessed was the huge grouper Ernesto accelerated toward him and then veered off at the last second.

Henry, out of his element and feeling out of breath and a little unnerved by Ernesto's game of chicken, kicked hard toward the surface. He heard the muffled sound of an engine grow suddenly louder and the bottom of a jet ski traveling at a high speed passed about five feet directly over his head. He surfaced just as the jet ski hit a large coral head, flipping it and sending both riders flying.

Neither rider appeared to be wearing a life vest, so Henry went for the woman first, who was screaming almost incoherently in a language Henry wasn't familiar with. She was hysterical but appeared unhurt. Henry gently put his arm under one arm and across her chest, pulled her onto her back and side-kicked with her over to the jet ski that was floating upside down about 20 feet away. She grabbed ahold and Henry struck out for the man, who appeared to be struggling to stay above the surface. As he swam, he heard Carter, who had surfaced a hundred or more yards away, yell his name. Henry stopped for a moment, waved, and pointed emphatically to where the woman was hanging onto the jet ski.

The man was bleeding profusely from some kind of wound to the top of his head. He struggled to stay afloat. He was huge, thickly built, with powerful arms and shoulders, so Henry approached cautiously, knowing how dangerous it could be to try to assist a panicking man of this size in the water. Henry managed to circle around behind him, got an arm around his neck, and began to side kick toward shore. The man struggled at first and protested in what sounded to Henry like Russian, but relaxed quickly and seemed barely conscious as they made slow progress.

As they approached shore, Henry yelled for help. After a moment Ricky and one of the other men came out of the Palmeres and ran across the beach and into the shallows. Henry reached them, got his fins off, and then the three of them half-dragged, half-carried the man onto shore. They laid him on his back and then Ricky ran back to the Palmeres to get the first aid kit.

The effort of both staying afloat and hauling so much dead weight had left Henry exhausted. He collapsed on the beach, and then rolled onto his back, gasping for breath. When he heard a jet ski start up, he managed to sit up. Carter had righted the jet ski and gotten it started, and he and the girl were slowly making their way to the beach. Out beyond the breakers, a Zodiac with three men on board was running parallel to the reef, trying to find a passage in.

Ricky returned, used a towel to wipe the blood from the big man's face, and began working to sterilize and bandage his wounded scalp. Henry crawled over to them.

"How is he?" Henry asked.

"Flesh wound, much blood but nothing to worry about," Ricky said. "Heads like rock, these Russians. I warned them about coming inside the reef with the tide going out, but Comrade Volkov does what he pleases."

Upon hearing his name, the big man smiled, tried to sit up, but thought better of it and laid back down. He turned toward Henry, extending a hand. "Gregor Ivanovich Volkov."

Henry took his hand. "Henry," he said. "Looks like your passenger's all right, too." He pointed toward the jet ski that was now almost to the beach.

"In your debt," Volkov said in English. He seemed not to notice the arrival of the jet ski. "Be my guest for dinner tonight. I send boat."

Last Call on the Left Bank

"So, this is really where Fitzgerald and Hemingway met for the first time?"

"Oui, Madame, it is true," the bartender said, looking up from the drinks he was mixing.

"It is said that Hemingway carried Monsieur Fitzgerald out over his shoulder at the end of many nights."

"Either your man Fitzgerald couldn't hold his liquor, or he had a thing for Hemingway," Suzanne laughed. She held up her glass for a toast with Rose.

Suzanne and Rose sat on the tall red leather upholstered stools at the bar in the La Closerie des Lilas, sipping French 75s. Suzanne had agreed to slum it and come over to the Quartier for dinner and drinks at the famous brasserie. She wrinkled her nose at travel on the metro—"Have you smelled it?" she'd asked—but had arranged for her usual car and driver, now parked down the street within easy hailing distance. A good thing, too, Suzanne had said, since the French 75, her favorite Paris drink, was scrumptious going down but packed a near-lethal wallop.

The bar was very crowded but two good-looking Frenchmen had given up their seats for the women. The Frenchmen had stayed close for a drink or two, encouraged by Suzanne's friendly banter, which seemed even more flirtatious in French, and the pheromones that she seemed incapable of not producing around men. But when it became clear that Rose had no interest, the men had wandered off toward other quarry.

"So, how goes it with Cisco?" Suzanne asked. "Still in the honeymoon stage, or trouble in paradise?"

Rose laughed. "Are those my only choices? It's been good, what little I see of him. Polo, the ponies, team meetings, it's been crazy. We did spend a nice day yesterday at the d'Orsay, but then he had to go up to Deauville for the next few days."

"Had to see a man about a horse?" Suzanne laughed. "The d'Orsay. Pretty artsy for a polo player. How'd he like it?"

"Not sure," Rose said. "I think Manet's *Olympia* got his attention, and he really liked Delacroix's *The Lion Hunt*. He didn't think the Van Goghs were very well done. Said he could probably do better than Gauguin."

They laughed. "So, to paraphrase Aristotle, what news out of Chicago?" Rose asked. "How's Victor?"

"Aristotle? My, aren't we the Left Bank intellectual," Suzanne chuckled. "Victor? Same as always. Something big going on right now, judging from the game face he's got on. Haven't seen that look since before his one and only start at Lambeau. All very hush hush."

She paused for a moment, then gently took Rose's hand. "Rosie, Victor told me something before I left that I think you should know. It's about Cisco."

"Cisco?"

"Well, you know Victor does his homework, and he has his clients' best interests at heart, even more so when they're also close friends."

Rarely had Rose seen Suzanne looking so uncomfortable. The mild sense of dread that she'd begun experiencing earlier that day during the tarot card reading began to return. "Go on," she said.

Suzanne lowered her voice. "Look, Rosie, nothing to worry about, but Victor thought you should know that Cisco's benefactor, his patrón as they call it down there, is a man known as Don Hector. Emphasis on the *don*."

"The don?" Rose said, shaking her head. "Not sure I follow."

"Rosie, Victor says Don Hector is head of a Colombian drug cartel. That kind of don. Victor said you should be really careful. I've learned over the years that if Victor says there's cause for alarm, then it's serious. He doesn't know what role Cisco's got in this—but why take chances? Maybe it's time for you to come home. You've had a nice adventure, now let's get you settled in with somebody safe, rich, and boring. Perhaps a rapprochement with Henry? You could do a lot worse, now that he's worth half a billion."

Rose stared at Suzanne, incredulous. She was reeling from what Suzanne had just told her, and her thoughts seemed to be coming to her in slow motion through the fog that had enveloped her after a third French 75. She suddenly felt a little sick to her stomach and pushed the drink away.

"That night at Bunny's place, when I met Cisco," Rose said, finally. "Always wondered about that. Wasn't an accident, was it, Suzanne? You set that up." Rose could tell from the look on Suzanne's face that she'd guessed right. "So, want to tell me about it?"

"Look, Rosie, it seemed harmless enough. Good-looking polo player meets beautiful older woman. Happens all the time down there during the season. I didn't think a little push would do any harm. Lord knows you needed it. How's that any different than the time I slipped Eddy Reynolds that fake note in anatomy and physiology class, saying you wanted to dissect his hot body? And anyway, who cares?" Suzanne said, forcing a laugh and seeking to diffuse the situation.

"So, when you pointed Cisco in my direction did the fact that I was worth half a billion come up?" Rose, in a cold fury, whispered. "Or were my hot looks enough to do the trick?"

Rose stood, swaying a bit as she sought to get her balance. She looked down at Suzanne, a contemptuous half-smile on her face. She bent down suddenly and grasped Suzanne behind her neck with both hands, pulled her face forward, and kissed her full on the lips. "Suzanne, you're my oldest friend and I love you," she said. "But don't ever get involved in my love life again."

Rose turned and walked slowly and unsteadily out of the Closerie.

Friends for Life

There was a rough sea running and as the Zodiac tender slowly rounded the stern of the ship and pulled alongside the swim platform off the transom, Volkov stood in a blue blazer and khaki Bermuda shorts, hands on hips and powerful legs planted wide apart, providing stability. He seemed none the worse for wear and had only a small bandage on the top of his shaved head as an indication of the mishap earlier that day. A few crewmembers stood behind him, waiting. *Ursus Major* and Nassau were painted in large gold letters against the dark blue hull. The Big Dipper, which Henry knew formed part of the constellation known as Ursus Major—the Great Bear—was artfully connected to the ship's name.

The tender pilot got Henry's attention and pantomimed the throwing of a line, and Henry picked up a heavy black line tied to the aft starboard cleat of the tender. Now the pilot expertly backed the tender so it butted gently against the swim platform and Henry threw the line to a crewman on the transom.

"Give me your hand," Volkov yelled, as the bobbing tender rose on a swell to about the level of the transom. Henry grasped Volkov's outstretched hand and was pulled with an effortless power out of the tender and onto the transom.

Volkov laughed and gave Henry an enormous, crushing hug. He waved an arm toward the enormous transom behind him. "Welcome aboard," he said. "You like ship? Not so bad for poor Russian farm boy, eh? Show you around, then dinner, drinks. Start in engine room. Twin diesel Cats, 6,000 horsepower. Cruise at 25 knots, no shit! Eighty-five meters, nine staterooms, sleeps 18, crew of 25. What's wrong?"

"We're moving," Henry said, and now he could hear the deep hum of the *Ursus Major's* engines as the ship slowly began to swing so the bow was pointed out to sea. As the stern swung around to face the beach and the crew power-winched the tender up the ramp onto the transom, Henry could just make out Carter Banks in the twilight standing along the edge of the surf, hands on hips. Henry waved but got no response from Carter. The tender pilot had furiously shaken his head no when Carter had tried to follow Henry and climb into the Zodiac earlier, indicating with hand signs he would return for Carter. The small Zodiac was filled with gear and it had looked to be a tight squeeze, particularly with the rough surf that had come up, so neither of the men had complained.

"Captain says bad anchorage here, so we move," Volkov replied. "We have old saying in Russia. 'Trust in God but watch for shoals.' Don't worry. Have you back in no time, year, two years tops," he said, and roared with deep laughter.

He put an arm around Henry's shoulders and began guiding him toward the stairs leading up to the next deck. "Come, see ship. Then dinner. Stole French chef off The Octopus in St. Barts. Made offer he couldn't refuse." He held a pointed finger against Henry's temple. "Tonight, eat like czars. Maybe you find woman you like?" He winked at Henry.

They'd reached the top of the stairs and the pool deck. Eight or nine young women, most topless and wearing only their bikini bottoms, were lounging on the chaise lounges or enjoying cocktails in the pool. A heavily tattooed crew member who had been sitting on the edge of the pool chatting up one of the women got quickly to his feet and made a hasty exit into what looked to be a lounge or disco.

"Ladies, meet Henry, my American friend," Volkov bellowed. Then he repeated what Henry guessed was something similar in what must have been Russian.

The women waved, and one yelled, "C'mon Henry, do have a drink," but Volkov waved her off. "First, see ship, then find cabin. Time enough for beautiful women, eh, Henry?" And Henry found himself half-carried, half-pulled along in Volkov's powerful bear hug away from the pool and toward the lounge.

Volkov sat at the head of the massive oval dining table in the open-air main deck salon with a dozen guests. Several of the crew were serving shrimp cocktail and oysters and lighting more candelabra. The conversation was boisterous and seemed louder than one would have expected at a dinner party or restaurant on land, and most of the party seemed very drunk. U2 played in the background and Bono was singing "When Love Comes to Town" in a duet with B.B. King.

A few hours earlier, Volkov had given Henry an exhaustive tour of the *Ursus Major*, during which the two had consumed the better part of the bottle of Stolichnaya that Volkov carried with him. "You like the Bear? Won her in high stakes poker game, like wild west," Volkov laughed at one point as they were working their way slowly from the lower decks aft to the main and upper decks, bridge, Volkov's stateroom, and finally, to Henry's guest suite.

Along the way, Volkov displayed what Henry found to be an amazing knowledge of even the most arcane aspects of the super yacht's design and exquisite architectural details: "Range? Fifty-five-hundred nautical miles at 15 knots, but make stops for women and vodka . . . Towels? Italian linen from Frette, so no complaints from soft Amerikanski." And so on. It seemed to Henry that Volkov viewed his ship with both deep affection and incredulousness, like a homeless man who finds himself living in a luxurious penthouse with Gisele.

Henry had then hurriedly showered and dressed in the ordinary crewman's uniform of striped Breton's jersey, navy Bermuda shorts, and white belt that he'd found laid out for him in the guest suite he'd been given.

The party ignored him as he emerged tentatively from the dark. There was a perceptible roll now that they were well underway, and Henry was more than a little drunk. As he walked rather hesitantly up to the table, a woman lazily reached up and handed him an empty champagne flute, evidently seeking a refill. Henry glanced at Volkov, gave a short bow to the lady, and began filling the glass from a bottle of Krug on ice in a stand nearby. Volkov roared with delight and clanged a spoon against a bottle of vodka, and the others at the table gradually fell silent. Volkov stood, motioned for the other diners to stand, held a small glass out, and offered what Henry would learn was typical of a Volkov toast.

"Nineteenth century. Białowieża Forest. Now in Belarus but then, royal hunting preserve. Russian czar hunting on foot wounds, mother of all boars. Very dangerous animal, 200 kilos, tusks like razor. Boar charges czar. Czar good as dead. Russian history changes in a heartbeat. Romanov line ends. No revolution. No party. No Putin." He chuckled. "No Volkov. But before boar can get to czar, shot rings out. Boar falls dead. Czar's life is saved. Serf with rifle emerges from forest. Penalty for serf caught hunting in royal forest? Death by hanging. But czar is reformer, and grateful. He has serf shot instead."

Henry looked around. The diners all stared at Volkov, unsure of how to react. Then Volkov threw his head back and laughed. He said something in Russian, slugged back the glass of vodka, and threw it over the open half wall to the sea. The diners, most of whom had been waiting uneasily to take their cue from Volkov, broke out in laughter, and most followed suit with their drinks and glasses.

Volkov walked over to Henry and put his arm around his shoulder. "Meet Henry," he said loudly. "My new American friend. Friend for life!"

There was some mild applause and a few half-hearted 'Welcome Henrys,' but the guests seemed generally uninterested as they began to sit and resume eating and conversation. A waiter pulled a chair out at the opposite end of the table from Volkov and motioned for Henry. As Henry was about to sit, Volkov suddenly stood and bellowed, "Nyet! Everyone stand." He waved an index finger theatrically, tallying up the number of diners. "Thirteen. Unlucky." The diners again rose to their feet and Henry saw several surreptitiously roll their eyes as if they'd been through this or something similar before.

Volkov turned to one of the staff and issued a short command in Russian. The crewmember did a short bow and walked quickly to a phone system on the wall, dialed, and spoke for a few seconds with someone on the other end. While everyone stood waiting, a fourteenth chair was squeezed in next to Henry's and a place setting added.

A trim, deeply tanned middle-aged man with blond hair and beard trimmed short and wearing a white tropical-weight uniform with short sleeves and shorts soon entered the room. Volkov motioned impatiently to the chair next to Henry's, and there were a few audible "Hurrahs!" and a "Thank God for Captain Peter Swan," and the entire dinner party now again returned to their seats.

"So, you're the American," the man said, turning to Henry. "Let me guess: friend for life?" He chuckled, nodding subtly toward Volkov, engaged in conversation at the other end of the table. He extended a hand and Henry took it.

"Henry Ball. You're Captain Swan? From your accent I'm guessing South African?"

"Good God no," Swan laughed. "Aussie. Couldn't trust a vessel like the *Ursus Major* to a South African. They'd bugger it up." He waved off a waiter holding out a bottle of wine.

"I apologize."

"No worries, mate," Swan said easily. "Glad to have you aboard. Nice that the boss has added an American to this menagerie."

"Not sure how long I'll be on board," Henry said. "Any idea where we're going? We left my friend on the beach back there. Any chance we'll put in at Havana?"

"Itinerary's subject to change on the boss' whim at any time but right now, a quick stop in the Caymans tomorrow and then here and there through the lesser Antilles," Swan said. "South of France for the start of the season, and then Cyprus, Suez, then east. No, Havana's out of the question, too much paperwork, too many hands out, mate."

Swan studied Henry for a moment and patted his arm. "Don't worry, your friend will make out all right," he said reassuringly. "Crew's well trained, mostly my people so whatever you need, just ask. First rate chef, very good cellar. Plenty to do on board. Excellent library. Don't bother, however, with the crew that are heavily tattooed. They're Volkov's and most don't speak a word of English. Wouldn't be very helpful even if they did."

He took a bite of salad, then continued. "You've no doubt seen the gym, plenty of water toys, some other interesting diversions." Swan nodded toward a few of the young women talking animatedly a few seats away. "Guests are the usual: Cypriot bankers, an English lawyer or two, a musician you might recognize, a couple of friends from Mother Russia and, of course, the girls. As the latest friend for life, you'll fit right in."

"You mean there've been others?" Henry asked, suddenly feeling a bit uneasy. But the woman next to Swan had draped a long, brown, be-jeweled arm around Swan's neck, drawing him close and asking when they'd be putting in at St. Barts. Henry turned away and beckoned for the waiter holding the wine.

Part II

Be bold, and let mighty forces come to your aid.

Bonjour, Madame La Guillotine

Carter Banks fell in and out of fitful sleep, with the sounds of trucks, hammering, power saws, hip hop, and laughter waking him throughout the night. The small room he had rented at Mama Lou Lou's for a reasonable 88 USD per day came with croissants, delicious local coffee in the morning, and a nice view overlooking the central square of Burondi, the PREA's capital city. It had also, until now, been relatively peaceful late at night.

While dawn had always been Carter's favorite time of day, he now felt unusually irritable with the lack of sleep, and surprisingly sluggish. He had, for the second night in a row, slept fully clothed, wearing even his boots. He rolled to a sitting position, pulled the Sig Sauer nine-millimeter from beneath his pillow, placed it on the nightstand, and checked the burner phone yet again for the one-word text he had expected to get two days ago from General Malik.

In an early morning routine that he'd deviated from only a handful of times in his adult life, he went through a rigorous circuit of exercises that helped lift his mood just a little. After a particularly violent series of push-ups, squats, lunges, burpees, and mountain climbers, he walked to the window and pulled a curtain back, expecting to see the usual straggling arrival of the merchants who manned the market booths that filled much of the square.

He peered through the curtains and saw that scaffolding and a large platform had been erected overnight in the center of the old French colonial square. Soldiers were struggling to lift something onto the platform with the help of a small crane mounted to the back of an army truck. Already a crowd was forming around the structure, and hundreds were pouring in by foot and on bicycle and moped from the streets that intersected the square like the spokes on a wheel. Here and there vendors were setting up their stalls and selling everything from souvenirs to live chickens to gourds of Buju, the powerful banana beer favored by the local tribes. Musicians had gathered here and there playing their steel drums and horns in a wild cacophony of discordant music.

Carter sat on the windowsill and swung open the old metal frame window. Two stories below, Mama Lou Lou stood on the sidewalk that fronted her café, dancing with a few of her waitstaff. They sang an old tribal song and Mama, with surprising grace for someone so large, swung her hips to the beat.

"Hey, Mama, *qu'est-ce que c'est?*" he yelled down to her.

She looked up, waved, and gestured out to the platform. "Monsieur Banks, rencontrer Madame Guillotine!"

Soldiers had succeeded in erecting what looked to be a large guillotine, glistening in fresh black paint but almost certainly a relic dating back to before the French colonial era ended in the early '60s. Several soldiers began pulling on the rope and the heavy blade slowly rose toward the cross bar at the top of the structure.

Carter stepped back from the window and checked the burner phone. Still nothing. Not a good sign, but coups d'etat tended to be messy and unpredictable, and it was entirely possible the general had been too busy or simply forgotten to text Carter the code word that Victor had insisted on for good luck: touchdown.

In any case, he knew in a matter of hours either General Abdul Malik's head, or that of President Mugabe, would be hoisted up by the executioner to the roar of the crowd. All he could do now was wait.

Miracles On the Côte d'Azur

"Je crois aux miracles...d'où tu viens, espèce de chose sexy."

Where had she heard that melody? Rose wondered. She couldn't quite place it, and her French wasn't yet good enough to make out the lyrics. She drained the last of her champagne and motioned to the waiter standing vigilantly nearby.

"Oui, Madame?" he asked. "Another of the Taitinger?"

She nodded and handed him her glass.

"That song, Alain, sing it for me in English."

He smiled and listened attentively to the song coming softly from the poolside speakers. "Hmmm. "I believe in miracles . . . where you from, you sexy beast."

Rose laughed. "That's it, Alain but it's *thing*, not *beast*." She began to sing softly along with the old Hot Chocolate tune. "Where did you come from angel? How did you know I needed you?"

Alain bowed appreciatively. "Beautiful, Madame." He swayed to the music for effect as he walked away.

She was at the end of a long line of identical white chaise lounges, all with umbrellas open to help fend off the mid-day sun, perched along the edge of the wall above the famous Hotel du Cap-Eden-Roc pool. She guessed that the ratio of waitstaff to hotel guests was about three to one, and the service was excellent despite a pecking order that had placed her farthest from the typical poolside amenities. She had been a bit surprised by the November heat and a hot southerly breeze brought the strong tangy Mediterranean smell mixed with an earthy, organic scent that Rose thought, rather romantically, must have originated in North Africa.

She leisurely applied another thin layer of the complimentary La Roche Posay suntan lotion on her thighs, stomach, and arms as she watched an enormous yacht with navy blue hull slowly motor into view about 500 yards offshore. Small pleasure craft bobbed suddenly up and down in its enormous wake and a minute or so later Rose heard the wake crashing into the base of the cliff that the pool was carved into. The ship came to stop and despite the considerable distance Rose could hear crew members giving orders as the anchors were lowered. Passengers had already begun lining up on the stairs leading down to the dive platform and a tender was being readied by the crew to bring the passengers ashore.

Rose lay back, yawned, and closed her eyes. She felt sleepy, even a bit lethargic. She had read somewhere that studies had found lottery winners almost inevitably reverted back to their pre-lottery level of happiness after just six months or so. While Rose was certainly not miserable, she had begun to feel the unease that, for her, had always come with a lack of purpose. Even now, drinking $50 per glass champagne poolside at one of the most magnificent settings on the Côte d'Azur and without a care in the world, she suddenly felt—dare she say it—bored? She smiled ruefully at the thought. Most likely a symptom of the hot early afternoon sun and, admittedly, the increasingly routine mid-day glasses of champagne, she reasoned. How shallow would one have to be to be bored with half a billion in the bank and traveling Europe on private jets with one of the world's most desirable men?

November was a bittersweet month in the northern hemispheres, and Rose suddenly felt a pang of homesickness as she thought of fall back home. She hadn't spoken to Henry in months, and even the lawyers were having trouble tracking his whereabouts. Somewhere in the Caribbean on a Russian oligarch's yacht was the last she'd heard. Serving him with divorce papers was proving more difficult than Rose had imagined it would be, and now she had a moment of regret about the gesture she had meant as a warning shot across his bow.

She found her iPhone in her purse, opened the flight tracker app, and searched for 1515 Tango Zulu, the 12-passenger Gulfstream GV she'd leased for the season. There it was, over the mid-Atlantic, speeding west at 538 knots and an altitude of 48,500 feet, well above the flight paths of most commercial aircraft. One of Cisco's ponies had pulled up lame at the French Open in Chantilly and now with the European season coming to an end he had asked for the GV yet again to make a quick hop to Bogotá to scout replacements.

Cisco. That was the issue, wasn't it, she mused. Did he love her? More importantly, did she love him? He was certainly the most exciting man she'd ever been with. The international high-goal polo season had been in full swing when she'd chartered the GV and crew late that summer and joined him for the HRH Prince of Wales Trophy at the Royal County of Berkshire Polo Club outside Windsor. "Cisco, do introduce me to your lovely friend," the prince had said at the reception, as he wrapped a friendly arm around her waist with a hand dropping briefly just south of what she and Suzanne used to call the 'no fly zone' for a gentle pat on her fanny. And so the season had begun.

But while his lovemaking was as pleasurable and ardent as ever, she had begun to detect what Henry would have called 'a disturbance in the force.' Was it the way he held her just fractionally less long after they made love? Or the fact that now he had begun taking the occasional telephone call at an intimate dinner rather than letting it ring? She had yet to confront him about his supposed ties to Don Hector, but Suzanne's warning in Paris and the old gypsy's fortune telling had, admittedly, caused her a few sleepless nights.

Oh, to hell with it, she said to herself, feeling suddenly very tired. She closed her eyes, the sound of the waves lulling her to sleep.

"Madame, your champagne."

Rose woke with a start. She looked up. It wasn't Alain but another man bending forward and extending a serving tray and glass of champagne. Since he'd addressed her in lightly accented English, Rose guessed that Alain must have told this new waiter she was an American. He was tall, fit-looking, and deeply tan, with clean shaved head, gold hoop earring in his left earlobe, and striped Breton fishing shirt with a name embroidered in what looked like Cyrillic on the upper left chest. His sleeves were pushed up, revealing a pair of sinewy forearms, and she caught just the glimpse of a tattoo before he stepped back, held the tray behind his back, and bowed.

"Merci," she said, taking the glass.

He turned as if to leave but then, evidently thinking better of it, turned and sat down on the edge of Rose's chaise lounge. It was so sudden a breech in protocol that it left Rose momentarily speechless and feeling a bit vulnerable.

"Madame, if I may be so bold," he said. "You are, as they would say in America—one hot mama!"

There was a pause and then the man burst out laughing.

Rose held a hand over her mouth. "Good God. It can't be. Henry?"

"The earring?"

"The Harlistas," Henry explained. "Cuban motorcycle gang. Kind of a rite of passage. Like getting paddled at a frat. Tried to buy my way out of it but the Harlistas weren't interested in money. Now, something of real value, like a genuine '49 Harley Hydra-Glide operator's manual, that would have come in handy."

Rose laughed. "And the tattoo?"

Henry pulled his shirt sleeve up a little further over his bicep to reveal what looked to be a single rose. "Wild night on St. Barts," he explained. "One thing led to another. Every sailor has one. Can't cross the equator otherwise. Neptune wouldn't approve."

"Goes well with the great new physique and haircut," she said. "My God, Henry, you gave me a shock. How the hell did you find me?"

"Strict radio silence," Henry said. "No one calls out, cell phones all put in a safe. Not sure why, something to do with security. Nothing to do on board, really, but read and work out. First time I've gotten to a phone in a month was when we landed here. Called Victor first, who then called Suzanne, who said you were here. Easy enough. Just looked for the hottest chick at the pool."

They'd decided to have dinner at the outdoor Eden Roc Restaurant, which offered a spectacular view of the Mediterranean as well as the privacy they both seemed to want. Dinner dress was a bit formal, but Henry had borrowed a blue sport jacket from the hotel. Earlier, he'd had a drink downstairs, leaning against the bar to offset the unsettling feeling he was still on the rolling deck of the *Ursus Major*, while Rose went back to her suite to shower and change.

Rather uncharacteristically, Rose had found it hard to decide on what to wear, trying on three or four outfits before ultimately deciding on a simple black dress cut to accentuate what she knew Henry considered her best features: her legs and particularly shapely rear end.

The temperature was still in the low 80s but there was a nice light breeze coming off the Mediterranean. Earlier, they'd commented on the spectacular sunset to the west out over the Mediterranean to the waiter when he'd wheeled up with their dinners. "Oui, the sirocco," he'd said. "Carrying the sands of Africa. Magnifique. Now, blue lobster for madame, and monsieur, the steak Diane."

Between courses the waiter lit the table candles and candelabra by their table. They fell into their old, easy manner, catching up on the four months they'd been apart. Neither seemed anxious to open any old wounds. They were like two seasoned diplomats from rival countries with a long history of waging both war and brokering peace and perhaps having an affair or two along the way, excited to begin yet another round of negotiations which both hoped would be productive.

They talked about Zach's rather spotty performance as a newly-minted poker pro in Vegas and how much it was costing them to underwrite it—"Cheaper to pay off the other poker pros just to let Zach win," Henry joked; the latest gossip about Victor and Suzanne—"Not sure what Victor's been up to but they're going to put up a new statue of Suzanne and her shopping bags in front of Cartier in Paris,"—and a dozen other topics.

But midway through dinner and with the effects of a nice bottle of Provençal rosé beginning to kick in, Rose reached over and took Henry's hand. "Henry, I don't know if anyone from Waxworth Barnes reached you during one of your island stops, but . . ."

Henry held up a hand. "Rosie, no need to explain. Yes, a courier did deliver a package when we landed in St. Lucia, which I glanced at and subsequently tore up and scattered out on the gulf stream. You can't get rid of me that easily. I got some good advice too from Volkov, my Russian host, quite the ladies' man I might add, about marriage. Seems that there's a Russian proverb covering just about every aspect of the human condition. 'Henry,' he said to me one night when we were lamenting the mistakes we'd made in our lives after a lot of vodka, 'A man without wife is like vase without roses.'"

Rose laughed. "Volkov sounds like a charmer," she said. "How'd you meet him?"

"Oh, saved his life down in Cuba," Henry replied, nonchalantly. "Now 'Henry friend for life.' It's been quite a ride. Had to part company with Carter Banks in Cuba, but he'll land on his feet. I'll make it up to him when I get back to Chicago."

"Victor's man?" Rose asked. "Yes, I got the impression last time I saw Suzanne in Paris that he and Victor were cooking up something big. Hope it all works out. So, tell me all about life on board Volkov's ship. And more wine, s'il vous plait?"

Heads Will Roll

The 'come to Jesus' meeting.

That's what Victor and his partners called it when it was time to confront an overly conservative client keeping too much of his or her wealth on the sidelines in cash, or an underperforming associate needing a well-deserved kick in the ass. As Victor's two senior partners suddenly arrived together at his office and closed the door behind them, Victor suspected that Jesus had indeed arrived and boy, as the bumper sticker says, was he pissed.

He guessed that they'd come at him in classic good cop, bad cop fashion. Bad cop was Bobby Fitzgerald, the tough, street smart, beefy, red-faced third generation working class Chicago Irish who had seen Victor's potential some 25 years before and helped nurture his rise and eventual partnership. Victor liked to say Bobby was the older brother he'd never had, and indeed they had a close relationship forged over years of business triumphs, late-night celebrations, bedding some of the same women—and knowing what closets the other's skeletons were hidden in. The good cop was Hal Stone, socially awkward and particularly nerdish by comparison to Victor and Bobby and considered a bit of a third wheel by outsiders looking in, but he had the savant's ability for seeing investment opportunities and was truly the brains to his partners' brawn.

Victor stood and gestured to the chairs by his desk. "Didn't see this meeting on my calendar, but I've got just about five minutes before . . ."

"Let's cut the bullshit, Victor, shall we?" Bobby Fitzgerald said, and Victor thought his face seemed even more red than usual as he sat heavily in the chair facing Victor. Hal, looking suddenly even more uncomfortable, took the seat next to him.

It was obvious to Victor from their demeanors that they likely had the goods on him. He knew his world was about to unravel, and his options were limited: either feign a massive heart attack, a ruse that might work on Hal but Bobby would never go for, or alert Olivia, his executive assistant, to what they jokingly referred to as a Code Blue. It was a desperate measure he had employed only twice before: once when a spurned mistress had produced a Beretta from her handbag and put a couple small holes in his prize brown bear; another time when confronted by a furious Bears linebacker who'd lost millions almost overnight on an investment Victor had said was, 'Like treasury bills, only a lot safer.'

He casually reached under his desk for the hidden button that, when pressed twice, would signal Olivia with a barely audible buzzer at her desk to rush in with the news that Suzanne had been in a terrible car accident and Victor was needed at Rush Memorial because it wasn't certain if she would make it, buying Victor just a little more time.

But Bobby beat him to the punch. "Don't bother, Victor, I fired Olivia just before we walked in," he said. "Hal?"

Victor slumped back in his chair and raised his arms in a gesture that suggested incredulity. He knew the only option left was to try to bluff his way out, so his facial expression now suggested irritation bordering on anger.

"Victor, there seems to be a bit of a discrepancy in our accounts," Hal began, voice quavering a little. "We're sure there must be an explanation, but something like $4 billion and change is unaccounted for. I should say was, since the forensics boys in London finally traced it to several accounts in the Caymans." He looked at Victor expectantly.

Victor gave Hal an icy stare. He was bluffing, but his only play now was to go all in. "I am shocked, shocked to find gambling going on here," he said sarcastically. "Accounts in the Caymans? No shit. You'd better have your facts straight, Hal, or I'm going to take a fucking flamethrower to the firm that I helped build!"

Victor glanced over at Bobby. There was a subtle appeal in his expression, and the very real telepathy that close friends, spouses, and business partners develop over the course of many years. *After all we've been through, all the money we've made together, all the money we can still make together—you're letting this little shit do this to me?* Victor telepathed to Bobby. *Come on, let's forget the whole thing, go get drunk, and chase some pussy.*

But Bobby was having none of it. He nodded at Hal. "Get on with it," he growled.

"Now here's where it gets interesting," Hal said nervously, but warming to the story. "With the help of our, ah, friends in the Caymans, we learned that most of the money from these accounts had been wired to a series of shell corporations and blind trusts meant to throw us off the trail, but we eventually determined that all roads, so to speak, led to a certain General Abdul Malik of the People's Republic of Equatorial Africa. The forensics boys couldn't find any actual fingerprints, but there were some minute traces of DNA. Your DNA, Victor."

Bobby's fist slammed down on Victor's massive sequoia desktop, sending a few of the crystal 'tombstones' that commemorated some of the more spectacular of the firm's leveraged buyouts and public offering successes flying. "Goddamn it, Victor, where's our fucking money?" he roared, rising half out of his chair as if about to spring across the vast expanse of Victor's desk.

Victor leaned back in his chair, put his feet up on his desk, linked his fingers behind his head, smiled, and shook his head at the apparent preposterousness of Hal's tale, and the conclusion they'd come to. He looked out at the Chicago skyline, and the casual observer would have surmised that Victor was taking his time with, and even relishing, what would be a complete and thorough denunciation of their absurd indictment. He was of course buying time, but he also sensed there was still a bit of doubt in the minds of his partners. Now, how to play it?

Wasn't it Hitler who had said that the big lie, told repeatedly, was more likely to be believed? A plan began to form. Maybe, just maybe, he could buy some time. Sure, he'd have to throw Carter Banks under the bus, but small price to pay. If he could hang this on Carter, there was still a chance he could walk away with just a stiff fine from the Feds. Hell, he was so good a rainmaker his partners would likely overlook any transgression short of the *Tribune* uncovering something really embarrassing, like a history of serial bestiality.

Victor shook his head. A wry smile began forming. "Of course, how could I be so stupid, the son of a bitch," he said, as if to himself. Then he looked at his partners. "Carter Banks."

"What about him?" Bobby asked, and while there was a skeptical look on his face, Victor could sense from his tone that Bobby would be happy to throw Victor a lifeline if the story was plausible and he could sell it.

"Banks flew to Africa two, maybe three times in the last six months," Victor said as if a lightbulb had just gone on, warming now to his tale. "Didn't think much of it. Banks said he was helping out some old Special Forces buddies. My guess is it won't be hard to trace his movements to that African shithole you mentioned, Hal. But how the hell did he find a way to divert that much money without someone in this firm getting wind of it?" He looked pointedly at Hal, who shifted uncomfortably in his chair.

"I never trusted that bastard," Bobby said, slumping back into his chair and now there was a look of relief on his face and his tone suggested that, yes, if they could hang this on Banks, Victor and the firm would live to fight another day, despite the painful losses. "Too smooth by half, if you ask me. Never did believe that story about Banks bagging that Iraqi general from two miles away. Where is he now?"

Victor gazed out the window for a moment, as if formulating a plan. Then he smiled. "Leave Banks to me, boys. I know where to find him and what buttons to push. He'll play ball and, most importantly, go quietly. We'll need Waxworth Barnes in on this too, so we can finesse this with the Feds when they start sniffing around, and then spin it with the media when it's time to offer up Banks. Let's plan on a strategy session tomorrow so we can think this thing through."

Then Victor looked at his partners and slowly shook his head. He'd bought some time and yes, he thought he might be able to get Banks to agree to holding the bag in exchange for a plea-bargained light jail sentence in one of those federal country clubs for convicts and a seven-figure severance package parked somewhere offshore. Against all odds, Victor had pulled it off when just minutes before he'd been staring into the abyss so, what the hell, why not take a victory lap?

"You sons of bitches," Victor said angrily. "To think that my two partners, men that I'd trust with my own life, would come in here and make these baseless accusations without even a shred of evidence. I wouldn't know the PREA from the NRA, or General Abdul Malik from Kareem Abdul Jabbar."

Victor was interrupted by a sudden knock on the door. One of the secretaries meekly opened the door and standing just behind her was who looked to be a delivery man in a short-sleeved olive color jumpsuit holding a large box.

"I said no interruptions," Bobby growled.

The delivery man, a tall, well-built, and very dark-complexioned black man with two rows of diagonal scars on his face, pushed past the secretary and put the large and apparently heavy box squarely in the middle of Victor's desk.

"What the hell's this?" Victor asked, as he rose out of his chair.

"Special delivery for Victor Black, compliments of his many friends in the People's Republic of Equatorial Africa," the man said in a deep, pleasant voice, with an accent that bespoke of a French preparatory school education.

A pleasant smile began to form on his handsome albeit deeply scarred face. "I fear that the contents will begin to spoil if Monsieur Black does not open immediately. So please forgive the intrusion, which was at my insistence." He bowed in apology toward the secretary as he walked out of the office.

Bobby and Hal stared at Victor. Victor shrugged helplessly, like an amateur neighborhood magician being asked to perform Houdini's famous Chinese water torture cell trick. He used the letter opener to make an incision in the taped lid, opened it and, with some difficulty, pulled out a heavy, Styrofoam insulating container of the type used by Omaha Steaks or Lobster Gram to deliver a perishable food item in need of refrigeration. This too was sealed in heavy tape, and Victor began cutting through it.

"Something stinks," Hal said suddenly, and now they all noticed the faint odor of forgotten leftovers left toward the back of the refrigerator for a week or two.

Victor cut through the last of the tape and with an exasperated, "What the fuck," lifted off the top half of the container. General Abdul Malik's severed head stared up at him, eyes still frozen wide from the evident shock and terror of the guillotine blade's sudden bite. What looked to be a small plastic football with 'touchdown' written crudely on the side was stuffed in the general's mouth.

Victor staggered back. Hal half-kneeled alongside the desk, retching. Bobby, who had done a tour with the 26th Marines, 3rd Marine Division in Vietnam and seen much worse during the Tet Offensive, gave Victor a final, withering look, and walked out the door.

Ships Passing in the Night

"You'd give Sting a run for his money."

They lay exhausted in each other's arms. The light was just coming up and enough of a cold breeze was blowing in off the Mediterranean through the open balcony doors so that Henry reached down and pulled a sheet over them. They could hear the plaintive cries of gulls and the rumble of distant surf crashing along the breakwater. The quiet voices of waitstaff rolling a cart on the ground floor veranda below their room came and went.

"Three months at sea will do that to a man," Henry said. "I'm glad I wasn't lashed to the mast like Ulysses, you're quite the siren." He kissed Rose on the forehead.

Despite being surrounded by a bevy of beautiful, unattached women and the unabashed hedonism that characterizes life aboard a yacht, Henry had remained largely celibate and surprisingly uninterested during the months he'd been on the *Ursus Major*. There had been just the one time when, late one stormy night mid-Atlantic one of Volkov's Russian girls had come knocking quietly but insistently at Henry's door. Henry suspected that Volkov had sent her out of either sympathy or perhaps to see if he was gay, so Henry had decided not to send her away.

The long stretch of abstinence, however, couldn't explain why he hadn't seemed to be able to get enough of Rose and his lovemaking had taken on a new ardor and thoughtfulness and imagination that had surprised them both. Rose was shocked but somehow pleased when late into the night, after pouring her another glass of wine, Henry had leaned across the balcony table and kissed her slowly, deeply and in a way he hadn't in years. It was like they'd somehow gone back in time 20 years and shed the collective weight of countless petty grievances, worry, disappointment, and betrayal. She had felt a surge of love and a yearning for Henry she wouldn't have guessed still lay dormant somewhere deep inside.

Henry picked up his watch from the nightstand. "We've just enough time for a shower, breakfast, and then we should hustle down to the tender. Volkov is a fanatic about keeping schedules, and he doesn't like to stay in any one place too long. Hardly ever leaves the ship. Says it's his agoraphobia. Seems unlikely. The man seems about as sensitive as a grizzly bear."

"We?" Rose asked. She rolled to her side, looking at Henry.

"Come on Rosie, it will be fun," Henry said, excited now and talking faster as the idea formed. He sensed that after the night they'd shared, he now had a small but workable window of opportunity. "The Amalfi coast, Greek isles, Cairo, Suez, then on to Australia and New Zealand. Volkov's insane of course, but interesting, and the *Ursus Major* is unbelievable. Volkov stole the French chef from some hoity toity five-star restaurant in Paris. Great guy, big as a house of course, all the best chefs are. You wouldn't believe what it's like to be at sea at night, the stars are incredible. If we get bored, we'll get off and fly back to . . ." He saw the look on Rose's face and stopped suddenly.

"Oh, sweet Henry." Rose reached out and held Henry's hand. "I have missed you so. Didn't realize until last night. We've been such fools."

Henry leaned over and took her face in his hands. "I want you back, Rosie. Now we've got the money, the time. It won't be like before. You're the love of my life. Hell, I'll even go to the opera once in a while. Forget that polo player, he'll land on his feet."

There was a quiet knock on the door, then more insistent.

"Oui?" Henry said loudly.

"Weather coming, Mr. Henry. Boss says time to leave. Now."

Henry recognized the voice of one of the English-speaking Russian crew. He knew now that they must have been watching him all along and followed him to Rose's room.

"I'll be down shortly," Henry yelled, annoyed at the intrusion and now suddenly concerned that Volkov had for some reason put him under surveillance.

"What'd I tell you?" Henry said, jumping out of bed and hurrying toward the bathroom. "I'll jump in the shower, you get packing. We've got about ten minutes before the Russians bust the door down and I'm forced to defend your honor."

By American standards the shower pressure was surprisingly weak, but Henry barely noticed. He worked up a lather and began singing in a theatrical baritone bits and pieces of *Music of the Night* from Phantom of the Opera, a song he knew Rose loved and a sure sign of Henry's new-found sensitivity and enlightenment.

"Open up your mind, let your fantasies unwind . . ." he sang as he quickly toweled off. "C'mon Rosie, jump in and I'll call down to the front desk to get the bellhop to get your—"

He stopped as he came out of the bathroom. The bedroom and balcony were empty and Rose was gone. He sat on the edge of the bed and read the short note Rose had written on hotel stationary and left pinned to the pillow with a rose from the fresh bouquet that had come with dinner the night before.

'So we beat on, boats against the current, borne back ceaselessly into the past' . . . we will meet again, my love. Look for me in the spring. Stay safe. Love, Rose.

"Game of kings!" Volkov said and waved for Henry to sit at the small round table for two in Volkov's study later that evening, after the *Ursus Major* was well underway. The door to Volkov's suite was ajar and Henry could just make out a pair of shapely, very tan legs with a silver ankle bracelet hanging out over the edge of the bed. A large onyx chess set took up most of the table space. "You play?"

Henry smiled. It had been years but there was a semester or two in college when he and a few of his roommates had been consumed by the game. He'd gotten pretty good, often under the influence of a particularly potent hash oil that continuously oozed out of the homemade still that one of his roommates had built. The potent green tar-like substance seemed to give him both an almost supernatural prescience and a voracious appetite for late night pizza.

"Yes, but I haven't played in years," Henry said. "Got any hash oil?"

Volkov set a bottle of vodka and two glasses on the table next to the board. He squeezed himself into the other leather captain's chair opposite Henry, rubbing his hands together in anticipation.

"West against east!" he exclaimed.

"Good versus evil?" Henry said.

Volkov laughed. "Bourgeoisie against proletariat."

"Capitalism versus the collective."

Volkov looked at Henry, surprised, and then roared with laughter. "You are scholar! Harvard? Yale?"

"Cable TV."

Volkov laughed. He reached over and poured vodka into both their glasses.

"I've always thought of chess as a metaphor for what truly separated man from the beasts—his acquisitiveness." Henry wanted to impress Volkov, but also tweak the man's sense of supremacy a bit. "No wonder the Russians are so good at chess. Communism is of course just a clever way for the masses to take what they haven't earned, and don't deserve, by force."

Volkov stared at Henry, muttered something in Russian, and then slugged back his vodka. He took aim at the large open window across the study but missed and the glass shattered against the wall. One of Volkov's crew, the one with the Maltese cross tattooed across his neck who Henry considered to be the most evil looking, burst into the room with pistol drawn.

"Nyet!" Volkov bellowed, rising from his seat. The crew member looked around the room and, quickly sizing up the situation, tucked the pistol in his waistband. He saluted Volkov and withdrew, closing the door softly behind him.

Volkov walked over to a small bar, retrieved a new glass, and sat heavily back down at the table. He shook his head wearily. "I have need of men like that, ex-military, good with weapons. Even nice guy like Volkov has many enemies. You have bodyguards too, yes? The black man on beach in Cuba?"

Henry felt a moment of guilt, thinking of Carter Banks standing there on the beach in Cuba. He made a promise to himself to reach out to Carter through Victor as soon as they made their next landfall.

Volkov graciously invited Henry to play white. He guessed that Volkov would be expecting a very conservative game from a man who was almost certainly a novice, so he instead opened with aggressiveness. He attacked rashly, putting his queen in harm's way almost immediately, and was forced to beat a hasty retreat as Volkov easily parried the attack and then counter-attacked. It was all over after just 20 or so moves.

Henry knocked over his king in capitulation, leaned back, and sipped his drink. "Am I a hostage?" he asked, suddenly.

Volkov looked surprised. "Henry, no, guest. Leave whenever. But first—you must defeat Volkov at chess." He leaned back and roared.

Et Tu, Carter?

"Know much about the Civil War?" Victor asked.

"Not my favorite period," Carter said. "Why?"

Victor stopped and leaned against the railing that ran along the perimeter of the Lincoln Park lagoon. A cold front was sweeping down from Canada, and the brisk winter wind known in Chicago as The Hawk had denuded the last of the fall foliage. A forlorn pair of mallards hunkered down on the edge of the pond in the lee of the wind as if mustering up the courage to fly south. The park was all but deserted, which evidently was what Victor had hoped for when he suggested a meeting with Carter there rather than his office.

"Back then it wasn't uncommon for men, particularly on the Union side, to hire a surrogate to serve in their place." Victor looked out at the lagoon.

"Theodore Roosevelt's father, for example, paid a man something like $500 to take his place. Changed the course of history of course since his son did everything in his power to erase what he considered to be a stain on the family's honor."

Over the years Carter had grown used to Victor's need to be the smartest man in the room. He knew this history lesson would be related to the point he would eventually be making. He waited quietly. The punch line wasn't long in coming.

"Carter, the rich don't go to wars," and Victor paused for a moment and turned to Carter. "Or go to jail. The lawyers at Waxworth Barnes say you'll likely do maybe 18 months in a Club Fed and, most importantly, come out a very wealthy man. Think of it as a vacation."

Carter shook his head and laughed. "Shit Victor, rich been screwing the poor since around the time of Cain and Abel. White man been doin' the black man almost as long. You try to overthrow a government, and you're asking me to step n' fetch it?"

Victor shook his head in apparent amazement. "Carter, when things went bad in that African shithole, you didn't expect to walk away unscathed, did you? You know what they say about the best laid plans of mice and men. War vet like yourself should know that. We rolled the dice and lost. It happens. The general fucked up. The key is to live to fight another day. I'm offering you a chance to come away whole. But, if that's how you feel, we can just let the cards fall where they may: the word of a reputable investment banker and beloved ex-Chicago Bears tight end with three floors of Harvard lawyers against former cop gone rogue and his public defender." He turned to walk away.

Carter reached out and grabbed Victor's arm. For the first time in the years he'd known him, Victor saw what looked to be fear in Carter's eyes. "Looks like you're holding all the cards, boss," Carter said, a hint of resignation in his voice. "So, how's this going to play out? Lay it out for me."

Victor smiled sympathetically and put his arm around Carter's shoulder. "Trust me, Carter, it's for the best. Pretty simple, really. I sent you to the PREA to get the lay of the land, see if we should be investing, make some contacts, that sort of thing. All above board. Straightforward intelligence gathering. Investment banker doing his due diligence. Hell, no different than the trips

I've sent you on to a dozen other emerging markets. You got wind of a coup, sized things up, got overly ambitious, and made a sizable bet, unbeknownst to us, on the general. The paper trail begins and ends with you, including the travel, the transactions. Really, about all they can pin you with is embezzlement, but I will attest to the fact that I typically gave you a lot of latitude and, well, you just went a bit too far on this one. Waxworth has already tested the waters with the Feds, and evidently the State Department wants this to go away quietly." Victor stopped. "What?"

Carter stared at Victor, a look of incredulousness on his face. "You shittin' me, Victor? You send me down there with hundreds of millions to finance a coup, walk away unscathed, hang me out to dry, and then offer to testify as a character witness at my trial? You got to do better than that."

Victor leaned on the rail and looked out at the pond. After a moment he turned to Carter and there was a hard look on his face. "Carter, how many investment bankers went to jail in '08 when that subprime shit they were selling almost took down the world economy? Zero. Who got caught when they whacked Jack Kennedy in '63? A patsy. The system's rigged. Always has been, always will be. You can play ball, spend a few years honing your cooking skills and catching up on back issues of *Popular Mechanics* in a Club Fed with $10 million parked in the Caymans waiting for you when you come out—or roll the dice. But let me remind you: ain't never been a poor black man been able to beat a rich white man at his own game. Think it through. I know you'll come to the right conclusion." He turned and walked briskly away.

"Victor, wait," Carter called. "Victor!" He turned away and smiled. He'd played Victor just about right.

"Times have changed, Victor," he said softly, looking back over his shoulder. "Times have changed."

Carter walked south, out of the park, crossed North Clark and entered the Green Tea Japanese Restaurant. It was mid-afternoon on a Saturday and the lunch crowd had thinned. He went into the men's room, found it empty, and went into a stall. With the expectation that Victor might suspect he was wired and pat him down, he'd taken care earlier to conceal the small wireless microphone by implanting it carefully in the layers of a large Band-Aid and then adhering it to the inside of his left bicep. The microphone was Bluetooth-enabled and transmitted directly to the voice memos app on his iPhone.

He took off his jacket, rolled up his sweater sleeve and removed the microphone. Then he opened the voice memo app and breathed a sigh of relief when the recording played audibly and surprisingly clear. Far cry from the clunky, unreliable wires he used to equip his snitches with, and had gotten a few killed, he thought ruefully.

He glanced at his watch. He had about an hour to kill before his meeting was scheduled with Special Agents Modjeski and Reynolds and a lawyer friend from his days with Chicago PD. While he didn't feel like celebrating, exactly, he thought the occasion called for some sort of libation. He thought some warm sake might do nicely. He pulled his sweater back on, took a quick look in the mirror, and walked out to have some of the Green Tea's excellent junmai sake at the bar.

Points of No Return

They raced westward, chasing the sunset as it slowly gave way to dusk. Cisco and Rose lay fully reclined and under a blanket, the only passengers along with three crew on 1515 Tango Zulu, 48,000 feet above the Atlantic and just past the midway point between the Canary Islands where they'd been forced to refuel due to strong headwinds, and Bogotá, Colombia. Rose glanced at the monitor mounted to the bulkhead showing their flight path, altitude, speed, and estimated time of arrival.

The point of no return, Rose thought, that spot in a journey where it's no longer possible to return safely the way you came. True of ships and planes due to fuel consumption, Rose mused, but what about people? Had she passed the point of no return? Was there really no going back? She glanced at Cisco, head just inches from Rose's and breathing heavily in a deep sleep. Cisco had that enviable knack that the best travelers have of being able to fall asleep, cat-like, almost instantly anywhere and under any circumstance or conditions. Despite her best efforts, Rose had never been able to fall asleep on airplanes and needed at least one or two sleepless nights to acclimate herself to even the most comfortable of hotels.

Just one of their many differences, Rose thought ruefully, as she looked out the oval window at the night. Still, she'd finally given into his pleas to make the trip with him to Bogotá for Don Hector's 60th birthday. He seemed unusually melancholy of late, and she sensed he needed her by his side. She couldn't be sure, but she guessed his mood had much to do with the way the season had ended. First Chico and then the Black Cat had broken down in the final weeks, and Cisco's two favorite ponies had to be put down. The inevitability of science and the new ways was finally borne out when Cisco's team eventually conceded bitter defeat to Adolpho Cambiaso and his younger and seemingly indefatigable perfect ponies.

She'd written off the growing sense of dread she was feeling about the trip as irrational, and was somewhat reassured on the eve of their trip by Cisco's response when she casually let slip what Suzanne had said about Don Hector that fall night in Paris.

"You Americans!" He had thrown his head back, laughed, and draped his arms across her shoulders. "Sí, Don Hector is a powerful man, and wealthy, but no different than many American businessmen. He has many interests, real estate, investments in Eje Cafetero, the coffee region. A hundred other things. But the *coca*? Never. Don is only a title of great respect, nothing more. You will come to love him, Rose, *Dios quiere*, God willing."

Then Cisco had looked deeply into Rose's eyes. "Don Hector is my patron, Rose, the father I never knew. Imagine a boy, dressed in rags, living on the streets of Bogotá. One chance in a million to make it out alive. Then—" Cisco hesitated, searching for the right words. Rose saw, for the first time, tears welling up in his eyes. "*Una bendición de Dios*, a blessing from above, the man they call Don Hector sees something in this worthless boy that no one else can see."

Rose heard Cisco mumble something in his sleep in Spanish. It sounded almost as if he was urging one of his ponies on, and she guessed he was dreaming of a match. She studied his face for a moment, in repose appearing more boyish and very handsome. She was very fond of him, and they'd been good together. But now Rose realized that, more than anything, she longed for home.

And sweet, funny, predictable Henry. The lawyers had said Henry had tried to learn her whereabouts when he'd made landfall on Crete, and then again on a call from the Seychelles. She remembered the hasty note she'd written on that last morning in Antibes, telling him to look for her in the spring. She wanted to be back in Chicago when he finally came home. Her decision was made. A few days in Bogotá, a very fond, very final farewell to Cisco, and then on to Chicago.

She felt a sudden chill and pulled the blanket up to her chin. She glanced up one last time at the monitor. The jet's flight path was nearing the northeast coast of South America. Rose shivered. The point of no return. A point on a map, a time in one's life. How she longed for Chicago. She closed her eyes, hoping now for the rest she knew wasn't coming.

Beware of Bears

It had been six months since their last successful raid and now, God willing, their fortunes seemed to be finally changing. The mayday had come in on the emergency channel and there, sure enough, just a few miles off the Somali coast, was a very large pleasure yacht firing signal flares in the twilight.

Six of them hastily assembled on the beach, bringing the prized Soviet-era RPG and two extra rockets, a couple AKs with full magazines, and an old carbine. They decided to take Muhammad's motorized dhow because it was a bit faster and still seaworthy enough for at least this short trip. They loaded the weapons into the boat, and an extra gas tank, a six-pack of Tusker beer, a few pails for bailing, and together pushed the boat into the surf. Muhammad, who had a genius for all things mechanical, got the outboard going on just the first few pulls, and the others pulled themselves in over the gunwales and they were underway.

This was to be 16-year-old Abdi's first raid with his uncles, and he stood proudly in the prow as the old wooden boat finally picked up speed in the light chop and got up on plane.

Earlier, the six of them had sat on the beach at dusk, gotten a small fire of driftwood going, boiled tea, and chewed on the usual mouthfuls of khat for its mild stimulant effect. The talk was animated as Ahmed, the oldest and most experienced of the uncles, drew a simple plan of attack in the sand. The plan was typical of all the ones they had executed many times without mishap in the past, although in recent months the cursed American patrols had made life more difficult. But a pleasure boat of this size in distress was too good an opportunity to pass up. The great prize must be experiencing engine trouble, because every ship kept up speed through these dangerous waters, but by now word would almost certainly have reached the Americans or, less dangerous but still a threat, the Somali military. God willing, they would have plenty of time to reach the ship, threaten her captain and crew with the death and destruction that even their primitive weapons were capable of, and then pull up to the swim platform off the transom and board her.

Ahmed and the others were always surprised by how compliant the crews and passengers were, particularly the westerners who were unused to weaponry and violence, but to ensure cooperation, they pistol whipped a passenger or two right at the outset so that there was no doubt about the seriousness of their intentions or willingness to inflict harm. Two of them would hold the crew and passengers at gunpoint in the main salon while the others looted the staterooms, found and opened the safes, and put all the contents and the most valuable personal effects of the passengers and crew into pillowcases.

In the past they might also have taken one or two hostages and they had indeed successfully negotiated the ransom one time of a wealthy French yachtsman for 100,000 USD, but these days no one wanted to fuck with the Americans or run the risk of a drone strike or an American SEAL team dropping into their village one night out of nowhere. With this plan, it would all be over in less than 30 minutes and there would be no repercussions later.

The next day, in the safety of their nearby village, they would divvy up the Rolexes and diamond earrings and gold bracelets and western currency into the usual shares based on tribal seniority. Young Abdi would get the smallest share, but his reputation would be made. He would perhaps have enough now to buy the milk goats he needed to help woo the beautiful Fatima, whom he hoped to make the first of many wives.

As they neared the ship, they turned to run along her starboard side. Muhammad throttled back a bit to let Ahmed glass the ship with an old pair of field glasses. It was dark and moonless now with a bit of overcast, and it didn't appear they'd been seen. A few passengers walked along the lower deck walkway, and he could make out the silhouettes of who he suspected were the captain and one or two others in the dull light of the bridge. A crewmember loaded and fired another flare from the sun deck aft of the bridge.

All seemed normal, so Ahmed instructed Muhammad to approach the ship. As they neared within shouting distance, he told Abdul, who had the best English among them, to hail the crewmember. The others in the boat brandished their weapons, and Ahmed leveled the RPG at the bridge.

"Hey!" Abdul yelled, and the startled crewmember turned suddenly. He saw the small boat now and he reached for a walkie talkie on his belt. They didn't have to wait long because the man who must be captain opened the bridge's starboard hatch and came out onto the walkway.

"We board you now!" Abdul yelled. "Give us what we want! No one gets hurt!"

"You're wasting your time!" the captain yelled in reply. "We're in contact with the American Navy and a gunboat is only minutes away. They will blow you from the water. Save your lives and leave immediately!"

Ahmed, who knew only a few words of English, asked Abdul what had been said. "The usual bluff," Abdul said. He grinned. "Americans on their way. He says we should leave."

Rather than waste one of their few precious RPG rounds Ahmed set down the rocket launcher, took an AK out of Muhammad's hands, pushed the safety lever down from safe to fire, then pulled the charging handle back and let it go. He aimed the AK at the roofline of the bridge above the captain and fired three rounds in rapid succession. The captain dove below the rail line. He held a hand up and waved desperately in what looked like capitulation.

"We come on board!" Abdul yelled. "Fuck you! Fuck the Americans!"

The captain got up from the walkway. "Yes, we will cooperate!" he yelled. "Come aft, take what you want but for God's sake do no harm to my passengers and crew."

"Give us what we want. No one gets hurt, God willing!" Abdul gestured impatiently for Muhammad to steer toward the rear of the ship.

They idled slowly along the length of the ship. Half a dozen passengers had come out now on the various deck levels and were watching their boat. They reached the stern and Muhammad swung around to bring the dhow gently up against the swim platform. As they approached the Somalis who could read English saw the words *Ursus Major* and Nassau below it.

The lower deck beyond the swim platform was dark, but a crewmember standing at the top of the stairs leading up to the next deck level gestured for them to come aboard. Ahmed, holding a line in his mouth, made the short jump from the dhow to the swim platform first and covered the crewmember with the AK. The others quickly followed—all except Muhammad, whose job it was to safeguard the dhow by taking it 50 yards or so away from the ship.

As the others assembled on the swim platform, they heard what sounded like the low humming of the wings of some giant insect. As it changed to a higher pitch the last thing any of them ever saw was the muzzle flash from the darkness of the lower deck as the deck-mounted six-barreled, electrically-driven M134D gatling gun fired its 7.62 mm rounds into the Somalis at a rate of 3,000 per minute.

Muhammad, sitting in the stern of the dhow, had just enough time to throttle up and start to turn the dhow away from the ship when the tracers arched out over the transom and scythed through the back of the dhow, sending Muhammad flying into the sea and cutting the dhow practically in half.

The firing ceased and Volkov and a few of his crew emerged from the darkness of the lower deck. One of the crew produced a pistol and issued the coup de grace to one of the Somalis who was still alive and screaming in pain. The crew members began heaving the bodies of the Somalis into the sea.

"Let that be a lesson!" Volkov yelled in Russian, waving toward the Somali coastline. "No one steals from the Russian bear!" He turned and started up the stairs to the deck above.

"He's mad, isn't he?"

"Stark raving, mate."

Henry and Captain Swan sat in the dark on chaise lounges alongside the pool. It was a moonless night and the ember on the end of Captain Swan's cigarette glowed red as he inhaled. Henry, unable to sleep, had wandered down to the pool deck and found the captain alone and stretched out, having a drink and a smoke.

Despite being told to stay in their cabins just prior to the arrival of the Somali dhow, Henry and a few of the others had come out onto the starboard outer deck out of alarm when they heard the initial warning shot fired by the Somalis. Henry had leaned out over the deck rail and seen the dhow motor slowly behind the *Ursus Major*, and then the dhow being cut nearly in half and slowly sinking below the surface as the tracers poured into her. Others had come out on the outer deck too with the sounds of machine-gun fire and what sounded like a man screaming in pain.

Henry sipped on the drink he'd made himself behind the pool bar. He glanced over at Swan. It was the first time he'd seen Swan take a drink or smoke during the entire six months that he'd been on the *Ursus Major*.

"It was an ambush, pure and simple," Swan said, answering Henry's unspoken question.

"But why?" Henry asked. "What was the point? Why run the risk?"

"Boss gives the orders, I follow them, pure and simple," Swan said. "Can't afford not to, mate, if you know what I mean. Made a deal with the devil. Boss is on the run and wants the crew sharp."

"What about the rest of us? There are witnesses. That was murder."

Swan was silent for a moment, then turned to look at Henry. "You're the third Volkov 'friend for life' that's been on board since I've been captain," Swan said. "First one was Jennings. Very nice Englishman. Disappeared one night off Biarritz. Then came Thorsen. Boss owed him for some reason or another. Had an accident while spear fishing with Volkov in the Bahamas. You've lasted longer than most." Swan lifted his glass in a toast.

They were well into the Gulf of Aden now, and the intense heat coming off the Arabian Peninsula felt as if the door on a blast furnace had been suddenly opened.

"How long have I got?" Henry asked, finally.

Swan got slowly to his feet and looked down at Henry. "Must get back to the bridge, mate, nasty shoals here and there in these waters. Wouldn't wait too long, if I were you. Keep your head, you'll be alright." He flicked his cigarette over the rail and walked off into the darkness.

The Table is Set

It was Saturday evening, nine p.m., and the restaurant and bar areas of El Cielo, one of Bogotá's hottest new restaurants in the trendy Chapinero neighborhood, were completely empty of patrons.

A table had been set for 20 and Alejandro Gutiérrez, the restaurant's owner, nervously adjusted the stems of the orchids in one of the three table vases so the heights of the flowers were as close to perfectly aligned as possible. Earlier, he had lined up in single file the ten waitstaff who he'd hand-picked for the occasion days before, inspecting their hands for cleanliness, the length of their fingernails, the crispness of the freshly-pressed uniform black shirts and slacks they all wore, and making a point to stand close enough to each to detect even the slightest deficiency in their personal hygiene.

Then he returned yet again to the kitchen, where his Sorbonne-trained, Milanese-born executive chef Tomaso Maggiore, sous-chef de cuisine, and half a dozen line cooks and assistants were busy in that loud, thrilling, terrifying, chaotic but somehow tightly choreographed cross between ballet, high wire act, and battle preparation characteristic of the ramp-up to dinner in the world's best kitchens, but particularly those of Latin America. Alejandro Gutiérrez somehow managed to catch the eye of Maggiore, who gave him a quick thumbs up before swatting the back of an assistant's head who evidently was moving just a half step too slow for Maggiore's liking. Alejandro nodded and glanced at his watch. Good. All was ready. He had done everything he could in preparation for Don Hector's arrival. The rest he would leave up to God.

At exactly 9:30 p.m., seven black Mercedes G-Class SUVs pulled into the alley behind El Cielo. The first and last cars in the caravan each disgorged three large, beefy men packed tightly into ill-fitting dark suits, the signature uniform of security personnel worldwide.

One man knocked on the rear entry door and then entered the restaurant with another of the men, while the others fanned out and stood guard. A few minutes later, the door opened, and the two men emerged. They opened the rear doors on the rest of the Mercedes and Don Hector's entourage climbed slowly out.

The party was in no particular hurry. Judging from the noise, laughter, and hugging, the casual observer would have guessed that this was a particularly happy occasion, perhaps a birthday or anniversary, or the announcement of an engagement. The children ran excitedly into the restaurant ahead of the adults, followed by most of the women and a few of the men.

Two men and a woman hung back for a moment. The men embraced, and the taller of the two reached back to pull the woman, who has been standing off to the side, into the scrum.

From the rooftop three stories above, Captain Alfonso Guzman of the Colombian National Police lay flat on his belly on a spread-out raincoat, watching through his night scope. He identified the two men embracing as Don Hector and the famous polo player, Francisco Torres. He guessed the woman was the wealthy American known to be traveling with Torres, Signora Rose Ball, but he couldn't quite be sure. Certainly, she fit the description. Even at this distance and through the night scope she appeared to be either American or European and quite striking.

A romantic at heart, Guzman felt a sudden pang of regret. The reports said she was a civilian, an innocent bystander likely unaware that the older man embracing her was a ruthless killer responsible for the deaths of countless innocent men, women, and even children. And her boyfriend? While the level of Torres' involvement in the Ramos Cartel had been relatively benign to this point, there were signs he'd become actively involved in logistics and was being groomed to assume an important role in the family business.

Now Guzman watched as the three of them walked arm in arm and entered the restaurant. The door closed and three of the security detail remained outside. One walked up to the driver's side of the lead SUV. An arm extended outward to hand the man a cigarette, and then a cigarette lighter.

Guzman suddenly felt an almost overpowering urge to light the cigar he had in a jacket pocket, but he couldn't take the chance. He set down the night scope, rolled onto his back, and looked up at the night sky, now beginning to clear from an earlier rain. Even with the ambient city lights, the stars were unusually sharp at this high altitude.

Who was it who said, 'Nothing in life changes in a year, everything in ten?' Guzman wondered. Ten years ago, Ramos and the other cartel leaders were untouchable and ruled from their remote fincas like the gods on Olympus. No one could have imagined a change in status quo that seemed to benefit so many. How many of the others in his graduating class from the police academy had grown rich over the years just by looking the other way?

Now, power was shifting to a new generation of politicians bent on reform and eager to curry favor with the new American administration, and the good old days suddenly were coming to an end. Fresh from their success bringing the once irredeemable FARC militants to bay, this new breed of politician had set their sights on the cartels.

A few of the better behaved, lower profile cartels would certainly survive the purge, but the notorious Don Hector was to serve as an example of how a safe new Colombia, now open for business and American dollars, deals with criminals. There would be the usual collateral damage, Guzman thought, and who could guess at the fate of the beautiful American woman?

He sighed, craving the temporary comfort that smoking the cigar in his pocket would give him. *Only the stars remain constant,* Guzman thought, *only the stars above.*

Appreciating the Gravity of the Situation

"So look at me now I'm just makin' my play, don't try to push me just get out of my way, cause I'm back, yes I'm back, well I'm back, yes I'm back."

Victor sang at the top of his lungs and turned the volume up to ten on AC/DC's "Back in Black." With the sliding glass doors to the terrace wide open he guessed the music was even audible to the police officers and FBI agents that by now would have blocked off a section of Lake Shore Drive 25 floors directly below.

Someone in the FBI Chicago office had tipped off the lawyers at Waxworth Barnes that Victor's arrest would be happening within the hour, and the usual perp walk and media circus would be a drawn-out affair and made particularly humiliating if Special Agent in Charge, Wisconsin native and Chicago Bears hater Al Modjeski had anything to say about it. Modjeski had grown up in a neighborhood of blue collar, green and gold-painted bungalows literally in the shadow of Lambeau Field and still harbored a deep but, until today, well-concealed hate stemming from a late fall day 30 years ago when a reserve rookie tight end on the Chicago Bears had caught his only career touchdown pass on a fake punt play to win the game and knocked Modjeski's beloved Packers out of the playoff picture that year.

To say that Modjeski had subsequently earned his law degree at Marquette, risen in meteoric fashion up through the ranks of the Milwaukee FBI office, made a surprising request for a transfer to the despised Chicago office, and then begun his dogged pursuit of Victor Black all as part of some grand design for revenge would of course be more suggestive of Shakespeare than Cheesehead. Still, there were a number of agents that day that noted Modjeski's Green Bay Packers lapel pin and commented later it seemed like a curious sartorial choice for springtime. Yes, they all agreed, Packers fans were, at their very core, bonkers.

"We're going to the mattresses!" Jerry Barnes had said minutes before in a brief phone call to alert Victor. Barnes' friends at Justice had tipped him off earlier that day, indicating they had Carter Banks and he was singing. Now they were coming for Victor. Banks had evidently laid out a blueprint of the PREA scheme in precise detail, along with what Justice said was a 'shitload' of corroborating evidence. Victor had smiled at the thought of his panicking Waxworth Barnes lawyers declaring a legal Code Blue, scrambling to bring in publicists and a judge or two, hastily assembling legal briefs and putting all the other legal apparatus in motion that $1,500 an hour buys you. Now they were maybe ten minutes from arriving at his Lakeshore Drive penthouse and Victor didn't have much time.

He'd hurriedly scrawled a note to Suzanne and put that and a list of his few remaining offshore accounts with security and password information into an envelope made out to Waxworth Barnes so the Feds couldn't touch it. Then, just before sealing the envelope he paused, and dashed off another quick note that read: *To Henry and Rose Ball: someday you'll thank me.*

He stuffed the note in, sealed the envelope, and laid it on the corner of his desk. Then he had only one more fateful decision to make before the FBI arrived: AC/DC or the Stones?

Victor, who played a mean air guitar and had cracked up the Bears locker room on more than one occasion with an uncanny, if naked, impression of the manic lead AC/DC guitarist Angus

Young, leaped up onto the waist-high brick wall that enclosed the penthouse's terrace and began a prancing, head-bobbing, air-guitaring dance along its edge. A crowd had begun to gather along the perimeter that Chicago PD had established, and now there were cries of, "Look up there," arms pointing, and then the entire crowd seemed to gesture excitedly upward at the strange distant figure bobbing along the top of the building.

Special Agent Modjeski, standing by an unmarked squad car and discussing the logistics of the arrest with his Chicago PD counterpart, looked impatiently at his watch. He'd already stalled for time waiting on the arrival of all three network affiliates, FOX, and CNN, but his patience was wearing thin. He was about to order his agents into the building when a collective scream went up from the crowd and they began to push back away from the barriers. Just as Modjeski began to look up to see what all the commotion was about he heard a sudden rush of air and Victor Black landed with a tremendous bang just ten feet from him square on the roof of the squad car.

The bridge was illuminated by just the light from the instrumentation, and as Henry's eyes adjusted to the dark, he could see Swan at the wheel and Doyle, the first officer, next to him staring intently at the console and talking quietly on a walkie talkie. Swan raised his hand to acknowledge Henry but also to indicate for quiet. After a tense few minutes, Swan seemed to relax, and he turned to Henry.

"Better get some ice on that, mate," Swan said.

Henry reached up and gently touched the large, very painful knot that had formed just above his left eye. Just a few hours before, Henry had finally checkmated Volkov, and then rubbed salt in the wound by quoting a famous line out of the movie *Patton*, "Rommel, you magnificent bastard, I read your book!"

Volkov's sudden punch had sent Henry flying backward out of his chair, upending the chessboard and destroying the evidence of Henry's improbable and short-lived victory.

"Word travels fast on a ship, Ball," Swan chuckled. "Boss doesn't take kindly to losing. Got to admit, you've got a bigger set than most."

Henry looked out. It was a moonless night, and very dark, and the *Ursus Major* seemed to be idling along at a particularly slow speed. Henry was surprised to see what looked to be a dark land mass surprisingly close off the starboard side.

"Cannibal coast of New Guinea," Swan said, nodding toward the land. "Young Rockefeller tried to swim for shore somewhere near here back in the 60s. They never found the body, but natives said later they speared and ate him. Rumor has it they still like the occasional 'long pig' in these parts."

Swan pointed down at the large chart plotter screen showing the ship's position in the narrow channel running close to the coast. "Boss has got us running these buggering straits to save time. Good thing she only drafts about 13 feet. No markers, strong currents, reefs everywhere, and chart's not to be trusted." He glanced over at Henry. "Only a condemned man would make a swim for it in these waters."

Henry glanced casually down at the chart plotter for a moment and saw that the water temperature was 78 degrees, the ship was traveling at just six knots in about 60 feet of water, and the coast was a scant 600 yards off their starboard side.

He saw, too, from the imaginary course line that was plotted that the ship would be emerging from the narrow passage and into open water in about an hour. He didn't have much time.

"Doyle," Swan said suddenly to the first officer, "Move your aft watch to the port bow, we're coming up on a nasty reef and I want another man up there for now. You still here?" he said brusquely, looking over at Henry, and he reached out his hand for a quick handshake.

Henry descended from the bridge deck down the circular lobby staircase to the main deck lobby. He heard music and laughter coming from the disco aft as he went amidships to his cabin. Nothing seemed amiss, and whoever had gone through the dresser drawers and closet had been expert, but he noticed the top drawer he'd left slightly ajar was now completely closed, and his passport, which he'd taped to the bottom of the drawer, was missing.

Henry changed into a swimsuit, put on shorts and a T-shirt and deck shoes, decided not to drink any of the bottled water in the refrigerator, took a final look around, then quietly opened his cabin door.

He walked quickly through the main lobby and exited onto the deck outside and went aft, crawling below the disco windows and hoping no one would be in or around the pool. He stopped for a moment to let his eyes adjust to the darkness and then looked slowly around the corner. He needed to get to the stairs at the stern that descended down to the swim platform off the lower deck, but now he heard voices and in the low ambient light could make out two of the crew talking to a few of the new Australian girls in the lounge chairs by the pool.

Henry staggered out, tripped, and barely recovered, swayed a bit, and continued around the pool toward the aft starboard stairs. "Not well, gonna' be sick!" he slurred as he walked by the edge of the pool.

One of the Russians laughed. He looked over at the other Russian and gave a quick, almost imperceptible throat-slitting motion with his hand.

"Fella get a drink 'round here?" Henry said, as reached down, grinned, picked up a half-empty glass and drained in a few gulps what he hoped was water but turned out to be straight vodka.

One of the Russians gave Henry a lazy kick that sent him staggering toward the stairs.

"Not well at all," Henry said, almost under his breath. Then he stumbled down the stairs and out of sight of the Russians.

From the swim platform Henry could enter the area on the lower deck where the tenders and jet skis were stored, and while he knew his ruse wouldn't hold up for long, he decided to take a chance. He went in through the garage door-like opening into the dimly-lit area, lifted the boat cover from one of the tenders and climbed up over the transom. In the small cuddy cabin forward, he fumbled around in the near pitch black and finally grasped what felt like a duffle bag.

He hopped down off the tender and went back to the swim platform. He could see now he had the red watertight survival knapsack that he'd peered into casually on a day trip months before, containing survival rations, knife, fishing line and hooks, saltwater purifier, and assorted other items that might prove useful.

Henry felt a barely perceptible surge in the yacht and a few decibels higher pitch to the engine. The *Ursus Major* was slowly picking up speed. He stripped off his shirt, shorts, and shoes, stuffed them in the bag, slipped his arms through the shoulder straps, sat on the edge of the swim platform, and pushed off into the phosphorescent wake that trailed the ship. He struck out in a powerful crawl at right angles to the wake toward where he knew the mainland was just a few hundred yards away. But there was a surprisingly strong current that now made it impossible to make any headway toward land. Thankfully the current was also bearing him in the opposite direction from the yacht, so when the yacht finally stopped and a searchlight began sweeping the shoreline Henry was already a half mile away and being swept away from land toward open water.

He turned over on his back to rest a bit, cradling the backpack on his chest, which gave him a bit more buoyancy. He glanced at his watch and the big luminous hands indicated he had another couple of hours to find what the dawn would bring.

New-Found Friends

It was a late Sunday morning and the Mercado de las Pulgas de Usaquen was already crowded as Rose began working her way slowly from street vendor to vendor, stopping now and then at one of the booths with bright yellow awnings to admire an interesting piece of primitive hand-wrought jewelry or the works of a promising local artist or to sample a pastry or two. The flea market seemed to stretch on for miles. Cisco had business with Don Hector that he said would take all day, so she bought a big, brightly-woven bag to shop with, slung it over her shoulder, and prepared to make a day of it. Juan Carlos, the hulking driver that Don Hector had assigned to her, walked at a discrete distance behind.

Perhaps she'd had one too many pisco sours the night before, or maybe the light cool breeze was carrying a mildly stimulative pollen from the flowering coca fields that she imagined existed somewhere in the mountains nearby. Whatever the reason, it seemed to Rose she had stepped back in time 100 years and entered some strange, exotic mountain country. The thought reminded her of a favorite old Al Stewart song. "On a morning from a Bogart movie, in a country where they turn back time, you go strolling through the crowd like Peter Lorre, contemplating a crime . . ." She softly sang the few lyrics she remembered and hummed the tune.

The song conjured an old memory. It was an early spring evening way back in high school, and she was driving a carload of girls in her mom's old station wagon home from an after-school field hockey practice, WLS turned up loud on the AM radio and the girls all singing "Year of the Cat" at the top of their lungs.

The memory made her smile, but also feeling uncharacteristically wistful. She longed for home. Her mind was made up. She would talk to Cisco this evening. Then she would call the Hyatt and see if the crew of 1515 Zulu Tango could pull themselves away from the pool and the señoritas long enough to get a flight plan filed and the GV fueled and ready for a departure to the States sometime the next day.

After a few hours her shoulder bag was almost full: a set of heavy ceramic coasters for Zach; a pair of flamboyant terra cotta Maguey hoop earrings that only Suzanne could carry off; several bags of the strong coffee she'd become addicted to during her short stay in Bogotá; a colorful, intricately-woven origami pony for Cisco; some interesting looking fruit; and, finally, a finely detailed silver skull ring she thought the new, more daring Henry, in full biker mode, would like. She hadn't bothered bartering. Her Spanish was miserable, and she had a natural aversion for trying to take advantage of anyone she considered less fortunate. Instead, she simply fanned out her American money in various denominations and trusted the vendors to extract the correct bills and give her a fair price. Most had, but she'd almost certainly overpaid for a very fine filigree sterling silver necklace, and the hand-woven wide-brimmed Panama hat she now wore to ward off the hot noonday sun had cost an absurd 900 US.

Suddenly she felt a bit faint with the heat and altitude and began thinking about having lunch at one of the outdoor restaurants lining the large plaza bordering the mercado. Just as she began to turn away from one of the stalls to signal Juan Carlos, a man bumped into her. He was unshaven and dressed as a typical Colombian farmer with sombrero vueltia pulled low, so his surprisingly good English came as a bit of a shock.

"Señora, my apologies," he said, bowing slightly. He gently grasped her hand as if to shake it, and Rose could feel something placed against her palm.

"Be very careful," the man whispered, and then Captain Guzman disappeared into the crowd.

Rose slipped the note into her pocket. Juan Carlos had been chatting up a young woman at a nearby booth and seemed not to have noticed.

In his dream it was night. He was in the stern of an open boat filled with men and women. An enormous full moon broke from the scuttling clouds and there were hundreds of similar boats around them. There was the deep rumbling of surf on a distant shoreline and there were cries to turn the ship.

In the boat just ahead, a woman turned back toward him and he could see now that it was Rose. There was a look of fear on her face he'd never seen before and she screamed, "Henry!" and pointed ahead toward the white line of surf was now visible. He tried to move, but his legs seemed almost powerless.

"Hang on, Rose!" he yelled, and he felt someone jostling him as the rest of the boat passengers started to panic, and he was pinned by their weight against the side of the boat. Then he heard the roar of the breakers and the screams of the passengers as Rose's boat was upended suddenly and disappeared into the surf.

"Hey, yu bilong Aussie?"

Henry woke suddenly. He found himself lying in one or two inches of warm water and squeezed tightly against the rough sides of a narrow wooden dugout canoe. A black man with wild, wooly-looking hair kneeling in the stern of the canoe and wearing nothing but an old army web belt with a sheathed knife hanging from it gently shook Henry's legs.

Henry managed to push himself up into a sitting position. His swimsuit was in tatters. He saw now that his legs rested on top of several large sea turtles turned onto their backs with flippers still rotating in a weak swimming motion. He was relieved to see that his head had been resting on the red *Ursus Major* survival knapsack.

There was the strong smell of decaying fish and Henry turned suddenly, leaned out over the low gunwales of the canoe, and retched. After, he felt a little better, but terribly thirsty. He thought he must have swallowed a lot of saltwater during the hours he'd been in the water, and before this man had somehow spotted him miles from shore and dragged him aboard.

The man seemed not to notice. "*Nem bilong mi* Robert," the man said proudly, pointing to his chest. "*Yu bilong wanem hap?*"

There were just enough recognizable words in the phrases that Henry guessed the man was speaking some kind of coastal pidgin English in almost Yoda-like fashion.

Henry pointed to himself. "*Nem bilong* Henry," he said. "Water yu got, Robert?"

The man laughed heartily. "Yu orait, Henry," he said. Then he pointed toward the approaching shoreline. "Planti kaikai, Meri tenk you tru."

Henry turned and he could see that there was a fire going on the beach. A naked woman who he guessed was Meri was holding a naked child's hand and standing in front of a simple lean-to watching them. The beach and the jungle behind it seemed to stretch on for miles, and there was a low mountain ridge visible beyond the jungle a few miles inland.

Robert began paddling vigorously as they approached the line of surf, expertly steering the outrigger so it gently rose on plane, and then surfed down the gentle swell almost right up to the beach. He jumped out into waist-deep water and pushed the canoe forward until it ground to a halt with bow out of the water on the beach. Then he came around to the bow and dragged the boat even further up onto shore.

Henry lurched over the side into thigh-deep water. He slung the knapsack over a shoulder and took a few steps toward shore. His legs felt weak, and he thought for a moment that he'd be sick again. The woman and boy ran up to Robert and they talked rather excitedly in their language and Robert gestured occasionally back at Henry.

Henry walked unsteadily onto the beach and the woman and boy silently took his hands. The woman wore a leather necklace with seashells and had loops of wire through her ears with bright, almost neon blue bird's feathers suspended from them. Both the woman and boy's hair were pleated into dreadlocks.

They led him slowly toward the fire and lean-to. A dozen or so turtle shells and strips of meat hung from racks of long, horizontal poles. Robert unloaded the sea turtles from the boat.

As they led him away from the water's edge, Henry wondered if he would be the second multi-millionaire to wash up on these shores and be served up as a feast of fresh long pig, but he was too tired and thirsty to care very much.

Pride Goeth Before the Fall

It was midnight and the two men had stopped on their walk about mid-way across the pedestrian bridge spanning the narrow Tunjue-lo River that ran through downtown Bogotá. There was no other foot traffic, and it was as safe a place as any, with Don Hector's men guarding both ends of the bridge.

Don Hector took a last drag on what was left of the cigar and tossed the butt into the river. There was a sudden swirling around the cigar butt as some large predator rose out of the depths and struck at it. Don Hector leaned back, braced by his thick forearms resting on top of the iron railing. He was a short, swarthy, power-ful man who had risen through the ranks with great cunning and by cultivating a fearsome reputation for physical violence. Now, particularly on those rare occasions when he could be seen out in public, he sought to reverse the effect with the help of a pair of non-prescription designer glasses and the harmless attire of an affluent but conservative American businessman on holiday. He turned to look at Cisco. "What does she know?" he asked.

"Rose?" Cisco shrugged, nonchalantly. "Nothing. I am a hand-some polo player, good with horses. You know these rich American women. Easily entertained. I am, as they say, the flavor of the day."

Don Hector studied Cisco for a brief moment, then nodded. "Good. I thought by the way you were looking at her the other night at El Cielo that there might be more to this than a casual fling. And that would not be good. She cannot of course be trusted with anything having to do with the family business."

Cisco nodded, but now there was an awkward silence. After a moment Don Hector gently punched Cisco on the shoulder and laughed. "Do not look so worried, my son. Your Rose Ball is safe enough. We have other, much bigger problems. Look over there, that white truck along the riverbank." He nodded toward where a delivery van was parked, about a block south of the bridge. Its lights were off and there didn't appear to be a driver.

"Yes, police, watching our every move of late," Don Hector said, scowling. "In the old days someone would have been dead before the sun rose in payment for this impudence. Now we must wave and smile at the camera, and play their game, for a little while longer."

"What does it mean?" Cisco asked.

Don Hector shook his head slowly, a wry smile on his face. "Politicians and police. Always so predictable. We will need to offer a sacrifice or two to appease the government's new American gods, but they will have their hands out again, soon enough. In the meantime, we must be careful. Now would be a good time to send your American beauty back to her husband and family. No use in discussing it. The decision is made." He linked arms with Cisco, and they began walking toward the far riverbank where Don Hector's men waited beside their car.

"Why ship stop?"

Volkov staggered onto the bridge and reached for a hand hold as the *Ursus Major* rolled from one side to the other in a trough between the 20-foot waves. With a typhoon building to category 5 and bearing down on them just 200 nautical miles to the east, they'd been making the best possible speed north northwest to the relative safety of the Philippines. They had another 300 miles to go but Captain Swan had been confident, up until now, they could reach the big harbor at Sarangani Bay before the typhoon hit with full force.

Swan and his first mate were looking through binoculars out the portside. Swan had the 'Jane's Fighting Ships' reference book open on the chart table beside him. He pointed out to what looked to be a signal light flashing rhythmically, disappearing and then appearing again. He handed Volkov the binoculars. "There, about 30 degrees off our beam," he said.

Volkov snatched the binoculars away from Swan, braced himself against the roll, and looked out. After a moment, he swore softly in Russian.

"Russian frigate, big one too, probably Admiral Gorshkov class. Signaling us to stop," Swan said. "They must be mad. In this weather? What could they possibly want?" He glanced over at Volkov.

Volkov handed him the binoculars. In the two years he'd captained the *Ursus Major*, Swan had never seen Volkov nervous, let alone scared. Now the color had drained from his face and he was sweating profusely.

"Tried to raise them on the radio but they're not answering," Swan said. He turned to his first mate. "Get the signal gun, Doyle, we'll see what they want."

"Nyet," Volkov said, shaking his head vehemently. "We run." He pointed east, toward the ominous black wall forming across the horizon behind them. It was mid-afternoon but already the light had dropped to about what you would expect at twilight, with a low, dense ceiling of strange looking clouds oscillating overhead.

Swan stared at Volkov. "Boss, that's a Cat 5 typhoon, winds will be clocking at 125 or more and waves taller than a five-story building," Swan said, in a low, calm voice, as if reasoning with a tiger gathering itself to spring. "We go in there and that'll be the end of the *Ursus Major*. We've got to do what's best for passengers and crew." He nodded at the first mate, and said, "Get on with it, Doyle."

Volkov reached around for the pistol that had been tucked inside his wasteband against the small of his back and, without hesitation, aimed, and fired point blank into Swan's mid-section.

Swan staggered back and collapsed with a groan to the deck. Volkov aimed the pistol at Doyle. Doyle took a step back, hesitated, and then turned to the crewman standing at the wheel. "Helm, steer a course zero nine zero, ahead standard. Damn it man, now," he said, urgently.

They could hear the engines add power and a slight shutter went through the *Ursus Major* as she slowly turned, reluctantly it seemed, to face the oncoming typhoon. Volkov held the gun on Doyle. He glanced out the port side and there was the Russian frigate directly abeam beginning to close the distance.

The Simple Life

It had been a very lucky day.

First, they had come across a small grove of mango trees with the fruit just starting to ripen. The highly prized indigenous mangos were scarce along this stretch of the coast and considered a delicacy. Robert tied the machete around his son's waist and sent him scurrying aloft. The boy reached the top and began chopping the fruit loose. They fell heavily to the ground, where Meri gathered them and put them in a large bag fashioned out of old nylon fish netting.

The day got even better when they found a large feral pig trapped in one of the snares that Robert had concealed along the most promising of the narrow trails that the pigs made through the dense jungle underbrush. Robert approached carefully, and when the pig lunged at him and stretched out to the end of the rope that held a hind leg, Robert deftly delivered the coup de grace with his machete.

They gathered around the pig. "Yesa, Robert, God blessim, Meri cook kaikai pig, tenkyu tru," Henry said, pantomiming a large and expanding stomach. It would be the first meat other than fish or turtle any of them had had in the two months that Henry had been living with them on the beach.

"Yesa, Henry, pig kaikai long nait," Robert laughed, indicating they'd be having the pig for dinner, and he reached out to shake Henry's hand.

The boy dragged up a long, very stout tree limb. Robert used the snare to tie the pig's legs together, ran the tree limb between the pig's legs and indicated to Henry that he should pick up one end of the tree limb. Together, Henry and Robert hoisted the pig, balancing each end of the tree limb on their shoulders. Henry guessed the pig easily weighed 150 pounds or more, and the limb bowed a bit and sprang up and down as they walked single file with the boy and then Meri with the fishnet bag of mangos over her shoulder leading the way, down one of the pig runs toward the beach.

Henry smiled to himself. He was almost completely naked save for the palm frond hat the boy had woven for him and a shark tooth necklace Meri had fashioned; a fitting memento from the eight-foot tiger shark he'd helped Robert boat after an epic two-hour fight. His belly was gone, and he guessed he was at least 30 pounds lighter than he had been just six months ago. His bare feet had already toughened to the consistency of shoe leather.

He was certainly in the best shape of his life. Why, just the other day Robert had wounded another pig with a long and very lucky throw of his spear, and they had covered miles at a steady jog trying to run it to ground. Every day, the physical exertion of finding and providing food was enormous.

At night, after dinner around the fire and the inevitable story-telling—they seemed both fascinated by and skeptical of his descriptions of even the most mundane aspects of the civilized world—Henry would lie in his simple lean-to fashioned with branches and palm fronds, and fall instantly into an exhausted, deep, dreamless sleep that he hadn't experienced since childhood. At dawn, he would wake and join the family around the fire in front of their lean-to, where Meri would have a breakfast of baked palm flour pancakes and fruit waiting.

And then the day would begin again: the boy and Meri collecting fruit and fresh water from a small stream, Robert and

Henry netting fish inside the lagoon or, if the weather permitted, paddling hard over the breakers and out beyond the reef in search of larger quarry, like sea turtles and small shark. He was, Henry thought, about as happy as he'd ever been, save for the brief time he'd spent courting Rose in college.

Over the course of a mile or more Henry and Robert had fallen back a bit, and when they finally emerged from the jungle Meri and the boy were standing on the beach looking out toward the sea.

"Sip!" the boy said excitedly, pointing seaward, and there, anchored out beyond the reef perhaps a half mile out was a large sailboat. It was the first vessel they'd seen anywhere near shore since Henry had arrived.

With the scarcity of boats in these waters Henry had suspected early on that this section of the southeast coast must be considered particularly treacherous. But somehow this sailboat had worked its way around the dangerous shoals and sandbars almost right up to the reef. They watched now as a man dove from the bow of the ship, joining several other swimmers already in the water.

Robert, Meri, and the boy looked at Henry. Robert gestured toward the sailboat. "Henry laik go long sip em Port Moresby?" he asked.

The boy ran to Henry and hugged him tightly around the waist. "Henry em no gut, bilong here," he pleaded.

Henry smiled down at the boy and rubbed his head. He'd almost given up on the idea of trying to reach Port Moresby 300 miles to the southwest, knowing there was no way to travel overland through some of the world's most inhospitable jungle and a rescue by boat seemed unlikely. Now, with transportation back to civilization, and even access to a satellite telephone presumably just a half mile off, Henry realized it was time to go. He'd grown very fond of Robert and his family and the life they were leading. But he thought now of Rose. In her last note at Hotel Cap du Eden Roc, she'd asked that he look for her in the spring. While he wasn't sure what month it was, he guessed it was perhaps March or maybe even April. He had a strong, almost overpowering longing to be in Chicago before the end of spring.

On Second Thought, Plan B

She'd happily give half her fortune just to be sitting back at Starbucks in the Northbrook Court Mall sipping a tall latte right now, Rose thought, having just been jolted awake yet again with a sudden swerving and violent collision of the Mercedes hitting yet another crater-sized pothole.

The GPS indicated that Don Hector's finca in the valley just outside Pacho was another 20 miles ahead, but on these cursed dirt mountain roads that could take half a day. Still, Cisco was in good spirits now that the sun had risen, knowing that their safety was now all but assured.

Hector would have the Bell Jet Ranger fueled and ready, and that night they'd be flown out of Colombian airspace to Don Hector's private island resort a few miles off the west coast of Panama. A few days to enjoy the spa, beaches, clean sheets, and the exceptionally good restaurant and deep cellar, and then, well, on to wherever the lawyers said that the extradition treaties, banking laws, and, most importantly, Rose's great fortune would make them untouchable.

He reached over and gently rubbed Rose's neck. With an effort, she smiled. Her wrists still ached from the day before, when

Cisco had confronted her and asked for the note the Colombian police officer had slipped her at the Mercado. Don Hector's man Juan Carlos had evidently been watching her carefully all along.

Rose had at first denied the encounter and Cisco, in the first display of anger that Rose had ever seen except on the polo field, reached out suddenly and grabbed her by the wrists with such force that she'd cried out in pain. Rose had flushed the note down a toilet but told Cisco the truth about its contents: Make an excuse. Leave the hotel. Go to the American consulate. You are not safe with these men.

Cisco had stared at Rose for a moment, then left the room, evidently to strategize with Don Hector in the adjoining suite. Minutes later he returned and brusquely ordered her to pack. They left hurriedly by the back stairway, walked through the underground parking garage, then exited into a back alley, where the empty Mercedes was waiting for them.

She'd had a terrifying and mostly sleepless night with one jungle downpour after another reducing visibility to practically nothing and making the narrow two-track mountain road built for carts, livestock, and foot traffic even more treacherous. But given the suicidal driving conditions, it would have been impossible for the police to tail them, and Cisco had somehow managed to hug the inside of the many sections where only a few feet separated the road from what must have been a sheer drop into oblivion.

Rose shuddered, remembering how, on at least half a dozen occasions the rear of the heavily armored G-Series Mercedes had careened seemingly out of control toward the abyss. But somehow, either by luck or divine intervention, Cisco had gotten control at the last second, cursing and cajoling the Mercedes all the while like he was handling a powerful but very difficult polo pony.

"Damn it, what now?" Cisco said. Up ahead a cart pulled by a donkey had somehow flipped on its side, blocking the road. Whoever had been driving the cart had evidently gone off for help. The donkey, still in its traces, was grazing on vegetation along the roadside and waiting patiently for the return of its owner. Cisco slowed to a stop.

"I won't be a moment, my love." He got out of the car, leaving the door open and the car running.

He must have seen some movement out of the corner of his eye, or perhaps he sensed something strange in the sudden stillness of the surrounding jungle, but he turned back toward the car and started to run. The first bullet winged him and spun him around and he raised an arm and held out a hand in what must have been a futile plea for just a little more time. Then a fusillade of automatic weapons erupted from the jungle along the road.

It was perhaps 10 or 15 seconds before Commandante Perez finally got his troops to cease fire. The small team of 12 elite Colombian Rangers emerged cautiously, with several advancing now slowly toward the car. The others looked curiously down at Cisco, his legs and arms akimbo like a department store mannequin thrown carelessly to the ground, surprise on his face, and blood pooling slowly in the wet red Colombian soil around his bullet-ridden body. The men all had the nervous, happy, and relieved expressions that soldiers seem to have when they have engaged in battle, killed other men, and emerged unscathed.

"Easy, men," Perez said as he walked up to the car. Despite six months of training with the Americans, there was still no predicting how his men would behave in live fire conditions, and despite the fact that he'd instructed them that Cisco was to be taken alive, that idiot Sergeant Dominguez had fired first.

Perez drew his pistol and slowly opened the passenger side door. "Señora," he said, and he held out his free hand.

At the first shot Rose had flung herself down across the front seats. For someone hearing gunfire at close quarters for the first time, the sound had come as a shock, and she'd covered her ears and burrowed her head as deeply into the seat cushions as she could.

"Señora," Perez said, a bit more firmly.

With considerable effort, Rose pushed herself up on weak arms and into a sitting position. Through the front windshield she could see troops gathering around what was left of Cisco to take snapshots with their cell phones. Perez wrapped an arm around Rose as she began to weep and helped her gently from the car.

Down, But Not Out

The autumn moon lights my way . . . ramble on . . . gotta find the queen of all my dreams . . .

It was a different season—late spring—but he was reminded of a favorite Zeppelin song as a giant blood moon rose over the lake to the east and appeared just over the estate wall. He'd heard an astrophysicist lecture one time on this moon phenomena, an optical illusion believed to be caused when the human brain assumes the object is closer, and hence larger, when near the horizon. It was a theory proven by viewing the moon through a drinking straw or by holding an aspirin over it at arm's length, Henry remembered, either of which would show the moon to be identical in size whether on the horizon or directly overhead.

His old friend Arnie Schlecter had picked him up at O'Hare a few days earlier, when Henry had landed after an arduous string of flights from Papau, New Guinea, reluctantly funded by the notoriously stingy U.S. consulate in Port Moresby. Arnie, with all his usual tact, didn't ask about Henry's recent whereabouts, and if he was surprised that a former billionaire had arrived with only a backpack with the name *Ursus Major* embroidered on it for luggage, had no money, and needed a place to stay for a few days he didn't show it. Of course, Arnie had heard the rumors and a juicy expose in the *Tribune* after Victor's death concluded Henry and Rose's fortune had indeed been part of the funds Victor had used to finance the aborted coup in the PREA. But the topic never came up in the few days Henry had used the guest bedroom.

He'd slept almost round the clock the first day and then, when he sheepishly asked to borrow some of Arnie's old clothes, Arnie had volunteered to outfit him with a run to Walmart and lend him $5,000 until he could get on his feet again. A few days later at the Metra commuter train station, Henry gave Arnie a sudden and uncharacteristic hug goodbye and promised to repay his kindness as soon as he had taken care of what he called some unfinished business.

What a difference a year can make, Henry thought. He straightened up from pretending to tie his shoe and began walking. There was a rent-a-cop checking invitations at the front gate, and beyond that, the long drive and courtyard were filled with luxury cars, with more being parked along the street by the valets.

Henry had no idea who was now occupying his Lake Forest mansion, but it had been foreclosed on months ago and the new owners were tonight entertaining on a scale that was guaranteed to get a tabloid page or two of photo coverage in next month's *Lake Forester*, particularly with the town now breathing a collective sigh of relief that the ghastly 'Powerballer' was gone and the estate called Lake Cliff had been restored to its rightful place in the natural order of things.

Good timing, Henry thought, as he walked casually past on the sidewalk across the street from the entrance, obviously just a curious neighbor out for his nightly constitutional. When he was just opposite the southwest corner of the estate, he waited until a car had passed and turned into the drive, then sprinted across the street. The running start gave him just enough momentum so that he could grasp the top of the eight-foot brick wall that fronted the estate and pull himself up and into a sitting position. He smiled to himself. His stay in New Guinea had done a body good. He wasn't even breathing hard. He would have needed a ladder to scale a wall half that height during his brief tenure as lord of the manor. *Yes, what a difference a year makes.*

The ambient light from the mansion and full moon just rising over the lake to the east illuminated the grounds just enough so Henry could see there didn't appear to be any dogs or security patrolling. And while it was already mid-May, there was still a chill in the air, so the party was being held largely indoors. Henry guessed the motion sensors and other security devices that might otherwise be in use to safeguard the estate at night had likely been turned off.

He dropped down along the wall and now began to walk casually along the walled perimeter of the vast lawn toward the lake, reasonably confident he couldn't be seen from the house some 50 yards away. The party was in full swing and he could hear the horns and drum of a jazz band accompanying a female vocalist, and all the rooms on the first floor were filled with people.

Just as he reached the edge of the lawn and the trellis at the top of the stairs, he was startled by a young couple in evening wear coming up the stairs from the beach. Henry nodded and stood to the side to let them pass. The stopped for a moment at the top of the stairs while the woman caught her breath. The man took off his dinner jacket and draped it around the woman's shoulders.

"Phew!" the man said. "That's a climb! Tommy Archer." He extended a hand, looking at Henry for an acknowledgement that he recognized the name.

"Oh, yes, Mr. Archer, saw your name on the guest list of course. Just going down now to do a sweep of the beach." Henry said, hoping the implication that he was security might answer some of the questions he guessed Archer was having about his appearance, a black warmup suit and bright red knapsack.

Archer gestured at the mansion. "Nice party. Your boss got this place for a song, so why not celebrate? Jeanne said the decorating was right out of Trump Tower. They had to gut the place. Can't wait to see it."

"Whatever happened to that Ball fellow?" the woman asked, as she leaned on Archer, removed a high heel, and shook some sand out of it. "I rather liked the wife, the one time I met her. Pity."

Archer laughed. "Victor Black, that's what happened. Ball—what a douche, am I right?" he asked.

"Complete douche," Henry agreed, and he high-fived Archer's extended hand. The couple turned, linked arms, and began walking across the lawn. Henry waited for a moment and then started quickly down the stairs.

The stairs zig-zagged from landing to landing down the side of the steep bluff. At the second to last landing, about 30 feet above beach level, Henry stopped, listened for a moment, then took his backpack off. He removed a small flashlight, turned it on, put it in his mouth and climbed over the railing. He squeezed himself in behind the stairs, where there was just enough room for him to stand upright on a slight ledge and facing the bluff. The bluff was a hard, compacted sandy soil and loose rock, and now Henry began digging with his hands at about eye level.

"C'mon, damn it," he said out loud. He was breathing heavily with the effort as he reached about arm's length in depth, then felt something hard and cylindrical. He managed to get his hands around it, grasped it firmly, and pulled it out. He hugged the heavily duct-taped plastic Folger's coffee can to his chest and rested for a moment.

"Thank you, Agnes," he whispered. "You were right. The bastards found a way to get our money—but not all of it."

Henry slid out from behind the stairs, climbed over the rail, brushed off loose sand and dirt, and stashed what he hoped was about $2 million in loose diamonds, rare coins, and cash in his knapsack. Then, rather than taking any more chances on the estate grounds, he headed down the stairs to the beach. It would be a long walk to the public beach to the south, but less risky than traversing the estate again.

Besides, it would give him time to think. The moon had risen a bit higher now over the lake, and it was calm with barely a surf. He walked to the water's edge, bent down, rolled up his sleeves and vigorously washed his hands using sand as an abrasive.

"Ramble on, ramble on, the moon lights my way," Henry sang along softly with the old Zeppelin tune playing in his head. "Got to find the girl of all my dreams."

El Buen Madonna

"¡*Muere, hijo de puta!* Die you son of a bitch!"

The bullwhip lashed out suddenly and the tip, breaking the sound barrier and as loud as a pistol shot, intersected perfectly with the small lizard halfway up the wall, snapping its spine and sending it flying.

El Director de la carcel Mercedes Cruz laughed with delight, set the whip down on her desk, and resumed watching through binoculars as her guards herded the new arrivals off the bus. They ran a gauntlet through a throng of inmates gathered in the big prison yard. The inmates harassed the newcomers with the usual catcalls and jeering, and already bartering with offers of protection, drugs, or sex. The guards swung their batons here and there to clear a path to the receiving pen where the new inmates would be processed, stripped, de-loused, heads shaved, and then given their prison issue and assigned to a cell that had been originally designed for two but now housed as many as eight.

"Muy bien," Cruz whispered under her breath. She licked her lips. "Sí, that must be the rich gringa."

She followed Rose with her binoculars as she made her way off the bus and fell into line. *Pretty, sí, and haughty, a wild horse that needs breaking,* Cruz thought, her breath quickening a bit. And who better to break her?

Known as La Viuda Negra, the Black Widow, and greatly feared by inmates and guards alike, Cruz ruled over the infamous all-women's jungle gulag El Buen Madonna with a cruel and brutal efficiency. She and her small cadre of club-wielding guards were known to appear suddenly without warning anywhere in the prison day or night, with bullwhip lashing out at the smallest infraction or perceived slight or in punishment for a payment less than her fair share.

Sí, she ran a tight ship so no one at Justice in Cartagena seemed to care much that she was making a fortune taxing almost every transaction in the robust drug and sex trades and profiting handsomely from the extortion and protection games that constituted a big part of the prison economy. Cruz ran a vast network of stoolies, sycophants, and informants that would have made Beria, the notorious head of Stalin's secret police, proud. The sudden disappearance of inmates for even the most minor infractions was not uncommon, but barely made a ripple in the vastly overcrowded prison.

When the line of new prisoners had finally passed beneath her window and out of sight, Cruz called out for the assistant working in the small antechamber that adjoined her office.

The assistant knocked, then entered. The woman made a short, deferential bow. "Sí, Madame Director?"

Cruz sat straddling the edge of her desk, her long, muscular legs clad in her customary khaki jodhpurs and riding boots. She scanned a file folder open across her lap, then looked up. "Rose Ball, one of the new arrivals and yet another of these Norte Americanos seeking to soil Colombian honor and reputation with their filthy drug trade. Eight to ten years for conspiracy to sell narcotics. Hardly seems enough. We should make an example of her, don't you think?"

"Sí, Madame Director."

"Assign her to A block, and that cell with Chiquita Riva and the others from FARC. Those leftists will give her a valuable lesson in the evils of capitalism and attempting to profiteer at Mother

Colombia's expense. Let it be known that she is a rich *yanqui*, but nothing too terrible is to befall her just yet," Cruz said, waving her hand in dismissal. "Make it so."

Cruz picked up a compact from her desk and studied her face. No, not too horrible to look at, she thought, despite the black eye patch and the jagged white knife-wound scar that crossed from above where her right eye had been, under the eye patch, across the bridge of her nose and down her left jawline.

She reached up and brushed her luxuriant mane of long black hair off her forehead. Then she applied just a hint of blush and the dark plum-colored lipstick she favored that seemed to make her lips look even fuller.

She smiled at her reflection. Bueno. Sí, she was so looking forward to having Rose Ball as her guest.

Partners in Crime

The sun was just coming up, but they'd been on the water since well before dawn, so the big ice boxes were already about half-full. The two cousins, Big Jim and Little Jim, were heading still more shrimp from their last haul. It was late in the season, but there were still plenty of snowbirds and vacationing families on Hilton Head and Kiawah Island, so they had big standing orders to fill from some of the larger restaurants and resorts. Despite what some of the old timers would tell you, the white shrimp were still there if you knew where to find them, and Carter and the two Jims had been working what they called the honey hole right off Fripp Island with spectacular results for the better part of two weeks.

It was a good start to the day before Memorial Day, Carter thought, as he turned his boat toward the entrance to Port Royal Sound, St. Helena's Island, and home. He tied the wheel off with a short length of rope in a primitive but functional autopilot, then throttled back to about 1,500 rpm. They were still about ten minutes from the coast, so he could afford to relax for a few minutes.

Carter walked off the bridge and leaned against the starboard rail of the 60-foot double-rig *Miss Rosie Mae*. A synchronized flight of heavy brown pelicans skimmed low just off the bow, and a small pod of hunting dolphins forced a fleeing school of what looked like yellowtail to break the surface in a desperate attempt at escape.

Carter took a deep, satisfied breath of that lovely, tangy lowland marsh air so pungent you could taste it and smiled. He'd put what little he had left after the lawyers had picked him clean—his last $140,000 and change—into the *Rosie*, a 50-year-old boat with a lucky reputation. He'd had just enough money to outfit her with new nets, electronics, and rebuilt diesels, refurbish the cabin and galley, rent a slip at Booger's Wharf on Capers Creek, and start shrimping. If it all went well, he'd clear maybe $35,000 over the next year after expenses. He knew, however, that Cap'n Skunk McGhee and the other skippers, who all liked Carter and respected his military service, thought he'd most likely go broke in six months or less, what with all the damn government regulations, quotas, strange weather and, well, just because. Still, Carter thought, come what may, right now at this moment he'd never felt so content.

He went back onto the bridge and steered into the sound, threading his way between the green and red buoys marking the entrance to the channel. As Big and Little Jim worked to stow gear, rig lines, and bumpers, they sang an old Gullah spiritual with an African melody that dated back to the days of slavery. Carter joined in for a stanza or two with his big, over-the-top baritone, making the Jims burst out in laughter.

Carter made his way slowly up the sound and then turned hard to starboard into Capers Creek. There was still a light morning ground fog hugging the shoreline, and up ahead Carter saw what seemed like a ghostly apparition begin to form at the end of their dock at Booger's Wharf.

As they came closer, the figure took on the appearance of a man, made all the more unusual by the fact that the man appeared to be white. Carter throttled back, used opposite throttle to swing the boat 90 degrees and parallel to the dock, eased her gently against the tractor tire bumpers, and put the engines into neutral. Big and Little Jim jumped onto the dock and tied bow and stern lines to the cleats. Carter shut down the engines, and stood for a moment by the wheel, gathering his thoughts. What the hell was

Henry Ball still doing alive and here on his dock—and how should he kill him?

They sat out on the deck behind The Foolish Frog at a nice table overlooking the marsh, peeling shrimp from a bucket and halfway through a second pitcher of margaritas. It was still too early for the dinner crowd to arrive and they were the only customers sitting outside. Priscilla, their very pretty waitress, made an occasional appearance to ostensibly deliver more shrimp and drinks but really to flirt openly with Carter, whom she'd admitted to having had a crush on as far back as their days together in high school.

"Man, when was the last time you had something to eat?" Carter asked. Henry looked up from his plate, smiled sheepishly, and popped another shrimp into his mouth. He'd almost single-handedly polished off a pound of shrimp and most of the first pitcher. Since leaving Chicago two days before on a Greyhound bus, Henry realized he'd had nothing more than the bag of chips and a candy bar he'd bought at the Chicago Greyhound station. He'd also gone completely without sleep, and not left the bus at any of the wayside or restaurant stops they'd made along the way to Beaufort. Several travelers seated nearby, first a retired couple and then a sailor on leave, evidently curious about this strange man clutching the odd red backpack to his chest, had tried to strike up a conversation, but Henry had either feigned sleep or uttered a phrase in Russian in response that seemed to imply he had no understanding of English.

"When the *Ursus Major* went down with all hands somewhere in the South China Sea, I thought, serves that son of a bitch Ball right," Carter said. "It was typhoon season and the official story is the ship must have been hit by a rogue wave because there wasn't even a mayday. Thing is, I later heard through the grapevine from some friends at DOD that two Russian Navy frigates had been seen shadowing *Ursus Major* a week prior, so I'm guessing some old scores finally got settled. I'm also guessing you saw the handwriting on the wall and got off shortly after she left Sydney, am I right?"

Ball nodded. He took another sip of his drink. "Look, Carter, I'm sorry about the way things went down in Cuba."

Carter waved an arm dismissively. "I know, you meant to write," he said sarcastically.

The two men sat in silence, watching the setting sun. After a moment Carter glanced over at Henry. "Man, you left me high and dry and on the hook for something like $20,000 in expenses which, by the way, Victor refused to cover when he learned that you'd slipped your leash. And let me tell you, those Harlistas ain't playin. But what the hell? Now Victor's dead and he took all your money with him, am I right? I took a serious haircut too, damn near went to prison, and now I'm here, living the dream. Fate sure is a fickle bitch."

Henry filled both their glasses from the pitcher. "Which is why I'm here, to pay my debts—and ask for your help."

Carter stared at him incredulously. "Middle age white man down on his luck with just a backpack to his name comes south by Greyhound to ask for black shrimp boat captain's help." Then he broke into laughter. "Shit, not since Poitier and Curtis were handcuffed together in *The Defiant Ones* has there been such an improbable premise. What's that?"

While Carter was talking Henry pulled the red plastic heavily duct-taped Folger's can out of his backpack and set it down heavily on the table.

"Borrow your knife?" Henry asked, pointing to the knife hanging from Carter's belt.

Carter pulled the old commando fighting knife that he'd had since Iraq from its sheath and handed it to Henry. "Careful," he said. "I keep it very sharp."

"I would expect nothing less," Henry said. He began cutting away at the layers of duct tape wrapped around the lid of the can. He stopped midway through when Priscilla came out, but Carter indicated with a wave that they were fine. When she'd gone back inside, Henry resumed cutting. He finished, paused for a moment for effect, and then removed the lid. He slid the can over to Carter.

"Holy shit," Carter said, looking down. He looked up. "Ball, you ain't as dumb as I thought. How much is there?"

Henry shrugged. "Hard to say, exactly. Two or three million in loose, flawless diamonds. Another half million more in rare, highly collectable gold coins. Hundred thousand or so in cash."

Henry reached over and pulled the coffee can back. He reached in and pulled a thick roll of hundred dollar bills out and tossed it to Carter. "There's more where that came from," Henry said. "Consider it payment on my debt, and a down payment on our next job. If we succeed, whatever's left in this can is yours."

Henry reached back in, searched through the contents, and pulled out a pea-sized diamond. He flipped it to Carter, who caught it, and held it up between two fingers in the fading light.

"That would look nice on Priscilla's finger, don't you think?"

Carter stared for a moment at Henry. "Who do I have to kill?" he asked, finally.

"Not sure," Henry said. "Hopefully no one. Depends on who gets in the way when we break Rose out."

Out of the Frying Pan, Into the Fire

Sergeant Ramirez, sweating profusely in full riot gear and accompanied by two other heavily-armed guards per regulations, hurried down the narrow aisle that fronted the cells of A block, fearing the worst.

There would be hell to pay if anything had happened to the American woman. El Director had wanted her softened up but Ramirez, distracted by a near-riot, two stabbings, and a 24-hour lockdown, had let a week elapse before now checking on the woman's well-being. The three men hurried along in the dim early morning light, ignoring the usual catcalls and insults hurled at them from the overcrowded and still locked-down cells.

"Mother of God, what was Cruz thinking?" Ramirez muttered to himself, as he motioned for his guards to hurry. Even among the inmates, these last remaining members of FARC were still greatly feared. After the government and FARC had finally reached an accord after so many years of bloodshed, it had taken the military another year to run an unrepentant Chiquita Riva and these four other women, her last remaining lieutenants, to ground in the jungle, where they'd been living for months on nothing but nuts, berries, snakes, and monkey.

Riva was a Cuban-trained Marxist who, as a member of FARC's notorious Central High Command, was responsible for countless kidnappings, assassinations, and car bombings. Worst of all, she hated the Americanos to her very core and, in true Marxist fashion, traced all the ills of the world, everything from global warming to the common cold, directly to the evil la América del Norte. There was no doubt that by now she had taken her vengeance on this new arrival, but hopefully Rose Ball was somehow still alive. Ramirez had alerted the infirmary in advance, just in case, and the doctor and his staff were already waiting for whatever was left of her.

As they neared Riva's cell, Ramirez was surprised to hear laughter, and voices speaking in English. He stopped and held up a hand, gripped his riot stick a bit more firmly, and peered cautiously just past the edge of the bars into the cell. The six women were sitting cross-legged in a circle on the cell floor, where the concrete perhaps offered some cool relief from the sweltering heat of the cell block. Ramirez, whose English was very poor, couldn't make out what the American was saying, but the women seated around her seemed to be following her story with great interest. Then Chiquita Riva, sitting right next to the American, reached out and gently squeezed the American's arm in what seemed to Ramirez to be a sympathetic gesture.

Ramirez leaned back against the wall, exhaled quietly with relief, wiped the sweat from his brow, and made a hasty sign of the cross. Other than a welt under the left eye and a noticeable scratch across the bridge of her nose, the American appeared no worse for wear. These would be easy enough to conceal with a bit of makeup and a Band-Aid from the infirmary. Oddly enough, one of the FARCs had an arm in a makeshift sling, and another had an eye swollen shut. After a moment, Ramirez motioned for his men to move forward.

Ramirez couldn't have known it, but in the preceding days Chiquita Rivas had attempted to employ the same textbook tactics on the new gringa arrival that FARC had used to break even the strongest of their captives over the years. Rivas could only guess at Mercedes Cruz' motivation for placing this rare, and reputedly very wealthy, *yanqui* prize in their cell, but she intended on making the most of it—and as quickly as possible. Cruz was nothing if not unpredictable, and Rivas knew they would need to move fast if they were to extract maximum benefit. If the Americana really was as wealthy as they said, then who better than Chiquita Rivas to appropriate this fortune and put it to good use on behalf of the workers it had most certainly been stolen from?

Two of Cruz's more congenial lieutenants had approached Rose a few days after her arrival, working on the assumption the American would, like all the new arrivals, now be completely terrified by the hellish conditions and feeling extremely vulnerable. For the right price, these two new friends could offer the protection she would undoubtedly need, and access to a surprising array of material comforts to make her stay at El Buen Madonna if not pleasant, then at least tolerable. Without their help, *¡Dios mío!* she would not last the week. The regular monthly payments her lawyers would bring would keep her safe and in relative comfort until her inevitable release—and how far off could that be for a wealthy, well-connected, and completely innocent Americana woman who of course had been falsely accused of crimes she couldn't possibly have committed?

Rather than jumping at the opportunity, however, the woman had turned them down flat, explaining in rudimentary Spanish that she didn't have any money, didn't want protection, and had no interest in anything else they had to offer. Nor did she have any lawyers working on her case. The gringa had offered this explanation in such a matter-of-fact way and with so little emotion—as if having no concern whether she was believed or not—that clearly she was *muy loca*, the women said when they reported back to Rivas in the prison yard later that day.

Rivas, enraged by the American's intransigence and feeling the clock ticking, would send her two other less congenial lieutenants that night. They had tried the easy and least painful approach; now harsher measures would be needed. No matter. In the end, Rivas had broken all her captives over the years, even the toughest of the Colombian rangers they'd captured after a firefight or two.

The Americano would be no different. She would give them what they wanted.

They'd been stealthy enough, slipping out of their bunks and slowly crossing the cell to the American's bunk around three a.m. just as weak moonlight began coming through the cellblock's high skylight, but the woman had not been sleeping after all, and was ready for them. The FARC woman who went for the usual choke hold must not have expected much resistance, and the force of Rose's forearm to her attacker's brachial plexus, a bundle of particularly sensitive nerves at the base of the neck, caught her so completely by surprise and with such power that the temporary paralysis sent the woman crashing instantly to the floor.

The other woman hesitated for just a moment, but it was enough to give Rose the opening she needed. She pushed off hard from her bunk, landing a scissors kick to the side of the woman's head. As the woman staggered backward, Rose's front kick to the woman's solar plexus knocked the wind out of her and sent her flying backward. She went down on one knee and Rose was just about to issue the coup de grace when Chiquita Rivas jumped her from behind and held the shiv to her throat.

"Give me a reason why I shouldn't kill you now?" Rivas hissed in English in Rose's ear. She pushed the shiv in just deep enough to draw a little blood.

"Go ahead, do me the favor," Rose said. "Kill me."

Rivas felt the woman's body suddenly relax, almost as if welcoming the thrust of the blade at her neck. *Muy loca, sí*, but how best to play it?

"You pay us, I let you live," Rivas whispered, soothingly. "How much can money be worth, even to a *yanqui?*"

Rose laughed, a bit hysterically. "Money! Is that all you wanted? All you had to do was ask nice. Sure, you can have everything I own. Reach into my right pocket. It's all I have left in the world."

Rivas held the shiv to her neck and reached cautiously into the right pocket of Rose's prison issue dungarees. She pulled out a single coin and held it up to where she could see it in the dim light: an American dime?

"So, the American banker, the man you call Black, stole your great fortune?" asked the woman who had attacked her first, still rubbing her arms to try to get the feeling back.

The six women sat on the cell floor just as the early light of dawn began to filter into the cell. They passed a plastic water bottle filled with prison hooch to Rose. She took a healthy slug, grimaced at the turpentine taste to the delight of the other women, and passed it to Rivas.

The women, curious now about this crazy gringa and deeply impressed by her fighting skills and desperate courage, had taken Rivas' lead and quickly made their peace. Time, after all, in El Buen Madonna was a commodity too precious to waste on petty grievances or fruitless escapades. Nor could they have survived so many years in a running battle with the Colombian army without adapting to circumstances on the fly. If the Americana was truly without money, then so be it. If nothing else, her fighting skills would prove useful, and she undoubtedly had many interesting stories of life in la América del Norte to help relieve some of the monotony of prison life and pass the time.

"Yes, a billion dollars," Rose replied, quietly. "All gone. A cursed fortune as it turned out. Wish we'd never gotten that money."

"And what of your husband?" Rivas asked. "Can he not help you now?"

Rose was silent for a moment, and the women could see tears for the first time welling up in her eyes. "Henry? Lawyers said he was missing and presumed dead," Rose answered, finally. "He was on a ship that went down in a storm. I keep hoping but there's been no word. Anyway, the lawyers stopped taking my calls months ago, right after I got arrested. You know the old saying: no mas dinero, no mas lawyers." There was bitterness evident in her laughter.

The women nodded in sympathetic agreement. Rivas reached out her hand and gently squeezed Rose's arm. "We are your sisters now, you are safe with us," she said. "And, who knows, perhaps your man is still alive, sí? If I have learned anything in this life, it is that nothing is certain."

Just then they heard what sounded like a voice on a walkie talkie. The door of their cell unlocked and slid slowly open.

Ramirez and his men charged forward into the open cell. Ramirez ordered the women to lay face down on the cell floor. One of the women moved a bit too slowly and a guard swung his riot stick against the side of her head. Two of the guards grabbed Rose under the arms, jerked her roughly to her feet, and half-dragged, half-carried her out of the cell.

The Die is Cast

Carter unrolled the photo enlargement across the wicker table in the screen porch and anchored the edges with hurricane lamps and a bottle of Mount Gay's rum. He lit the lamps, poured two glasses of rum, and slid one across the map toward Henry. Henry sat heavily in one of the wicker rockers, leaned back, and sighed with contentment. He took an appreciative sip of the rum, a liquor he'd taken a liking to in Cuba and even more so aboard the *Ursus Major*. Now, after a few week's stay at Carter's, he'd begun welcoming it at the end of every day like the arrival of an old friend.

It had been yet another epic evening at the Banks' house, a small, tidy white-frame bungalow at the end of a narrow two-track that had been in the family since the late 19th century. Carter's mother, a cheerful woman with a booming laugh that her diminutive body didn't seem capable of producing had served up another massive low country dinner. After a third helping of pan-fried chicken, field peas, mashed potatoes, and corn pone, Henry began to politely decline the pecan pie that Miss Alice, as Henry called Carter's mother, put in front of him, but the barely perceptible shake of Carter's head made it clear that a refusal would be impossible.

Then Big and Little Jim came by with a couple of mason jars of the local white lightning, a fiddle, and an old six-string guitar. Over the course of the next three hours the four of them—both Jims switching off from fiddle to guitar depending on the song, Miss Alice (whose soulful contralto had, legend had it, once been complimented on by none other than Muddy Waters at a nearby juke joint), and Carter's surprisingly resonant baritone—covered everything from old spirituals to Stevie Wonder to a rousing dance version of "Michael Row Your Boat Ashore."

The Jims had finally said their goodnights—a long, belated affair interrupted with more storytelling, drinks, and a song or two a cappella—and Miss Alice had, as she liked to say, dragged her weary ass to bed. The two men drank now in silence, listening appreciatively to the sounds of the marsh behind the house. Henry recognized the husky, guttural insistent croaking of what he now knew was the legendary 14-foot bull alligator that everyone called Bubba.

Carter leaned intently over the photo, studying a detail. He looked up at Henry. "Amazing what you can find on the Internet these days," he said. "CIA couldn't have produced imagery with this kind of detail 20 years ago. Now, every inch of planet Earth has been photographed by satellite, right down to that black cat I see in the corner of the prison courtyard. We had GPS back in the day, but good old-fashioned aerial reconnaissance can't compare to what our boys got now. We would have brought hellfire down on Hussein's Republican Guard, that's for damn sure."

Carter leaned back and sipped his drink. "You sure you don't want to take Waxworth Barnes up on its offer?" he asked, finally. "This is ain't no *Shawshank Redemption*. We've got about a one in a 100 chance of pulling it off."

"That good?" Henry asked, with mock seriousness. "Hell, that's still better than the odds I'd get with Waxworth Barnes. They said it would take a million dollars and a year just to get Rose a hearing before a Colombian judge to consider a writ of habeas corpus and then, for another million, the merits of an appeal. But they assured me that the whole process could be sped up with another couple million to help push the right buttons down there.

They were just fishing to see if I had anything left after I turned up alive. Those blood suckers left Rose hanging out to dry when they realized Victor had robbed us and Rose was left with nothing. I'm not giving them another nickel!"

Carter smiled. "I feel your pain, my friend," he said quietly. "Waxworth Barnes ain't my favorite either. So, to the task at hand. Our options are limited."

Henry looked at Carter expectantly and rubbed his hands together for effect. "Good! We've got options. Do tell."

"El Buen Madonna," Carter said, reading from a legal pad. "The Good Madonna. Quite the misnomer. Roughly 2,800 women packed into an impregnable concrete and steel box designed for a maximum of maybe 900 inmates. This place makes Alcatraz look like a Four Seasons. A product of classic late 19th century Spanish penology. Combination of the cruel and the pious. Harsh punishment to cleanse the soul. That sort of thing. Surrounded by about 100 square miles of jungle. All run with an iron fist by a sadistic woman they call The Black Widow and her loyal cadre of guards, gofers, and other hangers-on, most of whom I'm guessing are hand-picked relatives and others from her village or the Hood. Here's the only photo I could find of El Director Mercedes Cruz."

He reached down and held up a grainy, poor quality 8-by-10 that appeared to be an enlargement of a photo from a newspaper article. A raven-haired woman with eye patch and noticeable scar running across her face stood with a few uniformed men. The photo had been taken just as the woman had glanced with evident irritation at the camera.

"She doesn't seem too happy about having her picture taken," Henry said. "Must have gotten her bad side."

"Something like 30 percent of the inmates that go into this place are never seen again," Carter continued. "The few Americans that end up in there, hippie types caught smuggling drugs, expats that run afoul of the federales, surfer chicks that cross a jealous girlfriend with connections, well, they fare even worse. If we're going to break Miss Rose out, we'll need to move fast and use unconventional means. You can throw out the prison escape playbook on this one. We can't tunnel or blast our way in, we have no one on the payroll on the inside, we can't even pick off the guards and land a helicopter commando style in the courtyard. Look here, they've strung cable overhead."

"So, unconventional means?" Henry asked, nodding his head hopefully in affirmation.

Carter leaned back in his rocker. "An old CIA spook, name of Hendricks, told me one time in a little hole in the wall bar in Mogadishu: 'Banks, in this trade, when all else fails, and all the technology goes to shit, which it inevitably does, just remember this. Every man has his price, and every woman can be seduced.' Or maybe it was the other way around. I was never very sober during that last deployment. In either case, we'll see which applies in Colombia."

Carter took a sip from his drink and pointed down at the map. "There's a small village, San Rafael, a little one-mule town with a couple of cantinas about 10 clicks from the prison that the staff frequents. Only watering hole for 60 miles. About 150 miles due west of Medellín. I've got some ideas, but we'll need to get down there, get the lay of the land. We'll need a cover story too. Got to be a good reason for two gringos to be snooping around in the middle of the jungle. I'm delegating that to you."

"A gay couple on their honeymoon, looking for some local strange?" Henry asked.

"Shit," Carter scoffed. "Totally implausible. No one would believe that I couldn't have done better."

"You're right," Henry said. "I'll come up with something. In the meantime, hang on, Rosie, please hang on."

No One Gets Out of Here Alive

Mercedes Cruz smiled and nodded approvingly.

They had cleaned up the American nicely and, per her usual instructions, applied just a hint of blush, dark eyeliner, and the pink lipstick meant to subtly accentuate the woman's lips. The uniform from Medellín's elite Sacred Heart of Mary Catholic School for Girls, a simple white cotton blouse and dark blue skirt would have been the very picture of chastity on the 14-year-olds it was designed for, but when worn by the American? *¡Dios mío!*

Cruz's breath quickened a bit as she walked around the table, already laid out with reasonably good government-issue china and silverware, fresh flowers, and candles in preparation for dinner for two. A cassette tape played the Beatles, singing in scratchy harmony on an old boombox sitting on Cruz's desk.

She walked behind the woman, glanced down at the shapely rear end wedged into a skirt several sizes too small and barely down to mid-thigh, and pulled the chair out for her. "You must be tired after your ordeal, and hungry, yes?" she said soothingly, her mouth just inches from the woman's ear. Cruz put her hand on the small of the woman's back and was happy to feel her trembling beneath the warm, moist cotton.

"Rose, a beautiful name. Sit, Rose, do not worry, your troubles will soon be over. Do not be afraid. We will be good friends, you will see."

Rose sat and stared grimly straight ahead, as Cruz slid into a chair next to her, close enough that Rose could smell the heavy, cloying gardenia fragrance the warden was wearing. A heavy-set male guard, squeezed into a soiled waiter's white jacket a size too small, knocked and then entered, setting the two bowls of soup in front of the women. Cruz nodded toward an open bottle of white wine on the table and the guard poured a healthy measure into the women's wine glasses. Cruz nodded approvingly and waved a hand of dismissal.

Cruz raised her wine glass to propose a toast. "Salud," she said. "Buen provecho. Eat, Rose, you will like it. Our cook makes the best ajiaco outside of Bogotá."

When Rose showed no interest in the soup, Cruz slowly set her spoon down. She smiled and reached out to take Rose's hand. "No? Perhaps our fare is not good enough for the rich Americana? Perhaps the music is not to her liking? She is used to better, sì, sharing dinner with a lowly prison warden is beneath her?"

Rose shook her head. "What do you want of me?" she asked quietly. "Whatever you've guessed, whatever you've heard, the truth is I have no money."

Cruz laughed. She shook her head, took a sip of wine, and studied Rose for a moment. Then she leaned in close enough to whisper in Rose's ear, reached up, and softly stroked Rose's close-cropped head. "But think about this, my little chiquita, what life is like for those at El Buen Madonna with money, and what life is like for those without. For those without, six months, maybe a year." She snapped her fingers for emphasis in front of Rose's face. "The Americanas, most don't last even that long. We do our best but the conditions, they are impossible, no? Ah, but for those with money, a special cell, food, medicine, protection, and, most important, friendship with El Director. Then visits from the lawyers, and in about a year, adios, back to America."

There was a knock on the door and the heavyset waiter carried in a tray with the next course. Cruz glared at the man and issued a few curt instructions in Spanish. The man hurriedly set down the plates of food, glanced at Rose, bowed awkwardly, and left, closing the door quietly behind him.

There was a hard look now on Cruz's face as she stared at Rose. She had tried to reason with the woman, but clearly other means would be necessary. No matter. She would take great pleasure in bringing yet another of these soft women to her knees. She would of course pay; they all did in the end.

The blond California surfers were easiest of all. It was usually just a week or two before one of the usual Bogotá attorneys, hired by the terrified parents, reached out and the regular wire transfers began.

The burned-out hippies used as mules by the cartels? The ex-pats seeking romance or adventure? It was just a matter of finding their weaknesses. Every Americana had at least one wealthy relative willing to help keep a daughter, niece, or cousin alive. And for the few that did not? *¡Dios mío!* The nuns would pray for their souls and light candles in the prison chapel after a hasty burial in the jungle beyond the walls.

But what to do about Rose, the greatest prize of all? She had millions, but how best to get it? Cruz had assembled the usual dossier on Rose, but the file folder was surprisingly thin. A copy of her official file from Justice. A few articles about the Powerball win of course, a story or two about Torres that mentioned Rose in passing, details of the trial and Rose's conviction published in the local papers. But the reports indicated no family members had appeared during the trial, and none had tried to make contact since. There was credible information that indicated the husband was almost certainly dead. But most surprising of all? The lawyers seemed to have lost interest.

Cruz stood, walked to her desk, and returned with the bullwhip. She stood next to Rose and then draped the bullwhip over Rose's left shoulder. It hung down to Rose's waist like the long, heavy tail of a deadly black snake. Rose remained motionless, and then Cruz quickly coiled the whip around Rose's throat and began to pull the whip taut.

As Cruz tightened her grip, Rose instinctively rehearsed her defense: lean forward to draw Cruz closer and then snap her head back into Cruz's face to stun her and dislodge her grip; then a spinning back fist to Cruz's jaw; a front kick to the belly to knock the wind out of her; and finally, a crippling sidekick to her kneecap. But then what? Escape was impossible. Instead, Rose let herself go slack, no longer caring very much whether she lived or died. As she began to lose consciousness, she felt Cruz loosen her grip.

"Ha, and they said you were tough," Cruz whispered with derision in Rose's ear. "Now I know you will pay, my little chiquita, after a month in the hole, you will pay."

It's a Jungle Out There

The red howler lay flattened along the outstretched limb of an enormous strangler fig tree. The big monkey peered over the edge of the limb and stared down with hatred at the men walking along a narrow jungle path 75 feet below. The howler had of course heard the men coming a full 15 minutes earlier and smelled the man in the lead at least five minutes before they came into view. He recognized the man by his familiar scent, the usual ragged sombrero vueltia hat he wore, and the bright red bandana around his neck.

What was left of the howler's tribe lay prone in the high jungle canopy around him. As the alpha male, he'd issued the warning cry earlier, but when it became clear the lead man held only a machete and was without his usual rifle, he'd decided the tribe should stay put. The fig leaves had now reached a delicious stage that was just too good to pass up, and so he'd decided to take the chance. Still, he knew the others, particularly the females with their young, were terrified. This was of course the man that had killed three of the tribe in recent months and had led groups of men with their loud tree-cutting machines deep into the jungle on a number of occasions. The big howler made a soft, barely audible sound meant to calm the tribe.

He watched as the three men walked past the base of the strangler fig. They stopped for a moment and the hated man in the wide brimmed hat cupped his hands and made a loud, harsh, repetitive bird-like call that the howler didn't recognize. The howler exchanged a glance with his oldest mate, the tribe's matriarch, lying flat on a branch a few yards away. He pursed his lips, and gave a soft, muffled howler laugh of derision. He looked down again and imagined what it would be like to drop down suddenly from the forest canopy and sink his teeth into the hated man's neck.

The man, an old guide named Diego and a full-blooded member of the local Embera Chami tribe, looked up again, cupped his hands, and made the harsh call of the great green macaw. It was a large, very rare bright green parrot he'd seen and heard only a few times as a child many years ago while living with his tribe along the Atrato river miles to the west. He knew the bird was thought to be nearly extinct and its habitat was never believed to have stretched into this part of the forest, but who was Diego to talk two rich American ornithologists out of spending 500 USD each day to chase ghosts? As he had told his young wife that night after his first day with these scientists: "If the gringos say the Easter bunny is out there, then yes, I have of course caught a glimpse of his large white tail on many occasions, come across a large chocolate egg or two, and know just where to find him."

The three men paused to hear if there was a reply, but the jungle was strangely quiet, as if all the creatures living there, curious about the old guide's absurd calls but also greatly fearing him, were barely drawing a breath. The two scientists with Diego scanned the forest canopy with their binoculars. One then made some notes in a small handbook. Because it was late afternoon, and the light was already beginning to fail, the men agreed now to turn back. They had at least two hours' walk along a labyrinth of narrow game trails back to the dirt two-track where their old Land Cruiser was parked, and then another hour of driving to San Rafael. It was the end of the rainy season and a brief but heavy downpour was likely at this time every day, so the two scientists first put on the ponchos they carried in their backpacks. Then Diego led the men back down the narrow trail.

It was well after dark and pouring rain when the men finally pulled up in front of the Casa Monitos, the only cantina along the single main street of San Rafael. The two scientists had taken their dinner there each night for a week after their daily expeditions with Diego. The fare was simple, but the *bandeja paisa* would have compared favorably to that of any Michelin-starred restaurant in the States that specialized in Colombian food. Both men had developed an appreciation there too for the *aguardiente, a* fiery licorice-flavored liquor that cast a nice, warm mellow glow over the day's events. It was particularly welcome after the typically long, wet hard slog up and down jungle trails with the indefatigable Diego.

Because it was late, they asked Diego to join them. Diego happily accepted, relishing a change of pace from the predictability of his young wife Rosalita's bland cooking, and thirsty for what would be a much better grade of *aguardiente* than the crude local product he would have at home.

Two open trucks and a van, all with government insignia on the doors, were parked along the street. As they approached the three men were surprised to hear loud music and laughter coming from the cantina. On all the previous nights, the cantina had been relatively quiet, with just a few of the locals taking their dinner and some of the old men playing dominoes at the bar.

A group of armed men in olive drab uniforms stood at the crudely-fashioned bar and around the old jukebox. They had the loud, exuberant, and slightly unsteady demeanor common to men everywhere celebrating the end of a stressful workday and just beginning to feel the effects of the alcohol. Diego and the two scientists squeezed their way through the small, crowded, and very warm room filled with cigar smoke to the last remaining table in the back of the room. Just as they sat a roar of recognition went up from the men as Van Halen's "Panama" began to play. One of the men suddenly drew his weapon, aimed at the corrugated tin ceiling,and snapped off three or four shots in quick succession. The sound of gunfire in the small room was deafening.

The room erupted in raucous laughter. Grinning broadly, the shooter holstered his weapon and accepted a drink from Ariana, the petite, pretty waitress who had hurried up to him right after the fusillade, evidently hoping to prevent any further gunfire. A few of the men, laughing hysterically, gestured toward the table where Diego was reaching down to help one of the scientists off the floor.

Diego had been surprised, and quite disappointed, to see that at the first sound of gunfire the larger of the two scientists, the black man built like a weightlifter, had dived under the table. As Diego helped the clearly shaken scientist onto his feet, a few of the uniformed men came over and slapped the scientist on the back and offered apologies. The American smiled a bit sheepishly, shook a few of the men's hands, and sat with evident relief back down at the table. "Sorry, but that scared the hell out of me," he said. "Didn't realize guns were so loud. Phew! Who are those guys, anyway, Diego?"

Diego smiled, patted the scientist on the arm, and sniffed. It was fortunate the Americano hadn't soiled his pants. But for 500 USD a day Diego could not afford to show his scorn and the scientists, while very soft like all Americanos, were pleasant enough.

"Prison guards, from El Buen Madonna," Diego explained. "It is, how you say, *muy malo*, a very bad place for female prisoners. The men, they mean no harm. You are safe here with Diego."

It was several hours later when Diego finally pushed his chair back, belched happily, and stood a little unsteadily. He was, admittedly, not used to *aguardiente* of this quality and the Americanos had ordered round after round. Now, he had a mile walk back to his small hut, most of it along a dark jungle path, and there was still the chance that Rosalita would be receptive despite the late hour and his drunkenness. After all, had he not just made another 500 US, with a month's work already agreed upon? He shook the scientists' hands, thanked them for dinner and drinks, and confirmed their usual pre-dawn rendezvous. Then, careful not to give offense, he worked his way carefully through the small room, now even more crowded with the new arrival of another truckload of prison guards.

When Diego was gone, Henry Ball turned to Carter Banks and leaned close enough to be heard over a cacophony of laughter, shouts, breaking glass, and the jukebox playing Shakira. "You're no Denzel Washington, but the dive under the table had even me fooled," Henry said. "Did you see the look on Diego's face? Pure scorn. I'm guessing there's a method to your madness?"

Carter smiled. "Who could be more harmless than an American scientist afraid of guns?" he explained. "We're just as advertised: a couple of typical gringo scientist pussies looking for birds. No threat there, no reason to dig any deeper."

The bullwhip cracked like a pistol shot just over their heads, and this time both Carter and Henry dove for the floor. The room erupted in uproarious laughter and yelling and the sound of plates and glasses crashing to the floor as a table or two were flipped over for no other reason than the irrational exuberance typical of a very drunken crowd of excited young men. As Carter started to push himself up off the floor, two legs clad in khaki jodhpurs and stuffed into the tops of knee-high, tightly-laced, highly-polished leather boots came into view just inches from his face. He began to look up, only to be pushed to the ground by the force of one of the boots planted firmly in the middle of his back.

Over the loud din Carter could make out only a little of the Spanish spoken rapidly by the owner of the boot pinning him to the floor, but whatever the woman had said it was clearly at Carter's expense, and the roomful of men applauded and whistled and yelled. She bent down and her face came suddenly into Carter's field of vision: a woman with long raven hair and a ruined face that Carter guessed might once have been beautiful before some hard, sharp object had scored the deep, jagged crease and taken an eye.

Carter could feel her hot breath on his cheek and smell tortilla and tequila and lime as she leaned in just above him. "You are a long way from home, gringo. What brings you here, so far from your Starbucks and shopping malls and the safety of your mamá?" she asked, dangling the edge of her bullwhip caressingly across Carter's cheek.

Henry pushed himself into a sitting position and started to explain. "We're from Cornell, ornithologists working to bring back one of Colombia's national treasures, Ara ambiguus, the great green macaw. A beautiful bird, not seen in the wild since . . ."

"Silence!" the woman said loudly in her low, husky voice, glancing over at Henry for the first time and giving him a withering look. She turned her attention back to Carter. "The American man. So strong, so impressive, but perhaps lacking the cajones, no?" She laughed with disdain. "Cowering under the table like a woman. But perhaps you would now like a chance to reclaim your manhood?"

She pressed the heel of her boot down hard on the middle of Carter's back one final time for emphasis, then took a few steps back and gestured for the on-looking guards to help Carter to his feet. Two of the guards grasped Carter under the armpits and hauled him up. They let go and Carter, clearly shaken, teetered a bit as if struggling to re-gain his balance. The front of his pants and shirt were stained wet and dirty with red jungle clay that had adhered to him from the floor. He brushed himself off, took a deep breath to regain his composure, and glanced up at the woman.

"Up north where I come from it's customary to give a lady what she wants," Carter said. "So, what do I have to do to make the señorita happy?" He reached down to the table, picked up a glass of *aguardiente* and took a healthy slug.

The woman laughed. "Ah, the Americanos. Always so full of surprises. Perhaps I have misjudged you. We will see."

She issued a few commands in rapid Spanish, and one of the guards rushed up and handed the woman a cigar. She put the cigar in her mouth and the guard struck a match and put the flame up to the end of the cigar. The woman took several heavy drags, got the cigar going, and then gestured for the onlookers to back away. She walked up to Carter, took him by the shoulders and turned him sideways. Then she put the lit cigar in his mouth.

"Okay, scientist, do not move." She walked backward about five paces.

She unfurled the bullwhip that had been coiled around her shoulder, held it in her right hand, and gave it a casual flick so it lay stretched out behind her. She hesitated a moment, gauging the distance, then took an enormous stride forward, almost like a big-league baseball pitcher, bringing the bullwhip up and over her shoulder and sending the whip's tip toward Carter's face.

It intersected with the midpoint of the cigar at supersonic speed, snapping the end off with a loud crack, but leaving the butt end clamped firmly in Carter's teeth.

The room exploded in a tumultuous clamor as the crowd of onlookers surged forward. Several of the larger guards struggled to hoist Carter onto their shoulders in celebration, lost their balance, and sent Carter to the floor once again. The woman reached him just as he got to his feet.

"Bravo, scientist, you have cajones after all," she said approvingly. "Not everyone has done so well right, Sergeant Morales?" and she gestured to one of the guards standing next to her.

"*Si*, El Director, poor Carlos flinched, and lost half his face, another, only his nose," the Sergeant said in confirmation. "Your aim was perfecto; those men lost their nerve."

"I can drink with a man such as you," the woman said, putting an arm around Carter's shoulders. "*Quiero mas tequila, por favor!*" she yelled. "Come, we have much to talk about."

She guided him toward a table. As they sat Carter saw Henry working his way through the crowd toward the door. Henry glanced back and gave Carter a thumbs up as he left.

Henry moaned, slowly rolled over, and pulled the chain on the small lamp on the nightstand by his bed. His phone alarm, set for 4:45 a.m., had just gone off in the room they were renting in a small but very clean casa just off the main street. Still groggy with sleep, Henry cast off the single sheet and struggled into a sitting position on the edge of the bed and rubbed the sleep from his eyes. Just then Carter came in, closed the door behind him, and sat heavily on his bed. He yawned, glanced over, and smiled tiredly at Henry.

"Judging by the time—I'm guessing phase one of the mission was a success?" Henry asked, hopefully.

"Yes, sir, we got the hook in, a record marlin played out and up to the transom, now all we have to do is put the gaff in and pull her aboard," Carter said, a note of satisfaction in his voice, and he lay down and stretched out on his bed.

Carter smiled tiredly and rubbed his neck. Henry noticed a large, fresh-looking red welt. "Damn! I've met some crazy chicks in my day, and dated more than a few, but I ain't never met one this insane," Carter said. "Got her believing I like pain as much as she likes dishing it out. Oh hell, Ball, it's damn near dawn. Are we going out looking for that damn parrot again? Alright, give me ten minutes to shit, shower, and shave," he said, and he rolled off the bed and started doing his push-ups.

What Doesn't Kill You . . .

Despite the intense heat, Rose lay shivering in a fetal position on the raised concrete slab that served as a bed in her tiny cell. During the night she'd grown feverish, which had brought on a series of random and very vivid memories. She remembered now watching a documentary on the war in Vietnam with Henry years ago. Henry as usual had control of the remote and Rose, who hated war but was deeply engrossed in a novel and didn't much care what Henry was watching, looked up long enough to catch an interview with an American pilot who had been shot down over North Vietnam. The pilot had recounted how he'd managed to survive in the jungles for several weeks before his rescue. The pilot had said one of the most amazing things was how quickly you lost your aversion for almost anything that could be considered edible. In just a day or two after being shot down, he'd said, he was scouring the jungle floor for the grubs, spiders, slugs, crickets and all the other insects that had made his skin crawl just a few days before, and that he was soon devouring by the handful.

Rose had been in solitary confinement now for ten days, in a sweltering cell that measured six foot by eight foot with a small opening high up the 20-foot wall that allowed a hint of fresh, jungle air, and just enough light during the day so Rose could make out the walls of the cell. Once a day a small, hinged trap door at the base of the old iron cell door swung open and a wooden bowl filled with rice and a plastic bottle with about a liter of water were slid into the cell. Then the door closed with a loud, heavy metallic clang. Later, the door would open again, and Rose, on hands and knees, would slide the empty bowl and water bottle out toward an outstretched hand and an old pair of military-issue boots.

Yes, Rose thought, the American pilot was exactly right. After just a few days, as the gnawing in her stomach grew and she could think of nothing but food, she'd begun to hungrily hunt the only source of additional calories available to her: the two-inch long centipedes, beetles, and, tastiest of all, an occasional locust that became catchable as they scurried across the cell floor in the first dull light.

At first, she'd smashed the critters into a sort of paste that, when mixed into the rice, helped to conceal the bitter taste and make the meal more palatable. But by day seven or so, she was simply pulling off the legs, wings and heads, piling the torsos onto the rice and, while holding the bowl carefully under her chin and using her fingers, eating the entire bowl as fast as she dared.

As the light in her cell grew to a sort of dull twilight, the trap door swung open and Rose heard the bowl and water bottle sliding into the cell. Then the trap door clanged shut. She rolled sluggishly off the concrete slab onto her hands and knees. She had a terrific headache. She steadied herself, feeling a bit nauseous. She waited for the dizziness to pass. Then she bent down, opened the water bottle, and drank thirstily. She reached down for the bowl. She felt along the base of the concrete slab, found the pile of insects she'd cached the day before, and began adding them to the rice. As she reached into the bowl, she felt something. She pulled out a tight square of folded paper. She unfolded the paper, held the note up, and angled it into the light so she could just make out the handwriting.

Two American scientists come to the village. One tall and bald. The other, el negro, and very strong. La Guardia say they look for parrots. Coincidencia? My experience tells me no. I have seen how the Americans work. The spies. The military. Stay alive Rose. Destroy this.

La Hermana

Viva Chiquita Rivas, Rose thought, staring at the note. Then she crawled over to the ten-inch diameter hole in the floor in a corner of the cell that served as a toilet. She ripped the note up into small pieces and tossed it down the hole. She leaned her back against the wall and began weeping silently.

In her fever she had a vivid memory of the gypsy fortune teller in Paris, and remembered her prediction, that she would live a long life and visit Paris many times in the future. For the first time in years, she put her hands together and looked heavenward. She had let her faith wither over the years like some long-forgotten garden, but now she said a prayer for Henry, and allowed herself to feel hope.

Jungle Love

"Did you know that the Black Widow kills its mate?"

They lay together after lunch on a Colombian army blanket spread along the banks of a shallow, swift running creek in a jungle clearing just outside of San Rafael. Sunlight streamed down through an opening in the canopy above. The jungle had gotten used to their presence and there was the usual loud cacophony of birds and the steady hum of insects punctuated by the angry cries of a foraging troop of squirrel monkeys battling for fruit somewhere overhead.

"Why do they call you that, anyway?" Carter asked, as he rolled onto an elbow, grabbed the wine bottle out of the picnic basket, and poured them both another glass. He'd done his research and carefully packed a picnic lunch for what would be their first real date outside of half a dozen very drunken dinners at the cantina. Sergeant Morales, in exchange for 100 US, had slipped him a list of what he believed Cruz might like for lunch, and he was relieved to see she seemed genuinely delighted with the various dishes he served, courtesy of the surprisingly imaginative chef at Casa Monitos.

Cruz laughed. "It is what you Americans would call my brand. Sí, like your Spider Man or Wonder Woman. I could not run *El Buen Madonna* without respect, without a reputation that is feared. It is, as you Americans would say, good for business."

She reached up and gently caressed a long, jagged scar running along Carter's left forearm. "For a scientist you have many wounds. It is a more dangerous business than one would expect, no?" she asked.

"Harpia harpyja, the Harpy eagle," Carter said, thankful that Henry had grilled him repeatedly on the genus, species, and characteristics of 50 or so of the best-known Colombian birds. "Mama didn't take kindly when I showed up at her nest 100 feet up to band her chicks. They've got talons about twice as big as my hand. Thought she'd lift off with me and drop me somewhere.

"How about you?" Carter asked, pointing to the four-inch gash that ran along her left bicep, only partially concealed by the serpent tattoo that coiled around her arm from elbow to shoulder. It was the first time he'd seen her out of uniform. Maybe he'd been in the jungle too long, but Carter had to admit she was quite striking to look at. He was pleased she'd evidently gone to a bit of trouble to soften her usually austere appearance and accentuate her femininity. She'd worn a tight, sleeveless leopard-print jumpsuit. Her hair was tied back with ribbon, and she'd put on just a hint of eyeliner on her one good eye, a bit of rouge, and the plum-colored lipstick she seemed to favor. She wore a man's Rolex and some loose silver bracelets on the other wrist.

"Accident in the kitchen, I'm guessing?"

She laughed. "Sí, something like that. You can never be too careful. But what is this?" she asked, playfully lifting up the edge of Carter's shirt and running her index finger along the puffy welt that had been scored in Carter's side by a hot piece of shrapnel in one of his first firefights. "Another angry bird perhaps?"

Carter laughed. "No, that one was a red-hot poker. Madame Natasha, as I recall. I was down in the Louisiana bayou looking for the ivory billed woodpecker and spent a few nights in New Orleans at Madame Natasha's. Hard place to find without an introduction if you know what I mean. You won't find it on the usual tourist maps." He slowly shook his head and whistled. "Tall gal, about your height, very strong. I had her dress in a red leather devil's outfit. Really took her work seriously, as you can see. I think you'd like her."

Cruz sipped her wine and smiled at Carter. "You are so full of surprises, scientist," she said. "Sí, New Orleans. I have heard much about it. Mardi Gras, sí? And Madame Natasha. We must visit her together. I will have the time soon, and the money, *Dios quiere*, God willing."

Carter leaned down and kissed her. "All this talk of Madame Natasha has me excited. When can I see your prison?" he whispered in her ear. "Where you do your best work?"

She pulled Carter's head toward her, kissed him, then took his lower lip between her teeth and bit hard. He let out a gasp of pain. She rolled onto her elbows and got to her feet. She smiled down at Carter.

"Sí, you will like El Buen Madonna, scientist. It will make you forget all about your Madame Natasha. I will send my car for you. Day after tomorrow at the cantina, around 2200 hours? Now duty calls. We must go. Such a pleasant time. How did you know I love the chicken empanadas? Was it Morales? He's ambitious, sí, and smart. Remind me to have him killed."

It was dawn, and as the light grew the low trap door clanged open as expected. Rose rolled off the concrete slab, crawled to the door, and when the tray failed to appear, she leaned forward on her knees and extended an arm expectantly. She felt hands suddenly grasp her forearm, giving her arm a hard, very painful twist that forced Rose off her knees and onto the floor. She looked out the small opening and could just make out her tormentor's knees, with the jodhpurs stuffed into the tops of two highly polished jackboots. Rose stifled a cry as Mercedes Cruz's long, talon-like purple nails dug deeply into her arm.

"So, you and La Hermana have been passing notes, like young schoolgirls in love for the first time," Cruz said, and she laughed. She put the heel of her boot on Rose's forearm and gave Rose's wrist a hard twist with both hands. Rose cried out and tried to pull her arm free but couldn't find the leverage.

"You have of course destroyed the note, you are very smart, but you will tell me what it said, sí? And if not, nombre de Dios, you and your girlfriends will suffer. So?" Cruz asked, expectantly, and twisting Rose's arm even harder for emphasis.

"It said to go fuck yourself," Rose hissed through clenched teeth, and she closed her eyes and braced herself for the inevitable pain that would follow.

Cruz laughed. She let go of Rose's arm and bent low enough so that Rose could see her face. "As you Americans like to say, something is up. I can smell it. We will find out, soon enough, American billionaire. Nothing happens in here without Mercedes Cruz's knowledge or permission. You will pay, all the rich ones do."

The trap door slammed shut, and Rose pressed her injured wrist to her mouth. "Hurry, Henry, please hurry," she whispered, and then wept.

A Case of Mistaken Identity

Henry, soaking wet from the usual early evening downpour and bone-weary after following the indefatigable old guide over miles of jungle trail, flicked on the lights to their room, and screamed.

A black woman, built like a wrestler, with long black hair and wearing an eye patch was sitting on Carter's bed.

"What the fuck?" Henry asked, realizing now that it was Carter.

Carter smiled. "It's on," he said quietly, pulling the wig and eye patch off and casting them aside. "Day after tomorrow. A good thing too. Not sure how much longer our cover will last."

Henry sat down on his bed. "So, you're in? And she doesn't suspect?"

"I'm in, but I might have fucked up."

"No way, you don't fuck up."

"At the very least the Black Widow's antennae are up," Carter said, leaning heavily back against the headboard and putting his hands behind his head. "My great grandmother Mama Violet had a word for people like that. Hoodoo she used to call them, people that practiced rootwork, what you'd call witchcraft. She used to see them everywhere. We'd be at the market and she'd suddenly point to someone, a little old man in his Sunday best or a pretty young woman working a food stand. 'There's one!' she'd whisper, and she'd take my hand and we'd hurry home. After a while I could pick up on it too. This chick has that hoodoo feeling about her."

Henry stared at Carter. He could detect a subtle note of concern in Carter's voice that he'd never heard before. Up until now he'd always been so analytical, so imperturbable, as if every problem could be overcome with good operational planning and force applied in just the right place.

"When you say you fucked up," Henry said, finally, "what did you mean?"

Carter waved a hand dismissively. "Oh, it's probably nothing. Didn't even think about it at the time. She's sending her car to pick me up at the cantina for a tour of The Good Madonna, day after tomorrow, '2200 hours' she said."

"So?"

"That's military time," Carter said. "Almost like she threw it out there to get my reaction. The problem is, I didn't react."

"Well, that's probably prison time too," Henry reasoned.

Carter sat up and pushed himself to the edge of the bed. He ran his tongue over his lower lip, still swollen and a bit sore with the deep bite wound that he'd suffered at the conclusion of his picnic with Cruz earlier.

"Man, I'm getting too old for this shit, losing my edge," Carter said. "Just remember, Ball, that it's the little mistakes that usually get you killed. Come on, we've got a lot of work to do. No more mistakes, that's for damn sure."

"It was as what you would expect to find with two American scientists looking for birds," Sergeant Morales said, looking down at a page torn from a notebook. "Camera equipment, a tent, sleeping bags, camp stove, dirty laundry, some food items, bird books. Our men were thorough and made sure to leave no signs. Madame Director, nothing appears out of the ordinary."

"That's what worries me," Cruz said, holding out her hand for the slip of paper Morales was reading from. She nodded and waved a hand in dismissal. When Morales had left, she stood, stretched, walked to the window, and looked out at the prison yard. It was early morning, dry, sunny but still cool. Hundreds of prisoners were taking advantage before the jungle heat became too stifling to exercise, play football, or gather here and there in small groups. Statistically, morning was the time of day when violence was least likely, and the prison yard was known by the prisoners to be the safest place to be at El Buen Madonna. The tower guards were all expert marksmen and anyone foolish enough to start trouble was inevitably shot down before it could escalate. Peaceful, sí, Cruz thought to herself, but she could sense something, like a subtle movement on the very edge of her peripheral vision, or the faint tremors one might detect on a seismograph a day or two ahead of an earthquake.

She had sent two of her best men to search the scientists' vehicle the night before. She had no reason to believe the two men were anything but what they claimed to be. Sí, she liked the one more than she wanted to admit. Perhaps that was the problem, no? *Dios mío*, had she not been burned time and time again by the men in her past? She reached up to her face, and gently traced the rough edge of the scar that ran laterally from above her eye patch, across the bridge of her nose almost to the corner of her mouth. If she had learned anything in life it was that no man could really be trusted. The man who had ruined her once beautiful face all those years ago had of course died a slow, painful death, but she had vowed never to let her guard down again.

And so, for both reasons of caution and convenience, most of her casual romantic relationships in recent years had been with women. More pliable, sí, and more trustworthy. Yet, there was something about this American scientist that had aroused her long-latent interest in men. She had even allowed herself the luxury of imagining what their life might be like together in America. While she despised most of the Americans that came through the prison gates, she had a fascination with the country and its many luxuries and freedoms dating back to when she'd been a young girl living in a small tin shack in the poorest of Medellín barrios. But it was clearly a country where one would need a great deal of money, no? She had amassed a small fortune at El Bueno Madonna, that was true, but she would need much more to keep them both living in style in America. She did not imagine that a bird scientist, even an American one, would have much of an income. Fortunately, she had an ace in the hole, as the Americans liked to say. It would not be long now before the Americana Rose Ball finally broke down and gave her what she wanted.

She picked up the business card from her desk. Dr. James Wilkins. Senior ornithologist, World Wildlife Protection Agency. She sat at her desk and opened the browser on her computer. His explanation for the various wounds that covered his powerful body seemed plausible enough. Still, it would not take too much effort to confirm his identity, provided she could connect to the internet this morning. The spinning cursor indicated that signal strength was, as usual, very poor.

After a few minutes she closed out of the browser in disgust. No matter. She would perhaps have Morales do more research on the scientist later in the day. She glanced at her watch. There were more pressing matters to attend to, right about—now.

There was the sudden boom of a single rifle shot, and then the echo bouncing off the far prison walls. She turned just in time to see the prisoners near the center of the yard begin to run in every direction. A prisoner lay motionless at almost the exact center of the prison yard, blood spreading slowly out from beneath her head. Cruz glanced at the guard tower nearest her where the shot had come from. The guard lowered his rifle and then glanced in the direction of Cruz's office window.

One of the gangs had somehow managed to raise the going rate to eliminate the leader of a rival gang. Cruz opened the folder on her desk. Isabella Rojas. A pretty name. So sad. Cause of death: killed while trying to escape. The document was already filled out, and Cruz signed it with her usual bold flourish. She smiled. A few thousand USD more for her 'Escape to America' fund. It wouldn't be long now.

This Shit Just Got Real

"So, when do we synchronize watches?"

Carter looked up from the map and gave Henry a hard stare.

"This isn't the *Guns of Navarone*, Ball. In about four hours, this shit's going to get real." He glanced down at his watch. "We've still got about an hour of light, so let's get busy."

Henry forced a nervous laugh. "Sorry Carter, truth be told, I'm scared shitless. Humor has always been my way of dealing with extreme nerves. Give you an example. I put a whoopee cushion on the proctor's chair right before the big SAT test senior year, and . . . sorry."

The two men sat side by side on the tailgate of the Land Cruiser. They'd driven a few hundred yards or so into the jungle down a narrow, rough dirt two-track about a mile outside of town and pulled into a small clearing. Earlier, at the intersection where they turned off the main road onto the two-track, Carter had jammed on the breaks, jumped out, and used the machete to cut a large wedge at about eye level out of a big tree that stood on the edge of the road. While the main road leading in and out of the village was lightly trafficked, they'd been careful to drive far enough up the two-track to be safely out of sight. Carter had then unloaded all the cargo from the rear of the Land Cruiser, unscrewed and removed the floorboards from the cargo area, pulled out a U.S. Army-issue duffle bag from the crude sheet metal box he had welded to the underside of the Cruiser, and laid it carefully on the ground.

They'd scouted the two-track a few weeks before, with the old guide, Diego. When Carter had casually asked if there might be an airstrip nearby where the additional supplies and equipment needed to extend their expedition could be flown in the old guide, sensing an opportunity, had winked and a sly grin had creased his saddle-leather old face. "Sí, hombre, a good one, not too far. Not used in many years, and not on any maps. Only Diego can show you."

Then Diego had laughed, shaking his head. "*Madre de Jesús*, those were wild days," he said, reminiscing. "Escobar's men, muy loco as you would expect, but the pilots? Flying in all weather, always at night. We would light the fuel drums along the airstrip, and then say a prayer. We made nothing, you see, if a plane crashed. When, finally, the gringo they called Wild Bill, who had lived longer than most, crashed into the jungle in a rainstorm they moved their operation. It was a sad day for Diego. A year's wages, up in smoke."

Diego had shown them the airstrip, a narrow, relatively flat clearing cut out of the jungle at the end of the two-track about 20 miles outside the village. Carter, who up until then had always taken the wheel had instead asked Henry to drive, and it had taken them all of an hour to carefully negotiate the twisting, heavily rutted road to finally reach the airstrip.

An old windsock still hung from a pole at about the midway point and a series of rusted out 55-gallon drums marked the perimeter of the airstrip. A few old shacks with their tin roofs caved in stood at one end. Scrawny goats and a few hens grazed on the edge of the jungle. The airstrip itself looked like it had been prepared for cultivation recently and burned clear of jungle undergrowth, but there was no evidence of people nearby.

Carter had paced off the length and width of the airstrip, taken some pictures with his phone at both ends of the airstrip, and then spent a few minutes making notes and sketching a rough drawing of the airstrip. Finally, he looked up from his notebook and shook his head. "Thank you, Diego, but this isn't going to work. I make this strip to be only about 3,000 feet long. The flight crew we hired told me they'd need at least twice that to land fully loaded and take off from a grass strip at this altitude. I guess we'll just have all our stuff flown into Medellín and drive it out. Too bad."

Diego, evidently crestfallen at the loss of a potential payday, had turned sullen and remained silent on the ride back to town. He'd seemed to cheer up, however, when Carter had tipped him 100 USD. From that day forward, on their daily jungle excursions and at the cantina at night, Carter had watched Diego carefully but if the old guide had any suspicions, he was careful not to show it.

Carter hopped off the tailgate, knelt down, and unzipped the duffle bag. He'd noticed earlier that they'd been through their belongings, but nothing was missing and there were no telltale scratches on the screws that held down the floorboards, so they hadn't discovered the duffle bag.

Carter reached up and handed Henry a manila envelope. "Here, put these in your backpack for safekeeping. Just like we drew it up on the blackboard. John and Melissa Volpe. A well-to-do Chicago couple returning from a second honeymoon in Costa Rica. Passports, driver's licenses, credit cards. Pilots will file all the usual paperwork with customs when we get stateside, and usually they don't even come on board private aviation. U.S. has no extradition treaty with Colombia so nothing to worry about downstream. Keep that good woman by your side, Ball, and no looking back."

Henry put the envelope in his backpack. He took a drink from his water bottle. His mouth had suddenly gone very dry. He looked down at Carter. "Realistically, what do you think our chances are?" Henry asked, finally.

Carter pulled the Heckler & Koch MP5 submachine gun out of the duffle bag. He sighted down the short barrel and smiled. It was a very good weapon, light, compact, reliable, and with a very high rate of fire. It wasn't standard U.S. Army-issue, but Carter had found it easy to carry as a sidearm along with his .50-caliber sniper rifle. For this mission he'd fitted it with a night scope and 100-round drum clip loaded with nine-millimeter tracer rounds. It made the weapon much heavier and a bit unwieldy, and it wasn't inherently accurate anyway, but when set on full automatic, the MP5 could effectively pin down an entire company of men inside 100 yards.

Carter wasn't particularly superstitious by nature, but the feel of the old familiar weapon in his hands had the effect of a talisman of sorts. On more than one occasion the MP5 had more than evened the odds in a firefight and gotten him and the team he was with out of a few tight spots where he'd almost certainly have been killed if armed differently.

"I like our chances," Carter said, laying the MP5 gently back in the duffle bag. "We've got the element of surprise, overwhelming firepower if necessary. You've seen what we're up against. The prison guards are about as well trained as a troop of boy scouts. Just do your part, and we'll be fine. Need you to be parked right here from 2200 hours on. If I don't show with Rose by 0100 hours, presume it's charlie foxtrot—a cluster fuck—and drive to the airstrip for the exfil at 0300. Remember to put these flashing strobes down on the corners and on the threshold of the airstrip like we discussed. If the strobes aren't there, Ted's going to fly right on by and back to Medellín."

Carter stood. He could see the slightly dazed, wide-eyed look on Henry's face that he'd seen on the faces of so many of the young volunteer soldiers going into their first action. Carter pulled the magazine from the Glock he was holding, checked that it had the full 15 rounds, and inserted it back in the pistol's grip. Then he racked the slide to chamber a round. He held the pistol out to Henry. "Glocked, cocked, and ready to rock. There's no safety, so just point it at your target and pull the trigger. It'll be loud. I doubt if you'll need it, but keep it close."

Henry, who had never fired a pistol, reached out hesitantly and took the Glock gingerly by the grip.

"Carter, if you and Rose don't show . . ." Henry left the question hanging.

"Simple, Henry. You get on with your life," Carter said. "Now, time to synchronize watches."

Rose slipped in and out of a fitful sleep. In her dream, made vivid from a mild fever, she was a young girl again. Her father, very handsome with those Irish blue eyes that she remembered most about his features, sat next to her at the dining room table. *Brigadoon* was playing on the stereo, her father's favorite stage musical, and he sang along happily in his sweet tenor. Her mother worked and sang along in the kitchen. There was the delicious, almost overpowering smell of turkey cooking, and she knew it must be Thanksgiving.

"Almost ready!" her mother yelled. "Dylan, come help."

Her father winked at Rose and disappeared into the kitchen. Rose waited expectantly but she had the sense that days had elapsed, and the kitchen had grown dark and very quiet when finally, with the hunger pangs in her belly unbearable, she walked cautiously toward the dark kitchen doorway. When she reached the doorway, she managed to step back just in time. There was nothing there but dark, empty space. She hugged the wall, paralyzed with fear. Finally, gathering her courage, she leaned slowly over the edge of the abyss and looked down. She cried out for her mother and father, her voice echoing back to her faintly from a long way away.

The door at the base of her cell door opened with a bang. Rose woke, sluggish and unsure where she was at first, and then recognizing her cell in the last low light of dusk.

She rolled onto her side. There, on the floor near the open door, was a slip of paper. She slid off the low slab onto her hands and knees and reached out for the paper. She held it up close and in the low, dim light she saw now that it was a copy of the short article that had appeared in the *Tribune* after they'd won the Powerball. At the top of the story there was a photo of her between Henry and Zach, and all of them holding an enormous foam core check made out to Henry and Rose Ball in the amount of $1.2 billion.

Mercedes Cruz leaned against the wall outside Rose's cell. She had worked on the problem throughout the day, like a stalking hunter trying to put the crosshairs of her rifle scope on a distant, fast-moving, and elusive prey. Sí, until finally, the idea had come suddenly into focus. When the old guide they called Diego had whispered to Sargent Morales last night at the cantina that he had something of great interest to tell him about the two scientists, but only at the right price, she knew her instincts were right. The old guide was too crafty to tell Morales anything more without payment, but that information would come soon enough.

In the meantime, the dots were beginning to connect. *Méter de Dios*, how had she been so stupid? An American woman of great wealth arrives at El Buen Madonna. Within weeks two American scientists also arrive: one with the unmistakable bearing of all professional soldiers, and the other? She had not paid much attention to the tall, bald-headed one, other than to note how odd it seemed that a bird scientist would be wearing a shark's tooth on a leather necklace. Fortune hunters, perhaps, hired by the family? Or the husband, what about the mysterious husband? They said he was dead, lost at sea. She had looked at him very closely in the one photo in Rose's file. A tall, happy man, a little heavy like so many American men, and going bald. Rose could have done so much better, she had thought in passing. But as she studied the photo more closely, she began to wonder. Sí, about the same height, although the scientist was thinner and better built. But it was the American's face in the photo, his smile that on close inspection bore at least a passing resemblance to that of the tall scientist.

Cruz knelt down and leaned toward the opening at the base of the cell door. "The happy family, rich beyond their dreams," she said. "The beautiful wife, sí, wearing her best dress and the men, so tall and handsome in their suits. So sad, the husband Henry dead, the money gone. Or perhaps not? Two mysterious Americans arrive in little San Rafael, looking for parrots." She laughed. "Tonight, we will see, my little chiquita, we will see."

Cruz slammed the door shut, stood, and put her ear to the door. Nothing. She turned and walked briskly toward the guard standing at the open door at the end of the narrow hall. She waved a hand dismissively at the guard. "Vámanos!"

Hearing her leave, Rose, who had bitten down on the sleeve of her prison dungaree to prevent Cruz from hearing her sob, lay back down and cried out softly. "Run, Henry, for God's sake, run. If you're still out there, save yourself."

You Never Know When Your Number's Up

Carter checked himself in the bathroom mirror. He wore a black guayabera shirt that hung loose over a pair of black jeans. A folding paratrooper knife was stuffed down into his right boot. He turned sideways, making sure there was no evidence of the Sig Sauer in the holster nestled against the small of his back.

He glanced at his watch. The ten-minute walk would get him to the cantina 30 minutes or so early. By now Henry would have reached the rendezvous point. They hadn't packed anything but there was nothing in the clothes and personal effects left in the room that could identify them. He picked up the backpack, slung it over his shoulder, took a final look around, and closed the door softly behind him.

Carter took his time and approached the cantina from the opposite side of the street. Nothing seemed out of the ordinary, but as he neared the cantina, he saw the guide Diego and Sargent Morales come out and stand together for a moment under the dim light overhanging the entrance. Carter ducked quickly into the dark doorway of a small shop. He watched as the two men shook hands and Morales got into the prison van parked in front of the cantina. He started the van, did an abrupt U-turn, waved, and said something to Diego, then sped off in the direction of the prison. Diego waved back, laughed, and muttered something to himself as he walked off in the opposite direction.

Carter had given serious thought to putting a bullet in the old guide's head as he and Henry followed him down a narrow jungle path a few days earlier. He'd had his pistol half out of its holster when he glanced back at Henry and saw the look of terror in his face. And, truth be told, it just wasn't Carter's MO to kill a non-combatant in cold blood. The decision to let Diego live had, at the time, filled him with a sense of relief.

Now, Morales was almost certainly hurrying back to tell Cruz about the airstrip. If they hadn't been blown before they were now, and Carter's weakness had more than likely gotten them all killed.

Earlier in the day Henry had asked, rather anxiously, what Carter thought their Plan B would be if things went wrong. "Hell," Carter had said, "we're like Cortez. We've already burned our ships. Nothing to do now but go forward."

Carter leaned against the door and looked up in the night sky. If they had anything going for them, it was the weather. The low ceiling was breaking up and as the clouds scuttled along, the full moon rising just above the cantina roofline. It was the relative dry season and weather this time of year in the tropics was at least predictable: a late afternoon shower followed by clearing. A good night for flying, he thought.

The fluttering in his belly and tingling scalp reminded him of the start of the night raids he had been on in the old days—the men saddling up, the nervous bravado, but also the confidence of knowing the odds were always in your favor. You had the intel, the gunships and overwhelming firepower if you needed it, and men you could trust with your life. Now he had—an accountant?

The thought crossed his mind that maybe there was a plan B. Abort the mission. Forget Rose Ball. The odds were she was already dead. If she was alive the cunning Mercedes Cruz would soon be doing the simple math: Americans and an airstrip plus billionaire American equals jailbreak.

Why not just get the hell out? Rendezvous with Henry, tell him the mission had turned suicidal, and drive on to the airstrip for the exfil. Then the short hop to Medellín, a quick walk across the tarmac to the private jet and former military crew he'd hired at the exorbitant 'no questions asked' going rate, and a 0600 departure for Charleston. By sun-up the next day, he'd be piloting the *Miss Rosie Mae* out to the fishing grounds with Big and Little Jim.

And what about Henry and the loose diamonds and rare coins still left at the bottom of the Folger's can? Probably worth a half million or more, he guessed. Sorry, but in the world of black ops and mercenaries, there was no such thing as a money back guarantee.

Carter smiled. He'd seen other men lose their nerve. He remembered Mac McConnell, a fearless bear of a man with a Purple Heart and two bronze stars to his credit. As they were boarding a chopper at the start of a particularly hairy mission, Mac had suddenly fallen to the ground writhing in agony, claiming his back had gone out. Later, a very drunk Mac admitted to Carter he'd been struck with an overwhelming sense of dread. "Banks," he said, "I just knew my number was up, simple as that. Saw Death sitting in the cockpit of that chopper grinning at me, just as plain as day."

A set of headlights came into view at the far end of town. Death was very likely at the wheel of this particular vehicle too, Carter thought. As a younger man he'd lived for years with the near certainty he would be killed on some battlefield or in some unpleasant way. But, increasingly of late, back with his people and with his own boat and working out on the open water, he'd allowed himself the luxury of dreaming what it would be like to reach old age and die in his own bed.

"You're a damn fool," Carter whispered. He straightened, took a deep breath, slung his backpack over his shoulder, and walked out into the street toward the prison van pulling in front of the cantina.

L'audace, L'audace Toujours L'audace

Audacity, audacity, always audacity. It was a good line. Carter said that Patton had used it when asked about his strategy going into battle. The more audacious the better. It was the last thing Carter had said before Henry had driven off.

Henry leaned against the back of the SUV and glanced down at the big luminous dial on his Rolex Submariner. Fitting that a watch should be the last vestige of his great fortune, Henry thought. A constant reminder of what was now his most precious commodity.

The jungle, gone quiet with Henry's arrival, had now gotten used to his presence and there was the steady, electric drone of insects and the occasional crash of larger animals in pursuit or in flight through the bush and jungle canopy overhead. Henry took a deep breath, inhaling the fragrant jungle air that smelled of orchids, earth, and recent rain. It was a warm, windless, moonlit evening, still quite humid. He realized now that, over the course of the preceding months, he had grown to love these wild places. Amazing how much had changed in just a year. The old Henry, like some sedate housecat wandering tentatively outside for the first time, would have been terrified at spending a night alone out here.

He had another couple of hours to kill, so he let his mind wander. He imagined seeing headlights and the prison vehicle appearing suddenly down the jungle trail, fishtailing a bit on the slick two-track and skidding to a stop alongside the SUV. Rose, looking more beautiful than ever and none the worse for wear, would climb out of the passenger side and leap into Henry's arms. Carter would make some caustic comment like, 'Get a room' or 'Let's move, ladies' and they'd drive on to the exfil, fly out, and in a few days resume their lives together without a hitch.

Wasn't it pleasant to think so? The plan, which had prompted Henry's nervous last-minute query about what the odds really were and Carter's *l'audace* rejoinder was like the best of magic tricks: deceptively simple to the observer but requiring a deft sleight of hand and even a bit of luck. Everything tonight hinged on Carter's ability to first convince the warden to produce Rose, whether through the suggestion of some twisted ménage à trois or, more likely, placing a pistol to her head.

Up until now, Henry hadn't allowed himself the luxury of thinking about what their life together would be like after the escape. If he'd learned anything over this last year, however, it was that simplicity was the real secret to well-being. If he could talk Carter into giving him at least one of the diamonds remaining at the bottom of the Folger's can, he could imagine buying a cottage on a small lake in northern Wisconsin, or a small cabin on the rugged Wisconsin peninsula that juts like a thumb out into Green Bay. He and Rose would make their stand there, living off fresh-caught fish, honey from their beehives, and a vast vegetable garden. The days would all end the same way: the two of them snuggled together under a Hudson Bay blanket in front of a roaring fire, finishing a nice bottle of wine made from their own small vineyard, an aria by Puccini playing in the background. For a little excitement, they would make an occasional foray into town for a Friday fish fry and a few too many brandy old-fashioneds with the locals—who Henry had found to be the most unpretentious of people who took pride in their Cheesehead moniker.

Henry smiled. If anyone could pull this off, it was Carter. But if they didn't arrive at the appointed hour, Henry would have only one choice. He reached down and felt for the pistol tucked into his waistband. No, he would not be going on without Rose.

Or Are You Just Happy to See Me?

"I like what you've done with the place."

Cruz's office was lit with only candles, and the conference room table was laid out with a white tablecloth and dinner place settings for three. A vase with tall flowers was centered in the middle of the table along with an unopened bottle of Patrón Silver tequila, a few limes, and three small glasses. A boombox centered on her desk played a happy salsa that Carter began to sway his hips to as he gestured for Cruz to join him.

Cruz, who had been drawing the curtains when he opened the door, now hurried across the room and flung her arms around Carter's neck. As they kissed Carter could feel her hands run searchingly down his sides and along his waist. He broke free from her grasp before she reached the small of his back and twirled her around. "Oh, mamacita," he said. "You are a sight for sore eyes."

Cruz laughed with delight. She had spent an inordinate amount of time getting ready, first with the prison beautician, and then trying on almost all of her limited repertoire of evening wear before settling on a camo print backless lace-up dress and a pair of black pointy-toe stilettos. For the occasion, she'd even changed her eye patch to the one that had always brought her luck: a hand-crafted, black leather model encrusted with small emeralds and diamonds to form a coiled serpent.

"A toast," he said as he opened the tequila and poured two glasses. He handed a glass to Cruz and they touched glasses.

"*Cuando el amor reina, lo imposible puede ser alcanzado. ¡Salud!*" he said.

She threw her head back and laughed. They both drank from their glasses.

"When love reigns the impossible can be attained. Sí, it is true," she mused. She reached out for the Patrón, filling their glasses. "Your Spanish surprises me, bird scientist. It is much better than I would have imagined."

"YouTube video," Carter explained. "Head of a Colombian cartel at his daughter's wedding. Spent a few hours with my Spanish-English dictionary and memorizing it. Thought you'd like that."

She smiled. "You are very clever, bird man." She reached out and touched one of the backpack straps on Carter's shoulder. "And what is this? A backpack? Full of surprises?"

"Sí, for later," he winked. "A few tricks that I think will amuse you." He slid it off his shoulder and tossed it casually into a corner of the room.

"Speaking of surprises, are we expecting someone?" he asked, glancing down at the third place setting.

He wasn't sure where she'd hidden the little two-shot derringer but in the split second he'd looked away she'd produced the weapon and had it aimed steadily right at his head. She backed away. He thought there was a better than even chance he could get to her without being hit by that notoriously inaccurate pistol, but it had plenty of stopping power and the woman was in all likelihood a very good shot. The die was cast. Nothing to do now but play it out.

Carter held up his hands and feigned a look of pleasant surprise. "If you wanted to get me naked, all you had to do was ask."

She smiled. "I could not be completely sure, bird man, until I heard your Spanish. Sí, very good but with a strong Panamanian accent. Like many of the American soldiers they sent here in the old days to train our men."

"No doubt," he said, easily. "Miss Sanchez, my high school Spanish teacher, was from Panama. Never would have guessed that I'd pick up her accent. Big woman, as I recall, fond of parrots. Why, one time . . ."

Cruz waved a dismissive hand. "When the old Indian Diego came to us with the story about the airstrip, there could not be much doubt. Your hombre, the other birdman, his real name is Henry Ball, no?"

Carter smiled and shook his head. He reached over and slowly poured two glasses of tequila. "Baby, not sure where you're going with this but it's working. Are you as turned on as I am? Can't wait to get you out of that pretty little thing you're wearing. But keep the stilettos on and hang on to that gun. I'm loving that."

She held the pistol on him and felt for the walkie talkie on her desk. She brought it up to her mouth and switched it on. "Morales."

There was some static and then, "Sí, Madame Director."

"Bring up our guest, rápido," Cruz commanded. She set the walkie talkie down.

"We will know, soon enough, bird man, what brings you to El Buen Madonna."

They had cleaned her up a bit and put her in new prison issue, but at first Carter wasn't sure it was really Rose when Morales gave her a rough shove through the doorway from the dark outer office area into Cruz's office. She was very pale and with her close-shaved head seemed much diminished from the lovely woman that Carter remembered had carried herself with so much poise when he had squired her and Suzy Black on a Michigan Avenue shopping excursion all those many months ago. Rose was visibly trembling and held herself tightly, as if either very cold or awaiting some terrifying physical retribution. But when she looked up slowly, Carter thought he saw just a hint of recognition when their eyes met.

Cruz kept Carter covered with the derringer as she slowly walked over to Rose. Morales backed away and stood off to the side, a grin forming as he awaited what was to come. Cruz put an arm around Rose's shoulders, and then held the derringer right up to the side of her head.

"Ah, my little chiquita, why did you have to make this so hard?" she asked. "Your knight in shining armor has come all this way, only to have it end so badly."

"Not sure what the hell's going on," Carter said now, sounding irritated. "Who is this lady and what does she have to do with us? The least we could do is offer her a drink." He took a step toward the tequila and began pouring three glasses.

"Ah, so you don't know each other?" Cruz asked. "Rose Ball, the American billionaire, meet the man who is here to take you back to your mansions, your pretty clothes and jewels, your fast cars, and big American life. And the dead husband? Sí, Henry Ball is here too, alive and well and waiting nearby. Another birdman. Two bird men to fly my little chiquita away." She threw her head back and laughed.

Rose's aim was a little off, so her knuckle thrust into Cruz's larynx wasn't lethal, but it was delivered with so much speed and ferocity that it dropped Cruz instantly to the ground in an unconscious heap. A split second before she delivered the blow, she'd grasped Cruz's wrist and twisted the hand with the derringer so violently and fueled by so much adrenaline and rage that she'd felt the wrist snap and the derringer drop harmlessly to the ground.

"Down!" Carter yelled to Rose, and while Morales was fumbling for his service revolver Carter had the Sig Sauer out and fired two quick shots center mass and Morales slumped quietly to the floor.

"You've done something different with your hair since I last saw you," Carter said, as he kicked the derringer across the room and reached down to help Rose up.

She got to her feet, wrapped her arms around Carter's waist and pulled him close. "Thank God, Victor's man," she said. She looked up at him. "Henry?"

"Ball's fine," Carter said. "You'll see him soon enough. He said you were a fighter, but I had no idea. Now, we've got to move.

These old prison walls are about ten feet thick, so the shots probably weren't heard, but we've got a plane to catch."

Carter took a few quick steps to the corner of the room and retrieved his backpack. He unzipped it, pulled a pair of zip tie handcuffs out, knelt down next to Cruz and roughly tied her hands behind her back and then her feet. Cruz moaned and mumbled something. Then he pulled a black wig and eye patch out and tossed them to Rose. "You're about the same height," he said. "When we walk out of here, there won't be anyone around, but pretend you're very drunk. You'll hold on to me for support, and I'll help you across the courtyard into the car. The guards at the gate know better than to ask too many questions. Get into these too." Carter handed her a black warm-up suit and a pair of sneakers. Then he pulled a bandana out of his backpack, bent down and tied a gag around the still-unconscious Cruz's mouth.

When Rose was ready, Carter grabbed the bottle of tequila, took a final look around, took Rose's hand, and led her into the outer office. He'd come up a back staircase that gave Cruz private access to her office from the courtyard where Cruz's old Mercedes was parked. At the bottom of the stairs was a metal key box where Carter had watched the driver hang the car keys. Carter had the Sig Sauer out as they went down the dimly-lit stairs. When they got to the bottom of the stairs, Carter opened the key box, pocketed the keys for Cruz's car, and grabbed the three or four other sets hanging there as well.

Carter reached out and gently pulled some hair down from the wig over Rose's face. "When we get out there, keep your head down as if you can barely stay awake. Ready?" Carter asked, tucking the Sig Sauer back in its holster.

Rose nodded.

They walked out into the dark courtyard toward Cruz's car. Carter could see one of the guards in the nearest guard tower watching them. Rose pretended to stumble a bit and Carter lifted the bottle of tequila toward the guard tower in a drunken salute. The guard waved. Carter roared with laughter as they came up to the car, opened the door, and worked to get a clearly very drunk

Rose into the passenger seat. He slammed the door shut, took a final, huge hit from the tequila bottle, and pitched it to the side.

Carter got into the driver's side, started the car, and began driving slowly out of the courtyard, around the corner of the administration building, and across the prison yard toward the front gate. He could see a light on in the small guard shack and a guard sitting inside. As the car neared the shack the guard, clearly surprised by the approach of Cruz's vehicle, sprung from his chair and came out to greet them.

Carter pulled the Sig Sauer from its holster, tucked it in the seat cushion next to him and rolled down the window about halfway. "Buenas noches, señor," he slurred. "Volviendo al pueblo con la señora directora."

The guard hesitated and bent down to get a better look into the car at Rose, slumped down in her seat.

"Vámonos!" Rose commanded, in what Carter thought was a surprisingly good imitation of Cruz's deep-throated voice.

"Sí, de inmediato!" the guard said, saluted, and walked briskly back into the guard house. The heavy iron doors began to slide open. Without waiting for the doors to fully open, Carter floored it. As they began to accelerate down the road, Carter glanced back to see if there was any pursuit, but the big doors had begun to close behind them. Rose pulled the wig and eyepatch off and pitched them out the window. Then she leaned over, put her arms around Carter's neck, and kissed him on the corner of his mouth.

Carter almost missed where the jungle two-track intersected the main road, catching sight at the last moment of the white gash he'd cut in the tree as a marker. He jammed on the brakes and almost rolled the car as he took the turn skidding and then up on two wheels. He held out an arm to steady Rose but when he glanced over at her she forced a smile and nodded to indicate she was fine. They bounced along the deep ruts of the two-track and when the car bottomed out once with a bone-jarring crash, Carter knew the old car's suspension was destroyed, because it now had all the handling characteristics of a sled on ice. But they were almost there and as they went slip-sliding around a bend in the two-track the headlights swept the SUV into view, and there was Henry standing in front of it, holding a pistol to his head.

Carter braked and rolled toward Henry slowly but before they came to a complete stop Rose was out the door and running to him. Henry lowered the gun and she leaped straight into his arms.

"My God, Rosie, what have they done to you?" Henry said quietly after a moment, tears streaming down his face. He could feel how light and frail she was, and he was careful not to squeeze her too tight.

"Just hold me, Henry, if you let me go again, I'll kill you."

"Never, Rosie, never again, my love."

After a few minutes, Carter, who had walked back down the two-track toward the main road, came running back. He held up a hand. "Listen."

Henry set Rose down. There was the sound of a heavy truck or trucks in the direction of the main road. The three of them stood in silence, waiting for the sound to fade. The sound diminished for a moment and then grew louder and whatever the vehicles were, they had now turned onto the jungle two-track and the noise was perceptively louder.

Suddenly Carter reached out and pulled Henry toward him in a fierce bear hug. "You've come far, pilgrim," he said softly in his ear. "You'll be fine if you keep your nerve."

He let go of Henry. "Now get a move on. You two will be back in the Chi by this time tomorrow playing Monopoly with the neighbors, or whatever it is that old white folk do on a Friday night."

He opened up the SUV's tailgate and pulled out the Heckler & Koch MP5 submachine gun. He checked to make sure a round was chambered. Rose reached out and held Carter's arm.

"There's nothing to say, Miss Rose," Carter said. "You and Henry find yourself down in the low country sometime, he knows where to find me."

The sound of trucks had grown louder and what looked to be a spotlight could now be seen probing the jungle just beyond the bend in the road behind them.

"Carter, no way," Henry started to say.

"Now go!" Carter yelled. He slung the machine gun over his shoulder and began running down the two-track toward the light.

Henry slammed the tailgate closed. He climbed into the driver's seat and Rose got in next to him. He started the SUV down the two-track. As they moved off there was a sudden burst of heavy, rapid gunfire. He glanced in the rearview mirror and he could see red tracer fire arc through the trees in the direction of their pursuers.

Answered Prayers

It was two a.m. and Rose and Henry were the only ones on the long people-moving conveyor in the underground tunnel that connected the O'Hare terminal with the elevator center that would take them to ground level and transportation to—where, exactly, Henry suddenly wondered. His focus had, for two months, been on a mission that even Carter had said had only a one in ten chance of succeeding. Henry, having seen too many strange coincidences in the last few years to ever again rule out the hand of fate, hadn't dared think ahead for fear of somehow jinxing the operation. Now, as he pulled Rose close and leaned down and kissed her on top of her closely cropped head, he allowed himself the luxury of the presumption of beginning to plan for a future with Rose.

Mid-way across the length of tunnel, the plaintive sounds of a lone violin began reverberating off the walls of the empty tunnel. Henry looked up and saw that there was one of the poor, itinerate musicians that can be found in any of the world's largest airports and train stations staking out the entrances and exits and playing for change. While most of those musicians were barely competent, both Henry and Rose recognized, as they neared the end of the conveyor, that this violinist, a young black man dressed simply in jeans and sweatshirt with a colorful scarf looped round his neck, played with unusual skill.

As they stepped off the conveyor and walked toward the automatic sliding exit doors, Henry reached into his pocket for the last of his loose Colombian coinage to throw into the musician's open violin case. The man began playing with particular enthusiasm bordering on ferocity, and Henry realized it was a virtuoso violin version of the famous Jimmy Page electric guitar solo from Zeppelin's "Ramble On." As the violin solo segued into the song's solo rhythm part, Rose and Henry applauded and the man took a slight bow but kept playing.

Henry threw the few coins he'd fished out of his pocket into the violin case. Rose gave Henry a gentle nudge and Henry reached back into his pocket. He felt what seemed to be two large pebbles deep in his pocket, and he pulled out what he recognized as the two matching flawless round brilliant ten-carat diamonds that the ancient Michigan Avenue jeweler he had bought them from said were among the finest he'd ever graded.

"Here, have a closer look at these beauties, if they don't bring you luck nothing will," he remembered the jeweler Meyer Weisz saying. When he slid the loop across the counter, Henry had seen the faint tattoo on Weisz's left forearm that they'd put on him at Auschwitz.

There's a man that knows something about luck, Henry remembered thinking, and he'd bought the diamonds on the spot for a cool $400,000. They had been among the largest of the diamonds Ball had poured onto the table behind the Foolish Frog on St. Helena's as part of Carter Banks' down payment. Henry now realized when Carter had suddenly and uncharacteristically hugged him in his powerful arms on that jungle trail what seemed a lifetime ago, he must have somehow slipped the diamonds into his pocket.

"Carter, that crazy bastard," Henry said, as he held out his hand, palm up with the two big diamonds for Rose to see. "Last of a once great Powerball fortune. A jeweler told me one time they'd bring me luck."

Rose looked up at Henry. She took them gently out of his hand. "They have, Henry, they have," she said, and she pitched the diamonds underhand into the violinist's case. They joined hands and exited out through the big sliding doors.

The violinist finished his song. The long tunnel and people mover were empty now. He set his violin down carefully with neck resting on the case and, out of curiosity, picked out the two diamonds from the meager change and a few crumpled dollar bills he'd accumulated over the course of four hours. Through the glass door he could see the couple had reached the elevator center down the hall, and as they waited for an elevator the man had pulled the woman close and was kissing her. It was a surprising display of affection from an older couple who were undoubtedly exhausted from their travels and this late at night. The violinist smiled in appreciation. Then he held one of the diamonds up to the light overhead. He knew diamonds this large and so unnaturally bright and sparkling couldn't possibly be real, but he had a friend that made jewelry, and these would make a nice set of the slightly audacious earrings that his girl was partial to. *A lucky night after all.* He began packing up his violin and bow.

Epilogue

St. Helena Island, South Carolina

It had been 40 days since Carter had thrown Big Jim the keys to the *Miss Rosie Mae* as they walked away from the dock. "Take care of her, and keep fishing, lord knows we need the money. I'll be back in a few weeks," Carter had said.

There hadn't been a word from Carter ever since. Big and Little Jim had carried on dutifully, going out well before dawn every day, weather permitting. This late in the season, though, most of the shrimp had moved farther out into colder water, and all the other shrimp boats had been tied up for weeks at Booger's wharf or been pulled out of the water for some long-awaited repairs.

The good-natured guffaws and whistles from the other captains, who gathered on the docks each day to share war stories, pass a jug, and get out from under their wives and kids, had tapered off of late. The Miss Rosie was a lot of boat for just two men to handle and watching the two Jims struggle to haul gear and return each day with nothing but ice in their freezers was a sorry sight indeed.

It was late morning when the Miss Rosie nestled up against the big tractor tire bumpers along Booger's wharf after what both Jims agreed would be their last run. The men were flat busted and fueling the Rosie for another futile run to the shrimp scattered somewhere 30 miles out was no longer in the cards. It was a still, overcast day, stifling hot and humid, typical of hurricane season.

Thankfully, the weather had driven the others indoors and the wharf was empty, except for a few pelicans perched on the pilings. As the Jims transferred gear onto the dock, they sang a sad Gullah spiritual with a melody that dated back hundreds of years to west Africa and the lyrics that had helped the field hands endure the cruel tedium of slavery on the plantations.

I've been in the storm
Too long
Lord too long
Lord, please let me
Have a little more time
I need a little more time to pray

Then the familiar over the top baritone joined in and there was Carter striding down the dock toward them, a ratty old duffle bag slung over his shoulder and a big smile creasing his bearded face. The Jims dropped the ice chest they were carrying and ran toward Carter. Big Jim, who was actually the smaller of the two, leapt into Carter's arms while Little Jim wrapped his big arms around the two of them and laid his enormous head on Carter's shoulder.

When they finally broke from their scrum, the Jims stepped back and looked Carter up and down. He must have lost 20 pounds and neither of the Jims could recall seeing Carter unshaven or looking so slovenly.

Carter headed off the questions he could see forming on the Jims' faces. He threw down his duffle bag, gave it a little kick for emphasis, gestured at the *Miss Rosie Mae* and said, angrily, "I leave you the finest fishing boat in all of the Carolinas and this is how you treat her? From what I'm hearing you two only been out on the water one day out of every seven. What little you've caught been paying for nights out with the Bailey sisters, am I right?"

The two Jims stared at Carter, mouths agape. "Now look here, Carter," Big Jim, who usually did most of the talking, began to say. Carter burst out laughing, wrapped his arms around both men. "You two are a sight for sore eyes. Come on, I'll buy you a beer. Lord knows you've earned it. Then we'll see what Miss Alice is planning for dinner."

The three men walked arm in arm down the dock, the two Jims flanking Carter, and then Big Jim broke into a boisterous old song that was always the harbinger of good times ahead.